THE

ROOK

TWISTED KINGDOMS BOOK 2

FROST KAY

Audiobooks

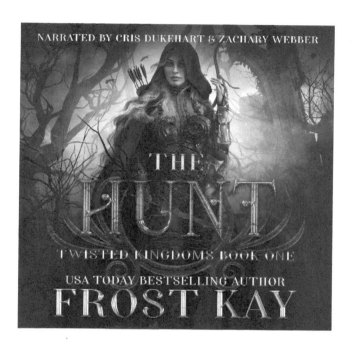

Are you an audiobook addict?

I am happy to announce that the Twisted Kingdoms are being produced!

The Hunt is now available!

ALSO BY FROST KAY

Indigo Alloy

ALIENS & ALCHEMISTS

(Sci-fi Romance)

Pirates, Princes, and Payback

Alphas, Airships, and Assassins

TWISTED KINGDOMS

(Fairytale Retelling)

The Hunt

The Rook

The Heir

HEIMSERYA

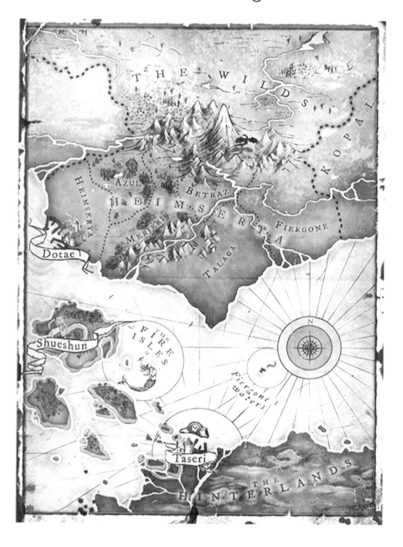

HISTORY OF THE KINGDOMS

Once upon a time… Elves, Shapeshifters, Giants, Dragons, Humans and Merfolk were all at peace—all equals. Their lands and kingdoms were prosperous, and their enemies didn't dare attack for their armies were formidable. Generations passed and the people began to forget what was most important—love, courage, loyalty.

That was their downfall—for in self-indulgent ignorance they allowed darkness to creep into the land like a thief in the night. It started out slowly.

The Merfolk let vanity take root deep in their hearts, the Dragons became greedy from the skies, the Giants grew bloodthirsty, the Humans covetous, the Shapeshifters prideful, and the Elves allowed apathy to squeeze compassion from their hearts.

It was said that the earth rumbled and cracked, shaking the

core of the world. When the tremors ceased, the Jagged Bone Mountain range surrounded the Elvish kingdom, cutting the elves off from every other living creature.

The Dragons abandoned their own kingdom and made their home in the Jagged Bones, threatening all who approached their lairs—making it impossible to pass through the mountains—though the Giants tried. As if the mountains of the Jagged Bones craved blood and hatred, many lives were claimed in the senseless violence there.

Upon witnessing such death, the Merfolk retreated to their watery homes, content to bask in the beauty of the sea and their own splendor, only occasionally consorting with pirates when it amused them.

Years passed and the myths faded from the world's mind.

The Elvish kingdom became the Wilds, the Giants sequestered themselves in their own kingdom of Kopal. The Fire Isle Kingdoms were forged by mercenaries—the offspring of pirates, Sirens, and Merfolk.

For a time, the Shapeshifters of Talaga held an uneasy peace with the Humans of Heimserya. The two kingdoms needed each other to survive, that all changed with the birth of a new plant and a royal son.

An extraordinary flower—the Mimikia—was discovered in Talaga. When distilled, it was a powerful drug capable of healing any wound. It was practically magical. The applications were limitless and its worth immeasurable. In their pride, the Shapeshifters boasted of their discovery, of their brilliance.

Word reached the Humans of this new source of wealth. They coveted this new miracle plant and the temptation proved to be too much for the newly crowned king who sought to enrich his kingdom. With his greed dawned a new era of bloodshed, prejudice, addiction, and depravity.

Welcome to the Twisted Kingdoms.

RECAP

"…Tempest? Tempest?"

Tempest blinked. Sitting at her first war council wasn't what she expected it to be. Exhaustion had plagued her for the past two days—it most certainly had to do with her fitful attempts to sleep and the nightmares that had chased her as soon as unconsciousness claimed her. *You only had two nightmares while you were gone.* The unwelcomed thought caused her to stiffen even as she nodded at Madrid.

"Yes, it was the southern village on the edge of the mountains that had been destroyed. I saw it with my own eyes. Everyone was dead," she said woodenly.

Madrid's face was grave, as were the rest of the men's expressions. They all seemed genuinely perturbed by her findings, which suggested that they were not privy to any kind of insider attack on the villages. Tempest wondered if she could risk telling them the truth of what she had discovered—that the shifters were not responsible for the sickness killing hundreds of common folk. That someone else was to blame.

But she couldn't.

It would be idiotic and suicidal. The men around her had been in power for a long time. They could all be very good actors.

Tempest inhaled shallowly, and she could have sworn the scent of death and the sickly-sweet poison wafted through the air. The scent that had come from her uncle's tent. She couldn't trust anyone. There wasn't any other choice but to stick to her lie she'd concocted with the Jester.

Her gaze darted to the king's seat, which was blessedly empty. Who knew what he had up his sleeve and how she could rebuff any more of his future advances? She needed to invent more excuses. It was also a relief that he wasn't watching her every move at the meeting. Destin was just as ruthless and observant as his forefathers. The longer he stayed away, the safer she was.

"What did you do, after seeing the village?" one of the men asked in a snide tone as if her presence offended his delicate sensibilities. Tempest did not, in all sincerity, know who he was. Nobody save Madrid seemed to appreciate her being at the war council meeting in the first place, which she expected, but it didn't make the palpable animosity any easier.

"I took out their leader, cut out his heart, and returned it to King Destin," she said, enunciating each word of her lie as if it was a vicious truth she was rightfully proud of. "I made sure to find out as much information about future attacks before I did so, of course," she added, as if in afterthought, in response to the shocked looks on the council's faces at her bloodthirsty confession.

All except Madrid.

He was watching her with an unreadable expression that she'd come to know over the years. It still unsettled Tempest greatly, though Madrid was normally an impossible person to read in the first place. But the blankness of his face against the other men in the room made him look almost sad.

No, not sad. It was almost as if he was disappointed in her, like she'd failed some sort of test. What did that mean? Was she reading him entirely wrong?

But the non-expression was enough for Tempest to open her mouth and almost confess that she'd been lying; that in truth she hadn't assassinated the Jester. That she was yet to kill a single human being in cold blood, and part of her clung to the wish that she would remain that way. Death was a part of life, but murder? That was something completely different.

You're an assassin. Death is your shadow.

Tempest kept her mouth shut.

When the meeting finished, she was fast to leave the room, her heart beating too quickly. Her lies felt thick and wrong in her mouth. She'd barely turned onto the narrow staircase a servant had shown her up earlier, when a hushed conversation in the stairwell stopped her in her tracks. She frowned and leaned against the wall, straining to make out whom the voices belonged to.

The hair at the nape of her neck rose.

King Destin.

"...that she took out their leader means we'll have to plan the next poisoning as if it was an emotionally charged retaliation," he murmured.

"Did you tell her to take the Jester out?" a second voice asked. Tempest thought it sounded like one of the men from the war council —but that wasn't possible. She'd beaten everyone in leaving the room so it definitely wasn't Madrid.

"I asked for her to bring me his heart. The bastard has been trouble from the beginning, and I knew exactly what type to send his way." He laughed, the sound sinister and sexy all at once. "I knew he wouldn't be able to resist her appeal."

Tempest jerked, sickened. He'd sent her not because of her skills but because he thought to use her as a tart. *Bastard.*

"This way the Talagans will have a far less organized front to defend against our attack once we strike."

The second voice chuckled. "I suppose that's correct, Your Grace. We should aim for a village closer to Dotae if we're going for a vengeful attack. Where was it that Lady Tempest was found as a child? We could orchestrate it to look like the shifters have gone after her personally. The people would rally behind her after such a thing. They already favor her."

All the blood drained from Tempest's face. Wicked Hell. What kind of monsters were they? She sagged against the stone wall and strained to listen to the rest of their conversation.

"That idea has merit. It will work for us twofold: she'll stay on our side *and* be completely devoted to her duty. She'll be so busy chasing ghosts, the poor little thing will be too exhausted to see the obvious," Destin murmured. "She is a sharp one, after all, so we must stay vigilant. Speaking of, where did my Lady Hound go? I was rather hoping—"

Tempest did not hang around to hear the rest of the king's sentence. She crept back up the stairs and glanced both ways. Not a soul.

Destin's voice grew louder and in blind horror and fear, she sprinted for the other parallel staircase. Temp hurled herself

CHAPTER 1: TEMPEST

The king's royal banquet had barely been going on for an hour, and Tempest was about to lose her mind. She did not know how she was managing to sit, quiet and obedient, surrounded by people who were conspiring to frame Talaga for everything that was going wrong. It did not help her nerves that she was serving as a double agent.

She ground her teeth together. Winter's bite, she hated how that sounded. She eyed the gilded merriment around her. If anyone knew that she'd aligned herself with the Jester... Tempest blew out a soft breath. Anyone associated with the renowned Dark Court was quickly executed without hesitation. If she wasn't careful, she'd find herself hung from the nearest pole.

"They should be exterminated," a weasel-like man with thick, caterpillar brows muttered to his group of companions.

Tempest hid her scowl and kept her expression blank,

taking a slow sip of her cider. It would be so easy to take out the blathering aristocrat. Her fingers twitched with the need to hold a blade.

Calm yourself. Killing everyone will solve nothing. Stop thinking like a Hound and think like a spy. Think like the Jester. What would he do?

Tempest bit back a laugh. She was reasonably certain that Pyre would waste no time in dismantling the king's court from within. He certainly had the skills and manipulation. But murdering Heimserya's war council and its royal family—particularly the king himself—would not help the Talagan cause. No, it would only make things worse. Talaga did not have the numbers to survive an all-out war against Heimserya, which was why Pyre and his band of shifters needed Tempest.

A double agent.

She set her goblet down and smoothed her hands over her silky dress, all the while studying the highborn murderers around her. She still could not believe she allowed herself to be caught in the Jester's intricate web.

One week had passed since she'd seen him.

A beautiful woman glanced in Tempest's direction and whispered to her companion. How long could Tempest keep her secrets? She wasn't overly worried about the gossips in court, but one of her uncles was bound to figure something out —Aleks, Maxim, or Dima. Tempest caught the eye of her fourth and final uncle across the table.

Madrid. Calling him her uncle was a bit of a stretch. He'd had a hand in training her, but he'd left the rest up to the other men. Not that she minded terribly. She was woman enough to admit that the head of the King's Hounds scared her. His gaze slid over the crowd, pausing briefly on her.

Tempest feigned calmness, even as her pulse sped up. The slight tension in her shoulders disappeared when Madrid's attention moved on. She needed to be wary of him. Temp had no doubt Madrid suspected, at the very least, that she was keeping something from him. But she hoped her obvious discomfort around King Destin was enough to distract him from the truth.

She examined the king's empty dais. It was a relief he wasn't in attendance tonight. It was difficult to hide her loathing for the man. Guilt pricked her. Partly, it was due to the king's betrayal of his people and his intent to frame the Talagans for the drug currently sweeping its way through village after village, killing almost everyone who consumed it. His alarming confidence, lusty appetites, and ruthless desire to gain whatever he wanted was problematic. Especially since he was determined to have her.

On the positive side, he hadn't sent for her all week. His chambers were not somewhere she wanted to be. Ever. Sharing the king's bed, or becoming his consort, was undoubtedly his intention. Her face twitched, and she clamped down on the urge to sneer at the thought. It seemed impossible to keep up the ruse that she was interested in him. And dangerous. He wasn't one to be trifled with. For a moment, Tempest worried over the reason *why* the king hadn't sent for her. Maybe he was capable of occasionally being too busy to deal with his hedonistic impulses. If only wishes came true.

Ladies simpered, and young men strutted about trying to catch the females' attention. It made her sick. A war was brewing, people were dying, and yet these people were drinking and eating like nothing was wrong.

"You do not seem to be eating much, Tempest," Madrid

murmured. He spoke so quietly that nobody took notice of their conversation. Even though he stood on the opposite side of the table, she heard his words.

She blinked. The man moved too silently for his own good. "It is difficult to eat when talk of war is filling the air," she replied.

"Never took you for someone with a weak stomach," a highborn man joked.

Tempest arched a haughty brow at him. "We could take this outside and I could show you how weak I'm not." That shut the pompous peacock up.

Madrid eyed her and turned back to the conversation at hand. Her other uncles pushed forward to listen in.

"Another village was hit yesterday," one of the members of the war council said. He was an aging man, with a lined face and graying hair. She didn't know for sure, but his nasally voice was too unique to forget. If she wasn't wrong, Temp believed him to be the man she'd overheard conspiring with the king to frame Talaga for everything going wrong in the kingdom. He was an ordinary looking sort of man. Unremarkable. It was hard to believe that such depravity lurked beneath the surface. What sort of man would kill women and children? She hated him.

"It was closer to the capital this time. Barely in the forest at all," Madrid commented.

The relief that washed over her was quickly followed by shame. People had died, and yet she was thankful it wasn't the village her mum grew up in. It was a wicked, selfish thought, but it was there nonetheless.

"This is concerning."

Tempest stiffened at the king's voice behind her.

The snake had slithered from his lair.

In a wave, the men bowed. Temp bit the inside of her cheek when the king's hand rested on her left shoulder, his thumb brushing her collarbone. He didn't look at her as he moved closer to the group.

"Before we know it, the shifters will be upon us in Dotae," he said. "It's only a matter of time before they prey on some of the more isolated villages."

The isolated villages... It was as if he knew what she was thinking.

She did not manage to suppress the shudder that ran through her at the thought. She glanced around. Thankfully, nobody was paying enough attention to her.

"There have been captures of the drug responsible for the deaths in several of the affected villages," Madrid said. The lead Hound was an observant man and only spoke when he had something of value to say. "Its roots definitely derived from the South Isles."

"Has Aleks had any further luck determining *what* exactly the drug comes from?" the king asked.

"Very little. The drug has been expertly purified. We have only been able to link it to the South Isles because of a few spies in the forest watching the trade routes," Madrid answered.

"It is only a matter of time before full-on war breaks out across the nation," the king replied, convincingly upset.

What rubbish.

"Obviously, we do not wish this to happen," he went on. "To go to war against the South Isles would ruin our relationship with them forever."

It was uncanny how easily King Destin could lie. He was the one who was orchestrating the entire disgusting plan, though hearing Madrid talk of *spies in the forest* made her stomach lurch uncomfortably. Did he know what his king was doing? He must. He was the lead Hound. As much as she didn't want to believe any of the Hounds had anything to do with the king's treachery, she couldn't let her affection for them cloud her judgement. It was almost her downfall before.

Framing the Talagans for poisoning villages in the forest was just the beginning of King Destin's plan. *Never mind the fact that most people killed by the drug were shifters.* Looking back on it now, she could not believe she had been so naïve as to believe the Talagans were responsible for destroying their own people. It had taken Pyre—the Jester—showing her what the villages along the border really, truly looked like for Tempest's eyes to open to the truth.

No, it took so much more than that.

Shame welled in her belly that she had not believed what she'd seen *when* she had seen it. It had been obvious the villagers were not fighters. She thought of Rina and little Aspen running their bakery without a care in the world. Except they *did* have a care in the world; all around them, their people were dying, the men going out to defend them and never returning. When all this was over—if there were any Talagans left at all— the number of women compared to men of marriageable age would be terribly out of proportion. It would be difficult to repopulate the Talagan people.

Perhaps their low female population had doomed the shifter race in the long term without any need for a war at all. A dark thought indeed. She glanced at the king from the corner of her eye. The fact that he planned to bring the South Isles into the mix was worrisome. She'd swallow her hat if he didn't have

Several heads nodded in approval, though Tempest noticed Madrid's face was just as impassive as she expected it to be, but there was also something in his gaze... If her uncle was letting that much show, he wasn't happy. *He does not like this plan.*

A soft snort to her left pulled her attention to the princess. The girl covered her mouth with her hand, shaking her head. "They are all empty-headed fools," Ansette muttered, clearly very amused.

Tempest's gaze shifted around them, searching for anyone near enough to listen in. There were none. One could never be too careful. "Whatever do you mean, Prin—Ansette?" Tempest corrected.

"I think you know exactly what I mean," Ansette replied, eyes wide and alert as she slanted a look Tempest's way. "Sending my brothers as ambassadors is going to cause more harm than good, don't you think? I mean, look at them. They aren't exactly... diplomatic material."

Tempest schooled her expression. There was no way she would ever admit how she felt about the princes. To do so was courting death. "As you say, my lady," she ventured.

Ansette snorted in laughter once more. "You're more intelligent than my father gives you credit for." She shook her head. "My father should be helping the kingdom as a whole, *especially* the shifters being disproportionately hit by the sickness along the Talagan border, instead of forming a treaty with a neighboring country, which will be an uneasy ally at best." Her expression darkened a touch. There was something about her father in her—an astuteness—that became glaringly apparent with such a look upon her face.

A ruler in the making. She was far more a monarch than her brothers already.

The royal's expression only grew more serious as she took a step toward Tempest. Ansette tilted her head up to stare directly into Tempest's eyes. "They will ruin this kingdom."

The whole conversation had teetered on the edge of treasonous, but that comment tilted it over. Tempest took a step closer to the younger royal. "Be careful, Ansette," she warned, speaking in low, furtive tones. "If you would permit me, I would advise against speaking of such topics in the company of strangers. You do not understand the danger of your words."

The girl chuckled, the sound managing to sound pretty and jaded at the same time. Tempest studied the royal. The princess was not yet fifteen, and yet she knew the girl had experienced more of the world than she should have. Ansette bore a shrewd and calculating mind already.

"I know much more than you think, Temp," Ansette replied. "More than anyone thinks. Don't think me ignorant. Being raised in the palace exposes one to all sorts of plots, machinations, and assassinations. Young I may be, but my soul is old and tired. I grow weary of the games."

"Don't we all," Temp murmured. "I always thought it more sporting to state your problems outright."

Ansette patted her on the arm. "A woman after my own soul." She sighed. "Alas, there are not more like us. I am so very glad I was able to make your acquaintance tonight. I feel like I may have found a kindred spirit in you, but only time will tell."

What did that mean? "Thank you for your stimulating company."

The princess nodded and turned to speak to a woman who'd approached them wearing a shimmering golden dress. Tempest tuned out as soon as the woman began to gush about new court fashion. Cocking her head to one side, Tempest regarded Ansette. The girl could be a formidable ally if she played her cards just right.

She blinked slowly and scanned the room, disgusted with herself. The princess might be shrewd, but she was still a child. It was Tempest's goal to spare the innocent, not embroil them in treachery and deceit. While the princess was not ignorant, she was an innocent, one Tempest had sworn to protect.

Madrid caught her eye, and Tempest wiped all expression from her face. She sighed, feigning boredom. He scowled, and she hid her smile. Needling the stoic man would provide some entertainment until she could be released from the hellish evening.

Winter's bite, she wanted her bed.

CHAPTER 3: TEMPEST

"*G*oing somewhere?"

Tempest grimaced and turned toward the door to face Madrid. "It did not seem as if I was needed," she said. No one had sought her out since the princess had drifted away in another conversation. While Tempest couldn't quite blend into the decorative wallpaper, not many dared to approach her. Which was fine with her. Most of the king's court, she desired no acquaintance with.

A flash of something almost like sympathy crossed Madrid's face, but, as quickly as it appeared, it vanished. "You will only gain more and more responsibility with every day you spend on the war council, Tempest. Was that not what you wanted when you sought a seat at the table?"

It had been, of course. For with responsibility came power, and with power came opportunity. The opportunity to discover who exactly was responsible for her mother's death thirteen years prior.

Do not think of that bastard shifter. He is in the past.

That was a bloody lie.

Nightmares from her childhood still plagued her years later. A shiver wracked Tempest's spine. Even with the challenges she faced, her mind didn't wander too far from the night her mother died or from the shifter she was certain had started the fire. One way or another, she'd exact vengeance.

"Tempest?"

"I am able and ready to accept any responsibility the council gives me. I'm at Heimserya's disposal." She forced a smile to her face and nodded at Madrid. "So, I am not to slip off to bed… What is it you need me to do?"

"It is not me who needs you. It is the king."

The food in her stomach curdled as she caught the king watching her out of the corner of his eye, that same smile on his face from earlier, but the gleam in his gaze was quite different. Possessive. Heated. Dangerous.

He wants you in his bed.

She swallowed, and sweat beaded between her breasts. There were many things she'd do for her kingdom, but becoming the king's whore wasn't one of them. It was all Tempest could do to keep her face blank as she obediently followed her uncle into an adjacent room. Several people from the banquet wandered about the room speaking quietly while sipping mead, whiskey, or wine. Her nausea abated. She wouldn't have to face the king alone. That she could deal with.

No sooner had the thought passed through her mind when the door closed behind her and heat pressed against her back.

"My Lady Hound," the king murmured, just for her ears. He

stroked a subtle finger down her arm as he moved around her, turning his body slightly so that nobody else in the room could see the blatantly personal gesture. Tempest bit back her flight or fight response, only just managing to stay rooted to the spot.

You can't stab the king.

"Your Majesty," she said, inclining her head politely.

"Did you enjoy dinner, Tempest?" King Destin asked. "You seemed rather tense."

"Merely tired, I must admit," Tempest said, unnerved that her discomfort must have been so obvious throughout the entire banquet. She needed to get better at concealing her emotions. Her lips pursed as Pyre's voice floated through her mind: *I can read you like a book.*

Stop thinking about him.

"Would you care to have a drink?" the king asked, proffering a glass of his preferred fire whiskey to Tempest in the process. "I know spirits are an acquired taste, but once you have developed such a palate, you can't go back to anything else. It is truly addictive."

The grin that spread across the king's face at the word *addictive* caused Tempest's skin to crawl. Did everything he say have an ulterior meaning? She swallowed. She knew what was really addictive: the damn drug he was spreading throughout their kingdom.

Tempest forced herself to look Destin square in his amber eyes. The faint lines at the corner of his eyes crinkled slightly, and he gave her an intimate smile.

None of that. She wasn't having any of his lusty looks, nor the alcohol that would dull her senses. The wine tonight was enough.

"I must, unfortunately, decline," Tempest said quietly,

Brine cursed under his breath before straightening up. "She would have killed you if she hadn't missed."

At this, Tempest burst out laughing and twitched against Brine's grip before she could stop herself. The nails on his hand began transforming into wickedly dangerous wolf claws in response. Winter's bite, that was creepy.

He growled into her ear. "What's so funny, dog?"

"Oh, nothing," Tempest replied, sobering. "It's just that—you honestly think I missed?" She caught Pyre's eye. He wasn't amused by her outburst so much as he was aware it was warranted. Tempest frowned. Why did she know that? She hated that she could read the tiny permutations of his expression. "Trust me," she continued, "if I wanted the Jester dead, he would be."

"And on that cheerful note, release her," Pyre said, repeating his previous order. "And leave us. Like she's said, if she really wanted to kill me, she'd have planted that dagger in my back."

The blade lingered at her throat for a few seconds longer and then disappeared. Brine squeezed Tempest's wrist until she was moments away from gasping in agony.

"Mind your manners, mutt," he whispered in her ear before releasing her in one swift motion.

That was rich, *him* calling *her* the mutt. Tempest swallowed the retort forming on her tongue and instead focused on rubbing the feeling back into her twisted wrist. The damn brute. Her wrist would surely bruise by morning.

Show no weakness.

Tempest pushed aside the pain and straightened to confront Pyre properly, who was still fussing over his outfit like a damn lady of court. She made no attempt to hide her distain.

"Don't give me that look. I spent too much money on these

clothes to have a dagger ruin the stitching," Pyre muttered, inspecting his shoulder critically for non-existent stray fibers along the seam. Both he and Tempest knew damn well her dagger hadn't touched him. "I need them to look perfect."

For whom? It was the middle of the night. She shook her head. Temp didn't want to know who he was entertaining so late or why the outfit mattered so much.

"Why am I here, Pyre?" she asked, impatience dripping from every word.

The Jester finished his inspection and reached for the dagger, pulling it from the mirror. Several shards of glass shattered to the floor. He prowled in her direction, the robe gaping the slightest bit, revealing a sliver of his burnished chest. He paused in front of her and held out the dagger, hilt first, to Tempest. She took it slowly.

Pyre dropped into a mocking bow. "You misplaced this, my lady."

"Pyre—"

"Relax." He sighed. "Can't you indulge in some niceties before we get down to business?"

"Not with you, no." Every moment she spent in his presence inspired feelings she didn't quite know what to do with.

He cocked his head to one side, fox ears twitching as if listening for changes in Tempest's heart rate. Unbidden, she thought of their tumultuous argument in the cabin and how it had led to his fingers trailing along her calves. She blinked. Why in the wicked hell was she thinking about that?

It had been a mistake. A moment of weakness. She gazed blankly at his chest. *For both of them.*

"Penny for your thoughts, love?"

She flinched, then arched a haughty brow, leaning back in

her seat. "You could offer me Destin's personal fortune and I still wouldn't tell you what's on my mind."

Pyre's smile slid from his face, and something predatory took its place. "Business it is, then. Do you have any updates from the war council?"

Relieved to finally be talking about something else, Tempest said, "King Destin is sending his sons to act as ambassadors to the giants of Kopal." She took a moment to recall everything she'd filed away. "Children from the capital are disappearing. He's blaming the Dark Court." She eyed Pyre. No expression. He remained impassive, patiently waiting in silence for Tempest to continue. Damn, he was hard to read. She sighed and rolled her neck. "And he ordered me to infiltrate the Talagan rebels and destroy them by any means necessary. It was implied to use my feminine wiles." She sneered the last word.

The Jester perked up at this. His lips curled into an amused grin, and she found herself resisting the urge to throw another dagger at him.

"I'm sure you didn't like that very much."

"How astute of you," she grumbled.

"Did you protest?"

"Of course not," Tempest replied, rolling her eyes. "It's the perfect cover to work with you to unravel the entire mimkia conspiracy. And I'm no fool; to protest Destin's commands would be a death warrant."

She pursed her lips, thinking about the blatant touch from the king tonight. He was becoming bolder. What if Destin commanded her into his bed? Her jaw clenched. There was nothing that would entice her to do so. Even the idea of letting him run his hands over her body made Tempest break out in a cold sweat. She flushed scarlet when she realized the kitsune was peering at her strangely.

She coughed. "Was there any information in particular that you were hoping I'd overhear?"

A weighty pause. "Not really. Destin sending his sons off is interesting, though. We might be able to work with that. Other than that, a few of my men were captured two days ago by the king's guards. They've been sentenced to death."

Her jaw dropped. "You should have led with that! What can I do to help? Do you want me to—I don't know—appeal for their release? Break them out? We can't leave them to—"

"That's *exactly* what we're going to do. We can't afford to break them out. It would do more harm than good for the resistance."

Temp blinked slowly and tugged on her left ear. Surely, she was hearing things. "You can't be serious."

"Deadly."

She swallowed. How could he so callously allow his friends and allies to die when he could very well save them? Her stomach turned.

You're not dealing with Pyre. He's the Jester now. Don't forget that for one second.

And then, as if they hadn't just been discussing the imminent and potentially preventable deaths of his comrades, the mercurial kitsune returned to his fractured mirror and smoothed down the fabric of his robe. He fussed with the collar and then untied the sash at his waist, exposing his chiseled chest and abdomen. Heat filled her cheeks. Why was she attracted to this criminal?

He raised an eyebrow at Tempest. "How do I look?"

"Like a drug lord with more money than sense," she replied,

simply to get a rise out of him. In truth, Pyre's finely made clothes looked as if they had been made for him and him alone. The gold robe and silk trousers accentuated the rich colors of his hair and complemented the amber tone of his skin.

The man's easy smile quickly faded, his mouth setting into a hard line, his first real sign of displeasure. Gone was the amused twinkle in Pyre's eye.

Good.

She only wished she could have investigated the mimkia problem, and the overarching issue of King Destin's lack of guilt over willingly sacrificing his subjects to mimkia to instigate a war, without the use of an underworld kingpin. But as luck would have it, that was not the case. It didn't mean Tempest had to like working with Pyre, nor make it easy for him to work with *her.*

Before the kitsune could fire back a retort or a warning, the sound of footsteps approaching pulled his attention from her. She huffed out a breath and turned in the direction of the newcomer. Pyre sauntered forward, leaning a hip against the back of her chair, effactually blocking her view from who'd entered the room.

She bristled. Stubborn man. Tempest craned her neck to get a glance of the person who'd entered. A man swathed in a plain, dark cloak paused a few paces from the exit. The ornate, silver chains clasping his cloak shut glinted in the candlelight. He lowered the hood of his cloak to reveal black, greasy hair slicked back from a sharply receding hairline. His pale eyes shifted around the chamber as if calculating the price of everything in the room. He caught Tempest's stare and smiled, exposing rotten, yellowed teeth.

Nasty.

"I see we are not alone," the man said, not looking away from Tempest. His gaze unapologetically roved over what he could see of her body.

Pyre ignored the statement. "What news do you have, Tam?"

Tam shrugged. "The guards have stepped up their security around the perimeter of Dotae. Some kids went missing, apparently. Don't know when we'll get the next shipment through."

Tempest eyed Pyre's silk-clad shoulders. *What kind of shipment?*

"We needed those drugs *yesterday*, and now you're telling me you have no idea when they'll get through?" The kitsune sounded less than pleased.

Tempest gaped at him in disbelief. Though she had only just called Pyre a drug lord, she hadn't really meant it or, at the very least, hadn't really *thought* about what it meant. That Pyre, as the Jester, was responsible for the drug problems she saw affecting the poor and homeless in Dotae so terribly. He might not have been the one peddling mimkia to the villages but that apparently didn't stop him distributing less deadly—but no less addictive—substances to the people of Heimserya.

Her lip curled, but she refrained from saying anything. Both men seemed to have forgotten her presence. All the better. She needed as much information as she could get.

"Ain't nothing I can do about the guards. It was your foolish plan," Tam said.

The Jester closed the gap between him and Tam.

Temp blinked at the spot Pyre had held prior. He moved so *fast*. What else was he capable of? She tucked her unease away as the Jester towered over Tam, a snarl rumbling in his chest. Her heart pounded in her chest as the kitsune began to shift, his face becoming more inhuman with every passing second. Maybe it was time for her to slink away. She inched away from her chair.

"That is what I *pay* you to do," Pyre growled. He grabbed a handful of the man's cloak. "All of your finery and fancy clothes are paid for by me. If you cannot get rid of a few guards—or find another route into the city—I shall find someone to replace you. And you won't like that... trust me."

Tempest paused. That was a death threat, if she'd ever heard one. Between this and Pyre's disregard for his own, doomed men, she wondered how much of the compassion and love she had witnessed back in the Talagan shifter village had been genuine.

Was it really all a ruse to convince her to work with him? An elaborate, disgusting set-up to force her to betray her own people? Her gut clenched. Just what had she gotten herself into?

Her head gave another painful throb, thanks to the Jester's henchman. Sweet poison, she needed some sleep and a headache tincture from Aleks. Tomorrow, after Destin's compulsory war council breakfast was over and she began her mission, officially, to reintegrate herself into the rebel alliance, she would pick apart the matter until she knew exactly how to handle Pyre.

Temp surreptitiously crept toward the exit of the cave, deciding it was better to slink away than address Pyre once more. Who knew what else he'd reveal tonight? She didn't have any more energy to try to figure him out. She slipped past a shadowed cove, making it past the Jester and Tam without notice, and got closer to her destination.

Just as she thought she'd made it free, a familiar hand grabbed at her shoulder and forced a bag over her head once more. Temp huffed but didn't fight Brine. No use incurring any more bumps or bruises. She knew when to fight and when to surrender.

"You really think I'd let you walk out of here alone, eyes open, did you?" Brine growled, jabbing his claws into Tempest's back to push her forward.

"Of course not," she mumbled beneath the bag, her mood souring even further. "Do you have to be so rough? What did I ever do to you?"

Brine didn't answer but at least she didn't feel the sting of his claws again as they moved toward what she presumed was Dotae. How far away was Pyre's den of extravagance from the capital anyway? Minutes? Hours? Her feet already ached, and they'd only just begun.

Fifteen minutes later, the bag was torn from her head, revealing to her the edge of the forest closest to Dotae's border. Thank the stars. She turned to face Brine, just as he grabbed the front of her dress.

His eyes seemed to glow as he muttered, "You might have the Jester fooled into believing you're useful, bitch, but you haven't fooled me. The first time I see you stepping out of line... well, it will be your last."

"I'll keep that in mind," she murmured.

He released her roughly and spun on his heel before moving through the trees as if he were made from the darkness itself.

Tempest rubbed the back of her neck. The Jester was a problem, but so was his wolfish protector. She'd have to tread carefully with that one. While Pyre played games and twisted words, Brine was honest and blunt. She didn't doubt him for one second when he said he'd kill her.

Another wave of pain stabbed her temple. Tempest winced

as colorful spots began to dance over her vision. It wouldn't be long now until the migraine slammed into her, full force. "Dumb wolf," she muttered. It was highly unlikely that she'd get any sleep now between the pain and the nausea.

Tempest trudged toward the city gates, rearranging her cloak and pulling her hood up to once more protect her ears from the cold. Then, she steeled herself for the long trek back to the capital city, to her bed.

CHAPTER 5: TEMPEST

"*S*tupid, strutting alpha males and their tempers," Tempest found herself reciting, over and over again like some kind of mantra. Her mood had grown decidedly worse by the time she finally reached the outer walls of Dotae—which was saying something, since her bad mood back in Pyre's cave had been considerable.

Reaching the city walls had been uneventful, other than having to battle against the incredibly cold night air and the pounding in her skull. She'd decided against entering through the main city gates—women traipsing about in the night received a certain reputation. While she wasn't exactly a proper lady, she still needed to keep her reputation somewhat intact. So, she'd skulked to the southeastern part of the city. The slums. The city wall there was crumbling and had been clearly overlooked for some time. In fact, she knew that the patrol tended to avoid this area, so it was never well guarded. She'd bet her best dagger this was how Pyre got his drugs into the city.

Using the loose and broken bricks, Tempest nimbly ascended the wall. A giddiness swept over her as she climbed higher and higher, almost whooping in satisfaction when she reached the top of the thirty-foot wall. Her dress and cloak whipped around her in the winter wind. She'd like to see any of her fellow Hounds accomplish such a task while wearing a gown.

The wall curved and smoothed out in the distance on either side of her. While she longed to walk around the perimeter of her city for a while, that was hardly inconspicuous, and she preferred to go about her business unseen.

She took a deep breath of freezing air that bit her lungs, wondering why she hadn't just gone straight through the city gates. Wanting to avoid the guards was a poor excuse—and largely a lie that she could not fool herself with. Ultimately, she knew, deep down, why she did not want to return to the Hound barracks. After everything she discovered over the past few weeks, Tempest felt less and less like a member of their ranks, and she could hardly stand to look at any of them.

Keeping secrets from her uncles pained her. She'd never lied to them. Every time she lied, it felt like she lost another piece of herself. Her entire life, all she'd wanted was a family and to fit in. Her uncles had created that for her. Now, it felt like it was on the edge of collapse.

Your so-called family might be murderers.

She shied away from that thought. Tempest didn't want to think—or want to believe—that this was the case, especially given how they'd cared for her. And what of Madrid? He'd never been one for speaking many words to anyone, much less to Tempest. She'd always assumed that was because he was the head of the Hounds and had far too much to do. He had no time to concern himself with the likes of a scraggly orphan girl who'd been too wild to be cared for within King Destin's court.

But it was becoming glaringly clear that Madrid actually paid more attention to her than she'd initially thought. Now, she couldn't help but wonder if that was because he suspected her of wrongdoing.

Like betraying your king and country.

Tempest jumped from the wall to the nearest building and traveled for another fifteen minutes across shanties and roofs. She paused and peered down from the edge of a rowdy tavern. Drunks laughed beneath her while others crept quietly through the shadowy streets. Though night was fully in bloom, the time of day never seemed to matter in the slums. The people here never quite went to sleep.

A whimper caught her attention. She scanned the street and spotted a nightwalker being accosted by a man who was two times her size. Tempest rose onto the balls of her feet, preparing to intervene, when the woman slapped the man across the face and stomped on his foot for good measure. The man held his hands up and back away.

"Get sober," the nightwalker hissed. "Or never see me again!"

The disturbance settled, and Tempest glanced at the small gang of children who had darted from the tavern below, crusty bread in their grubby little hands.

Tempest chuckled. She was quite certain, even from up here, that she recognized a couple of the children from the orphanage she often helped out at. The question was, had they stolen the bread, or had it been given? Probably the former. Little miscreants. An angry man ran into the street and shook his fist at the fleeing children. "If I catch you again, you won't like it!"

Stolen it was.

The children of this orphanage had always had a knack for thievery. Tempest had learned some of her best tricks from them; she owed them a great debt for bestowing on her their secrets. With a small smile, she cast her gaze to the southwest and the northeast: the merchant quadrant and the working-class quadrant. They were completely silent. Most of the residents would be in bed, likely exhausted from a hard day of work.

The final quadrant in the northwest was the most affluent part of the city, within which the palace and the seaport were situated. It, too, appeared to be dead asleep, but Tempest knew it was all a façade. The members of the upper class were secretly as rowdy as the slums, only they kept their business indoors. There were parties and violent revels and sordid affairs happening within every third or fourth grand building. The revelries wouldn't end until the sun rose, when the hedonistic upper class fell into bed only to repeat the same reckless behavior again the following night.

Dotae was huge. How many people did it hold? On the ground, it was hard to grasp the scale of the population of the capital city. Up on the roofs, however, Tempest had a bird's eye view of Dotae. She knew to triple the number of people in the slums compared to the merchant sector, and even that was a conservative estimate. All in all, Tempest imagined there were close to a million people living within Dotae's walls.

An intimidating city. There wasn't a city half as big, not for leagues and leagues.

While she enjoyed the city, even loved it, she wasn't a true resident of Dotae. In her heart, she was a forest girl. Daughter of a healer. Lover of all that was pure. It was all she had left that had been unsullied. By King Destin. By the Hounds. By the Jester himself.

Tempest was not entirely sure how to even reach the little clearing in the forest where her mother's cottage had been. It was but a faint memory, and it pained her that, with every day that passed, it grew a little fainter still. Her heart stung just as painfully as the bitter night air did her face. She was losing hold of the one clear, coherent part of her past that made her who she was. Forgetting her mother would erase the last piece of the forest girl from her soul.

Tempest could remember her mother's voice in scraps of stolen moments between dreams and wakefulness, but it was getting harder and harder for her to remember her mother's face. Did Tempest look like her mum? She slapped her cheeks to bring some heat back into them. But there was no one to answer her.

She wished there was.

Her head pulsed again, a sharp ache moving through her skull. She'd spent enough time outside. It was really time to retire to bed. She could not feel her ears, nor her fingertips. Her teeth were chattering so badly, she worried she might bite straight through her tongue. When had she gotten so cold?

On silent feet, Tempest slunk over the sea of roofs. She dropped to the street and veered to the left to take a shortcut to the barracks when a group of off-duty guards caught her eye. She resisted the urge to cover herself and held her head high as she attracted their attention. She felt naked out of her uniform. They moved in her direction before she could slink off down the street. Tempest scowled, then relaxed slightly when she realized Levka was among the group. Tempest was still not entirely sure if he was genuine or was merely using an opportunity to get closer to her now that she was on the war council. Regardless, she was relieved to see him. She would face no trouble or harassment from the guards with Levka in their presence.

"Where has our lovely Lady Hound been, then?" one of the guards asked. "The slums are not for the likes of you."

Her shoulders tensed at the name the king used for her. *A palace guard, then.*

"I could ask you the same question," Tempest replied, keeping her tone just as good-natured and jovial as the guard himself. "What are you all doing? It's so late, and we're in the slums, no less! Don't tell me you were visiting a brothel?" Her gaze slid to her friend. "Though surely not you, Levka." She made sure to emphasize his name and gave the Hound-in-training a pointed look.

Instead of blushing or turning away—which Tempest would have expected if he really, truly liked her—Levka looked indifferent instead.

Very telling.

"And what about you?" a guard whom Tempest *did* recognize fired back, grinning sleazily. "You're out just as late and in the same unscrupulous part of the city as we are. Don't tell me you have a lover here?"

There wasn't any way she was going to answer that. Either way, they'd all assume the worst.

"Oh, looks like the girlie is ashamed," a third guard said. "Don't tell me. Are you an *animal-screwer*? Is your lover a shifter? Most of the bastards in this area are. Why else would you be in the slums *alone*?"

Tempest flinched at the insinuation, not because of what it said about her, but because she now knew a fair share of shifters who were good people. She thought of Briggs, of Aspen, the fawn shifter, and his mother Rina, who had baked bread for Tempest. Most of them were good, honest people who did not deserve the ire they faced from Dotae every single day. The prejudices against the shapeshifter people were baseless and wrong.

"Bet she would like the hands of a bear or a wolf or a lion on her," the third guard taunted. "I mean," he slurred, clearly a little drunk, as they all obviously were, "she took on that beast in the ring easily enough. No *man* can handle her."

Her lip curled at the suggestion in his tone. "Well not *anyone*, to be sure. Only the strongest and brightest. Clearly, that doesn't include any of the likes of you." Not her best retort, but she couldn't stand there, silent. She arched her brow at the quiet Levka who said nothing, choosing to look at his feet instead. *Coward.*

Tempest was on her own.

"Considering your fondness for rabbit shifters," Tempest began, directing her answer at the palace guard, "and the unspeakable things you ask them to do to you, I'd say you're far more familiar with shifters in bed than I am." *Thank you, Juniper, for always gossiping with me about the goings-on in the palace.* Her smile grew as the man's face darkened. "You really should be more *discreet* about these things."

The guard did not like her response at all. "What do you think, Levka?" he asked, forcing the Hound-in-training to look up from his feet and answer the question. "You've lived with her since you were kids. Is she into shifters? Or do her tastes run even more *sordid* than that?"

Unbidden, Tempest thought of Pyre, then clucked her tongue in disgust. She stared at Levka, daring him to say something, anything.

"Well, let's just say I would never touch a woman who'd been sullied by such trash," he muttered without looking at her.

Tempest couldn't believe what she was hearing. Was he really insulting her right now? Putting himself above her? As if she was nothing beneath his feet? Was she not the Hound and he the trainee? Some days, she cursed being born a bloody woman. Had she not earned her place on the war council? But it didn't matter to them. They only cared about what body parts she hid underneath her clothing. As if that dictated her worth. While she didn't have feelings for Levka, it still hurt to have him dismiss her that way.

"No," Tempest said, firmly and slowly, so there could be no doubt about what she was saying. "I'm not an animal-screwer. Yet something tells me I would altogether prefer being one than screwing any of *you.*"

She threw a pointed look Levka's way and was once more disappointed when he did not respond. Without another word, she forced her way through the group of drunken guards and stalked back to the barracks. She was so tired and angry. Angry at King Destin, who wanted her to do *anything* to get into the good graces of the Talagan rebels. Angry at her uncles, who were likely responsible for spreading mimkia to all the villages. Angry at Pyre, who was the ruthless, cold-hearted Jester.

Yes, she was angry with Pyre more than anyone else.

She felt guilty—betrayed, even—that she had trusted him even an inkling when he clearly was no better than the people she was currently fighting against as a double agent. He was a rebel, a drug lord, someone who played with the lives of others.

What if he really was responsible for the missing children? How could she give him any of her trust at all?

Her shoulders slumped as she finally spied the door to the barracks, but it was short-lived. Her spine stiffened as Levka stepped from a shadowy corner and hovered near the door. How in the hell had he beaten her back? A tiny part of her was impressed by the speed with which he had returned to the barracks.

Long-legged bastard.

"What were you doing out all by yourself?" he demanded, though he had the sense to keep his voice hushed.

That was rich. Tempest crossed her arms over her chest, her patience about to well and truly snap. "It's none of your business, Levka."

"Right. You made that fairly clear." He sighed and rubbed at his brow. Levka's shoulders slumped, and he had the sense to look abashed. "I know you said you don't want to associate with me. I know you're not my property, and that I have no right to ask you to forgive me after what just happened. But I... I don't know what came over me back there. I don't. I shouldn't have acted like that, especially not in front of other people. It's disrespectful. I know I don't have any right to know where you were. I'm sorry."

Tempest almost caved and accepted his earnest apology.

Almost.

"I know it's easy to get wrapped up in peer pressure," she said, feeling as if she was talking to a child rather than a young man her own age. "But you should know better. We've spent most of our lives together. You should *want* to defend me, especially if you care for me, Levka. And even if you didn't know me, you shouldn't have let those men talk to me like that." She swallowed hard. "You joined in without much hesitation."

"Temp—"

"Saying sorry does not excuse your actions tonight, and you know it. If your behavior taught me anything, it taught me that you and I are not right for each other." She opened the door to the barracks and looked him straight in the eye. "We don't have a future together, and I won't change my mind about that."

Tempest stepped inside and slammed the door in Levka's face before he had the chance to respond. Her heart clenched at the pain that had flashed across his face. She leaned against the door, breathing heavily. She immediately felt terrible about her needlessly harsh rejection. *Don't think about it.*

"Next time you sneak in, don't slam the damn door," Dima muttered from his bunk.

"Sorry," Tempest whispered. She didn't mean to disturb the whole place. She crept to her bed and managed to kick off her boots and drop her cloak to the floor before crawling under the sheets, still wearing the dress and all.

Tomorrow, she'd deal with everything on her plate. For now, she'd sleep.

CHAPTER 6: TEMPEST

*W*inter's bite, she hated morning.

Tempest felt like death, yet she dragged herself out of bed to eat breakfast at the palace with the war council and the royal family. It had become a regular part of her routine over the last several days.

It was a mistake.

Her new morning ritual pained her to the point that she hardly ate anything. Sitting among scheming war criminals dampened one's appetite. Tempest rubbed at her eyes. Bloody hell, she was exhausted. What she wouldn't give just to crawl back into bed.

"Excellent!" King Destin said joyfully.

Her lip curled. Morning people. Depraved, morning people were a blight on the world. She wiped her disdain from her face and sighed, her gaze flicking toward the king. What had the monarch and his lackies concocted the night before once she'd been dismissed?

Destin stood, his chair scraping across the floor noisily. Tempest straightened as all eyes were riveted in the king's direction.

He smiled, his handsome face lighting up. "My sons will be leaving for Kopal in three days hence," King Destin announced.

That was sooner than expected. Such a trip took preparation and time. How long had the king been planning this? What was his end goal? With the rising rebellion, why didn't he want his sons close? Risking his sons' lives on the road was careless. Her mind flashed to what the Jester had said the night before—that knowing the princes were going to leave Dotae could be useful. Why would the king announce his sons' travel plans like he was? Moving his sons in secret was safer. Was he trying to flush out a traitor? If so, it was stupid to gamble with his heirs.

"It will do the kingdom some good," Destin continued. "It will be to our benefit to show that we are willing and ready to make alliances with other nations, especially in these trying times with the Talagans." He sat as his war council fawned over him.

Her skin prickled. Someone was watching her. Tempest glanced to her left and caught the attention of Ansette who was sitting beside her. How had she not noticed the princess before? She swiped a hand over her face. Stupid mornings.

The look in the girl's eyes told Tempest loud and clear that the princess did not think it was a good idea to send her brothers away so early, either, and that there was therefore something much larger at play right now. Ansette stabbed at a boiled egg on her plate.

Tempest slid her gaze to the king. Did he know his daughter was clearly unenthused with his decisions? That sort of discontent among royals was dangerous. The girl was going to get herself killed if she didn't start learning to hide her feelings. Tempest once again rubbed her temples, feeling sick and stressed. Between what the king had—and hadn't—said, the way Pyre had acted as the Jester the night before, and even how Levka had treated her, Tempest was rung out. Now, she also had a dissatisfied, intelligent princess to keep an eye on.

It was too much. She couldn't take being around people anymore.

Tempest stood abruptly, clattering her knife and fork onto her plate of largely uneaten food. She muttered an apology and fled the banquet hall before a single word could be said to keep her in place.

She needed a distraction from all the treachery, politics, and mind games. Tempest needed to fight.

Forlornly, she thought back to a few short months ago when all she had to worry about was her trial to join the Hounds. Everything had been simple then. Easy.

It had all been a lie.

Nothing was easy.

The next day was filled with Tempest training, training, training, until her body felt like it might break. But with every day that it didn't, it instead grew stronger and leaner and harder.

Tempest trained until she could almost ignore the fact that she was a double agent.

Almost.

Stars, she loved physical activity—how it suited her soul and made her feel in control of herself. But it wasn't helping like it normally did. Tempest snarled and violently shot an arrow. It hit the target and shattered on impact. She heaved in a breath, sweat dripping down her neck. That might have been a tad aggressive.

"Careful, Tempest," Madrid said sternly from his position overlooking the training grounds. "That's your third one this week. Surely, you do not want to ask the king for more arrows."

She stiffened at his tone. Uneasy, Tempest shifted, and her fingers tightened around her bow. What exactly did Madrid know about her arrangement with king? Anything? He had to know something. He was *the Madrid*—the King's Sword.

Heat rushed into her cheeks in embarrassment at the king's suggestion from the night before. She still did not understand why he had ordered her to do *anything necessary* on her next mission. His insinuation had been obvious, but if he was as personally interested in Tempest as he had previously let on, then why would he want her sleeping with the Talagan rebels? Perhaps it was all a show to make sure the other members of the war council knew that he was in control of her.

That soured her mood further.

Instead of verbally answering Madrid's question, Tempest nodded. He pursed his lips in a rare show of emotion. Clearly, she'd needled him. He turned from Tempest to oversee another group of archers who were gawking at her.

Time for Tempest to move on to something else. The sword.

She moved over to the circular arena preserved for close-combat fighting. There was nobody else there. Thank Dotae. Her mood was as black as the Jester's heart. Carefully, she leaned her quiver and bow against the post and pulled her sword from her scabbard before clambering over the ropes to begin swinging the sword in practiced movements. No one approached. A humorless smile touched her mouth. It seemed as if nobody would dare to spar with her in her current mood.

So, instead of sparring, she satisfied herself with moving through different stances and combat patterns until her temper was quelled somewhat and her transitions from one move to the next were as fluid as water. Losing herself in such movements brought peace and centered her. The world ceased to exist.

Sweat pooled beneath her corset, her arms ached, and yet, she carried on. Tempest swung but halted abruptly as she caught sight of a visitor who'd snuck up on her. A visitor that had the attention of the entire barracks.

She moaned softly. Why did he have to intrude on her peace now? She tried to catch her breath, chest heaving, and considered ignoring the observer entirely. But it wasn't possible. There were consequences to ignoring a king. Tempest sheathed her sword, all the while staring at the ground. Time to face the devil.

Lifting her gaze, she impassively eyed the intimidating figure of King Destin. Disturbing, really. He was splendid, even in a plain white shirt, high-waisted black trousers, and knee-high boots. She was struck by how much younger than his years he looked in such casual clothes. Even in simple garb, he commanded attention.

Destin ran a hand through his auburn hair and beckoned for her to come closer. That rankled her. He called her like she was a blowsy wench. Tempest pressed her lips together and forced herself forward, knowing she couldn't refuse. She paused just out of reach, a respectable distance. No need to give the gossips of the barracks anything more to blather about. Then there was the fact that, deep down, she was scared Destin would somehow smell betrayal on her.

The king smiled. "Why so far away?" he asked, the picture of politeness. But there was a glint in his eye that told Tempest he thoroughly enjoyed the challenge of putting her on the spot.

"Forgive me, Your Majesty," she said, bowing slightly. "I thought you would not enjoy the smell of me. Right now, I am soaked in sweat; it is not pleasant." She'd thrown down the gauntlet. No man enjoyed a smelly woman.

The king threw his head back and laughed, his tan throat exposed. He dropped his head, his golden eyes twinkling with mirth. "Humor me. Come closer, Tempest."

Damn it. Nothing to be done but obey—to openly defy him would be inadvisable at best—and so she slowly closed the distance between herself and Destin and climbed over the fence. No sooner had her feet touched ground, when he pushed her against a rough wooden post. He brushed a lock of sweat-drenched hair from Tempest's face.

Destin licked his plush lips. "I'd rather be the one to help you work up a sweat, all things considered," he said, voice low.

The dirty knave.

On purpose, Tempest misunderstood him. "That could be dangerous for your health, Your Majesty. I'm quite deadly with a blade, as you well know." She smiled as if she had genuinely misinterpreted the king's comment, but her ruse was no use. Tempest watched King Destin's Adam's apple move as he swallowed, a small smile playing about his lips.

"I am aware," he murmured. "I like a little risk."

Her eyes widened as she understood what he intended to do a mere moment before he did it.

The king kissed her.

She wanted nothing more than to recoil, but with the post behind her and everyone's eyes on them, she had no choice but to put up with the king's assault. Her stomach twisted, and she focused on the way the wood dug into her spine and pressed into the back of her skull. Her pulse picked up when he pressed his mouth harder against hers and swiped his tongue against her closed lips, evidently wanting her to open to him.

Like hell. Instead, she bit his lower lip. *Hard.*

Destin jerked and broke the kiss. Her chest brushed his as she tried to catch her breath. A small bit of blood dotted his lip, and bile burned the back of her throat. She'd marked the king. Others had died for such a trespass.

He flicked his tongue against his busted lip, and a slow smile crossed his face, his eyes heating further. Horror churned in her belly. If anything, he looked at her with even more lust than before. What kind of deviant was he? His amber eyes dragged themselves up and down her heaving chest and shaking legs— her weakness was fully on display. Did he enjoy being the one in control? His personality certainly suggested so. She supposed she should not be that surprised, given how many mistresses King Destin was known to have had. His sexual proclivities were not likely to be all that plain.

Not knowing what else to do, Tempest ducked under King Destin's arms, mumbling, "I have to go."

She knew the king's eyes were on her, so Tempest made sure not to run. She kept her steps slow and deliberate, leaving her back uncomfortably exposed. She had barely made it five feet from the man before he called out, "Don't have too much fun with the rebels."

Tempest shuddered. Despite what the king had said the day before about having her do *anything* to infiltrate the Talagan rebels, *this* felt far more like his actual order.

And it sounded like a threat.

Exhausted, with muscles crying from all the physical exertion and a near-permanent headache coloring her vision, Tempest stalked back to the barracks, thinking that she'd rather sleep the entire day away. She swiped her mouth with the back of her hand. Scrubbing the king's slobber off of her was top priority.

She missed a step when she spotted an interloper in the barracks. Her lip curled.

Pyre. The Jester. He lay sprawled across her bunk with a lazy grace that spoke of dark nights and silk sheets. Could she not catch a break? First, the king, and, now, the kitsune? Surely, a higher power was conspiring against her.

Tempest's hand flew to the hilt of her sword entirely on instinct even as she slammed her door shut to protect the two of them from prying eyes. Her brow twitched, the lingering headache on the verge of becoming a full-on migraine simply from looking at Pyre smoking a pipe without a care in the world while he so clearly watched her reaction, with twitching fox ears and amused, golden eyes.

A bloody pipe.

"Just what in the name of Dotae are you doing here?" she hissed, glancing around the empty barracks as if there was someone lurking in the shadows.

"Can't I miss you?" he crooned.

CHAPTER 7: PYRE

*I*t had been several years since Pyre had entered the city walls of Dotae through a proper entrance. Nobody knew him there, so he could very well have walked straight through the city gates without much trouble. All he would have had to do was resist the urge to show off, hide his shifter features, and keep his eyes downcast so nobody noticed the shine to his golden irises. But he'd never taken the easy route. It had become a game of sorts, finding new ways to infiltrate Heimserya.

And today was no different.

His reluctance to use the city gates this time around had some relation to his work. Tam was a problem. At one time, the smuggler had been as trustworthy as a smuggler could be, but the man was cagey. Well, cagier than normal. Something wasn't right. Pyre was determined to figure out what was afoot. Earlier, he'd sauntered into Dotae through the slum quadrant without a problem. So how in the blazes had his men been caught? There hadn't even been any guards for hours. It had been an easy journey over the ramshackle roofs of the slums.

Even though it had been years since he had been in Dotae, Pyre still knew perfectly well where the Hound barracks was. He traipsed through the city, taking in every sight, sound, and smell. Sewage permeated the air of the slums. The poorer district hadn't changed since his last visit.

The pleasant smell of baked bread drifted by him as he crossed through the merchant quarter, though Pyre was proud to admit that Rina's bakery in the forest smelled better. He hated the merchant quarter. It was full of crooks and too loud for his ears. Merchants were the worse. They paraded themselves around as honest folk while robbing people blind. They were the real thieves. At least Pyre didn't pretend he was something he wasn't. Anyone who came to him knew exactly what they were getting into. He did not hide his nature, never had.

The barracks came into view, and he scanned the area. This was where he needed to exercise extreme caution, mindful of any approaching footsteps. Infiltrating the Hounds was easy, but it paid to be cautious. It had saved his life many times.

Pyre sniffed the air. A small rumble escaped him at the tell-tale female scent.

Tempest. His Hound.

His lip curled. The Hound. She wasn't his.

Yet.

Her scent was faint at first, for the air was full of the sour stench of sweat from training members of the Hounds, the tang of metal swords clashing against each other and the overwhelming, acrid bitterness of smoke from a fire. Pyre nosed in and out of various rooms in the barracks, unable to help himself from pilfering a few weapons and interesting items that took his fancy. They wouldn't miss them.

A dagger with a carved bone handle. An ornate key that was so expensively made it had to be protecting something valuable. Pyre loved a good puzzle, and he would enjoy discovering what the key unlocked. He discovered a map of Dotae with several seemingly innocuous areas of the city circled in bright red ink.

Another puzzle.

Lastly, Pyre stole an emerald ring from the barracks. It was too slender to fit upon his fingers, which meant it was likely a keepsake of some female relative of a Hound. Pyre felt no sympathy for the Hound who would discover it gone. They were paid murderers.

He neared the final barracks building. Tempest's scent was stronger. A thrill of excitement caused his heartbeat to quicken. The smell of the female Hound always caused such a physical reaction from him. What was it about her that riled him? He used to resent it, but now he had grown to accept that some visceral, animal instinct in him was irrefutably drawn to the woman.

Pyre glanced around and quickly scaled the side of the building to peek inside. It was a long rectangular room full of beds with a large fireplace at one end and a door at the other. Completely empty. Excellent.

Quickly, he picked the lock on the window and slid the glass pane out of the way, before carefully slipping inside and closing the window behind him. Pyre dropped to the stone floor, landing on the balls of his feet. He scanned the room once more for any hidden enemies. He found none. It was a drab room—

all utility and no luxury. Beds ran along the two, long parallel walls with weapons scattered about.

This was where his enemies rested. A surge of energy and adrenaline rushed through him. He was in their den, and they knew nothing of it.

His men hated him putting himself at such a risk, and, in truth, Pyre agreed with them. If he was in their position, he would not want the Jester crawling through Dotae simply to nose around the barracks of the king's assassins.

Tempest's scent grew stronger still, and he paused by the only bed with a privacy wall next to it. He ran his fingers along the chest at the end of the bed and then across the plain blanket covering her mattress. The urge to roll on her bed pricked him. He squashed it and froze when a noise outside the window gave him pause.

He stepped onto her bed and looked through the glass window above. The hair along his arms rose, and his lip curled back from his teeth. King Destin in the flesh. The bastard's attention was pinned to the female in the ring who moved like water and sin, her periwinkle hair whipping with her movements.

Tempest.

Pyre looked on, observing the macabre scene as the king waved Tempest over. At first, it was funny, the way Tempest clearly did not want to come close to Destin even though she was being commanded to, but then Pyre noticed the genuine fear flitting across her face. That was dangerous. Pyre knew the king could smell fear miles away. He fed on it. Enjoyed it.

The king pinned Tempest against a wooden pole and kissed her.

A snarl formed in the back of Pyre's throat, and his claws

pierced the skin of his fingers, lengthening. The obvious desire in King Destin's face when Tempest bit his lip sent Pyre into a confusing rage. How dare that mongrel touch what was *his*. His entire body hovered on the edge of rage as the king's gaze roved over Tempest like she was his property, his alone.

Mine.

His claws dug into the window frame. He could do nothing about the situation and had no right to interfere with whatever was going on.

Get a hold of yourself.

The practical part of him filed what he'd seen in the back of his mind; it could prove useful in the future. Though Tempest had been cagey about answering any questions about King Destin before, Pyre had always known that there was more to her feelings for the king than mere fear for a manipulative ruler. Now, he was beginning to grasp just exactly what was going on.

Whether Tempest enjoyed the attentions or not, he pitied her. The king's advances were not something he'd wish on his worst enemy. He'd seen the effects of what Destin's attentions begot. Pyre stopped his thoughts there. No need to go down memory lane.

He forced himself to release the windowsill and frowned at the claw marks he'd left. That was unfortunate. Nothing to be done. Tempest ducked underneath the king's arm and moved toward the barracks. Pyre smiled to himself as he caught the look on Tempest's face. She didn't look pleased. That brought him more pleasure than it should have.

Chuckling quietly at himself, he sat down and then stretched out across her bed. From her expression, she looked as prickly as a porcupine. Their next interaction would be spicy, and he couldn't wait. Her scent teased his nose, and he couldn't help but roll around on her bed, rumpling the cover and spreading his scent everywhere.

You poor sod. Knock it off.

Pyre frowned at himself. He could not afford to care for the Hound. She was useful to him, and he was useful to her. Their relationship was one of business. So why couldn't he get the last time they touched out of his head? Instead of attacking him when he was weak, she embraced him. Why? What did she seek to gain? His trust?

Familiar footsteps approached the door, and he shook the thoughts away. He had to be every inch the arrogant, charming, self-serving fox shifter Tempest knew and loathed. A smirk twisted his lips. She would hate to see him on her bed more than anywhere else. For that fact alone, it was worth creeping into Dotae just for the expression on her face.

The door opened, then closed so violently that its hinges rattled. Tempest blinked slowly when she caught sight of him, then flames leapt in her gaze, and his heart picked up pace. This was what he craved. The banter. The fight. With her.

The Lady Hound was rattled.

"Pyre," Tempest said, so quietly it could barely be counted as speaking. The horrified, furious look on her face was priceless. Pyre's mouth split into a grin immediately. "What the hell are you doing here?"

CHAPTER 8: TEMPEST

"*D*on't make me repeat myself," Tempest hissed. "What the hell are you doing here, Pyre?"

The fox shifter twisted around until he was lying on his front, chin resting on his hands. "I thought you might have missed me," he mocked and batted his long lashes. God, he set her teeth on edge. "It has been so long," the Jester lamented.

"I saw you *yesterday*," she bit out. "Or did you forget about the fact you had me dragged to your bloody cave in the middle of the night?" The back of her head throbbed with pain at the memory.

Pyre waved a dismissive hand. "You left without saying goodbye," he complained. He pouted, his lush bottom lip sticking out. "It offends me that you felt the need to sneak out, love."

She was *not* his love.

"It offends me that your man clubbed me over the head like

a barbarian."

He smiled, flashing just a little fang. "Can't help it, love. All my men dream of dragging a delectable female back to their lairs. You, on the other hand, have been very rude." She flushed when he sat up and swung his legs over the side of her bed, then leaned back, lounging on her bed like he owned the thing, legs apart. The picture of self-indulgent nobility.

Bastard.

"Get off my bed," she demanded.

He ran a hand over her coverlet. "While plain and a bit crude, I like my current spot. Now tread carefully, or I might take offense at your inhospitality."

"Inhospitality?" Tempest muttered. She shook her head. What was she doing bickering with him in the middle of the Hound barracks? Someone could walk in at any moment. She stomped to the end of the bed, scowling at him. "What are you doing here, Pyre?" she repeated. "Your presence here could ruin everything I have been working so hard for. This is careless, even for you. What is so important that you—"

Pyre pulled an ivory card from inside his leather waistcoat and held it out to her, cutting off her sentence. She eyed it like it would bite her. He poked her in the arm with the sharp edge, and she reacted on reflex, slapping it out of his hand. It fell to the ground with a dull thump. The surface was silvered. Was it an invitation?

"Why did you do that?" the kitsune asked. "I wasn't going to slit your throat with it."

She glared at him. "Why. Are. You. Here?" she demanded through gritted teeth, resisting the urge to slap the man. He was on her last nerve, and all she wanted to do was brush her teeth and wash her face. She swore she could still taste the king.

Pyre eyed her, a devilish twinkle in his eye. "Is your tetchy mood something to do with the time of the month?"

He didn't.

"Excuse me?"

His gaze narrowed on her chest. "Your breasts are bigger, and you're prickly. Plus, your scent is sour."

Her vision turned red, and she launched toward him. His eyes rounded as she crashed into his chest and then tumbled him back onto the bed. She straddled Pyre and pressed her dagger beneath his chin, breathing hard. He smiled at her and arched a brow, like he was amused with her antics.

"Why is it that every time a woman has a valid point, the male species finds a way to make it about the perceived weakness of the female body? Being angry at you isn't a product of my moon time, but of your stupidity," she growled, pressing the blade of her dagger a little harder against his neck. Pyre shifted and Tempest froze as a dangerously sharp claw prickled the soft skin under her chin. Damn shapeshifter. "Do you have any idea of the pressure I'm under right now?" she asked, ignoring the claw. "From all angles, I'm given commands and orders which I either have to obey or decide to ignore. Every choice I make has repercussions for those around me. I'm putting my life in jeopardy as well as those I love." Traitorous heat pressed at the back of her eyes. Like hell would she cry. "*And* I'm getting no sleep because people like *you* keep dragging me off in the middle of the night. So, the least you could do, is answer my questions!"

She flinched when he removed his claw from her throat. Her breath caught in surprise when he touched her cheek so softly. The pads of his calloused fingers and the tips of his claws running along her skin caused her to shiver. What was he doing?

"Sorry," he said, very quietly. "I'm sorry, Temp."

Her anger drained away as quickly as it came, and she sagged against him. At least he sounded genuine—until he ruined it.

"Though," he continued on, in a completely different tone of voice, "if your instinct is to climb all over me when you're angry, then I can't really be all that sorry about igniting your temper." A slow smile curled onto his lips, and the air seemed to heat around them. "If you wanted to get me on my back, all you had to do was ask."

Tempest snarled and rolled off him. "You're such a pig." She couldn't get away from him fast enough. She hovered at the foot of the bed as Pyre sat up, rubbing his neck.

He chuckled and shook his head. "Kitsune, not pig," he corrected. "Open the letter. You'll get your answer."

She glanced at the invitation where it lay abandoned on the floor. Tempest reached down to retrieve it and used her dagger to open the envelope. Her brows furrowed when she unfolded it. The card was blank. What the bloody hell?

She frowned at Pyre. "What is this?" she asked. A secret form of communication?

Pyre tsked. "So curious. I like that about you."

Tempest rolled her eyes and frowned as he gracefully climbed to his feet on her bed and glanced out of the window. "What are you doing?"

"I'd think it was obvious?" He cracked his knuckles and rolled his neck.

"You're leaving?" What was going on?

"You need to pack," he said, his gaze focused on something

in the distance. "We have to leave. There are so many things to do."

She waved the invitation at him. "Tell me what this is," she insisted. "How else am I supposed to know what it is? It's *blank*."

Her eyes rounded as his nails lengthened, and he used them to easily open the window. *Too* easily. They needed better locks on the windows. Pyre perched on the sill and sniffed the air in a decidedly foxlike manner. He turned slightly, cocking his head to one side as he stared down at Tempest. He had to be the most exasperating creature in the world.

"Was this all a show?" she hissed. "Just to let me know you could get to me any time you wanted?"

"You're much too suspicious for someone so young," he commented.

"That's a little like the pot calling the kettle black, isn't it?"

A slow grin spread across his face. "Bring something nice to wear. And I mean *really* nice, not your reluctant approximation of nice."

Tempest gaped at him. Rude. She had excellent taste and style.

"What for?" she demanded. "Pyre, either you answer my questions or so help me—"

"Leave the city as soon as you can," he interrupted. "I will find you soon." Then, he leapt out the window, disappearing from sight at a speed completely impossible for a mere human to achieve.

What had just happened? She blinked slowly. Once. Twice.

"Unbelievable! He is completely impossible!" She glanced around the empty room and back to the window. Tempest had more unanswered questions now than she did before. What was this visit *for*?

CHAPTER 9: TEMPEST

He'd disappeared like a bloody specter.

Tempest stared out of the window, trying to figure out how he managed to ghost the Hounds' training yard without being caught. Wicked hell, he drove her nuts. Her fingers twitched at her sides, aggravation pulsing through her veins. His dramatic visit had thrown her off kilter. Why would he risk so much by coming here? Was it a test? Was he spying on her? Was it a test of mental warfare?

She dropped to her bed, bouncing. Tempest leaned back against her pillow. Pyre's smug expression was burned into her mind. Or was his visit just an adrenaline high for the cocky kitsune? Surely, he wouldn't be that stupid... Had she really bruised his ego the night before when she'd disappeared? He couldn't have been that offended if his wolf had escorted her out. Plus, what was she supposed to have done? He'd been in the middle of intimidating a creepy subordinate. Nothing could have convinced her to hang around and witness more of his act as the Jester.

"And besides," she grumbled, closing her eyes against the headache that never seemed to leave her these days, "the argument we'd been having wasn't exactly one that would be good to have continued."

Stop talking to yourself.

Exhaustion and anger were not the best companions while she was trying to outmaneuver the enemy... Well, Pyre was an uneasy ally, at the very least. He wasn't the hero, and last night proved that even further. He all but flaunted his position of authority in the underworld. Their conversation from the night before still chilled her. Lives weren't worth anything to him—even the lives of his own men.

How much do you think he values your life?

A wry smile twisted her lips. *Not much,* she mused. Their relationship was tenuous at best; after last night, Tempest had wondered how they'd interact with each other going forward. With the way Pyre had just treated her, it seemed he had no qualms about going back to the way they were before she knew his identity. What did that mean? She didn't know if it was a good or bad thing. Regardless, she'd have to tread carefully. Pyre was playing games with her. He wasn't the jovial fox from the forest. He was the Jester. A dangerous criminal with ties to the Dark Court. She didn't doubt for one second that he would plant a knife in her back if need be.

Not if you get him first.

She stared at the ceiling as her annoyance crept in. He hadn't explained a single thing to her. Her brows furrowed. Apparently, he didn't have any important news to pass on, so did that mean she was a side quest? Irritation pricked her at the notion. Tempest scowled at the ceiling and shoved the feelings down, not wanting to examine why it bothered her so.

Why was he really in the capital?

Tempest breathed in deeply, trying to center herself. Pine, spice, and a male scent swirled around her. She jerked upright and glared at her pillow. Even without a shifter nose, she could scent Pyre on her sheets. What had he done, rolled all over them? She huffed. Why did he smell so good?

He smells of home.

Too enticing.

"Bloody male."

She forced herself out of bed, hating how her thoughts kept circling back to Pyre, no matter how she tried to wave them off. Tempest yanked the bedding from her mattress. There was no way she was sleeping in a bed that smelled like the Jester. She dropped the linens at the end of her bed and eyed the blank invitation sitting on the trunk. She plucked it from the surface and held it up to the light, inspecting it carefully.

It couldn't truly be blank.

She turned the card this way and that. And then, between one blink and the next, the invitation caught the last ray of sunlight streaming through her window. Tempest squinted. Etched into the card in an impossibly intricate fashion was, unmistakably, a mask.

"What do we have here?" she whispered.

The handiwork was beautiful. She'd never seen anything like it. Tempest ran her finger over the mask. She couldn't feel a difference between the art and the card stock. What sort of trickery and magic was this? What was it for? Pyre had said to wear something nice. Could it be for a party or event? Maybe a gathering of rebels? She smiled. If that was the case, there's no way he would let her near it. She knew he trusted her about as much as she trusted him.

A criminal gathering, then.

It would be so easy to just ignore the Jester's orders and stay right where she was. He didn't have any authority over her, but the king did. He'd given her the order to leave on her mission. Glancing around the empty barracks, she sighed. Better to leave now before Destin checked up on her.

She tucked the card into the top of her steel-boned corset and adjusted her shirt, so she was properly covered. Next, Tempest packed her bag—two changes of practical clothing and many more weapons—purposely leaving behind anything that was feminine. The kitsune didn't get to dictate what she wore.

"I'm a Hound. An assassin. A warrior."

She'd be damned if she was going to play dress-up for anyone, let alone her enemy. She and Pyre may well have had a common goal, but that didn't mean they were on the same side. She'd be mistaken in thinking they were true allies. At the end of the day, they were enemies down to their very core.

And war was coming.

She eyed the empty tub at the rear of the room. It would have been nice to bathe before she left, but it wouldn't be practical. Traveling was a dirty venture. No need to waste more time. She clasped her cloak around her throat and tossed her knapsack over her shoulder. Time to go.

Her steps were steady as she exited the barracks, intent on heading to the city gates and procuring a horse. She paused as Madrid pushed from the side of the barracks and into her path.

Her heart leapt. How long had he been standing there? Did he know she was a traitor? Oh god, she was going to die. She swallowed and forced herself to remain calm. If he had proof, she'd already be in chains.

Tempest approached him, her gait even, as her heart galloped. She paused before him and waited for him to say something.

He didn't. How typical of Madrid.

He merely nodded at Tempest and indicated for her to follow him, then proceeded to wind through the city.

The silence between them stretched on for what felt like forever. Her nerves were now somewhat calmed, but she kept a close eye on the street. The Hounds were trained to be invisible. If they wanted, they could haul her off the street without anyone noticing. It used to comfort her. She felt safe and protected. Now, it only brewed unease.

That's what happens when you betray your kingdom and family.

She sucked in a sharp breath and ignored Madrid as he eyed her. They neared the tunnel parallel to the merchant docks—an exit out of Dotae reserved only for those with special permission from the king. One moment, she could hear the waves crashing against the jetties. The next, Tempest dutifully followed Madrid into the darkness of the tunnel, which swallowed all sounds but the echoes of their boots on the stone. Was this how she died? Her fingers moved to the daggers at her hips. She couldn't fight off Madrid, but she wouldn't go down without a fight. If this was the end, she'd die as a warrior.

Nothing happened.

Her nerves were frayed and raw by the time they stopped a little way outside of the city walls. Madrid turned to face her, his expression as implacable as ever. It was as if the man had no feelings. She eyed the nearby forest. Had they set up an ambush for her away from the city?

You're becoming a paranoid freak.

He rolled his neck and then focused back on her. "Remember your training, Tempest. Don't be rash. Serve your kingdom well."

She nodded.

He opened his mouth and then closed it, an emotion flashing through his eyes too quickly for her to decipher. She blinked. That was odd. What was bothering Madrid?

He nodded and then spun on his heel, the black tunnel swallowing his retreating form. She stared over her shoulder. What had that been about? She slowly turned around and looked forward. Time to march into the proverbial lion's den of the rebels.

When you dance with the devil, you risk becoming the devil yourself...

If dealing with the Jester directly—if only playing along with his game—was the cost Tempest had to pay in order to figure out what the hell was happening to her kingdom, then Tempest would gladly sell her soul.

She could only hope it would never come to that.

CHAPTER 10: TEMPEST

Tempest shouldered her pack and skirted the edge of the forest which tapered off onto a white, sandy beach. She inhaled deeply, enjoying the scent of the salty sea and the crashing of waves against the shore. The icy wind whipped her cloak around her boots as she picked her way along the shoreline. It would have been easier to cut through the trees, but she needed a moment to collect her thoughts, and she wanted to avoid any of the little villages that ran along the outskirts of the woods. Who knew what was lurking nearby. And Tempest, herself, was hardly inconspicuous.

Black clouds loomed in the distance, hovering above the sea like buzzards over a carcass. A burst of wind slammed into her, yanking her hood from her head. That was her cue to leave. She didn't want to be anywhere near the coastline when the storm hit. Winter storms were the worst. Every year, the storms sank ships, ripped trees from the earth, and destroyed parts of the port.

Tempest turned east and moved through the trees, their boughs waving high above her in a pagan dance. Her tread was soft on the bed of pine needles beneath her boots. The woods thickened, and she pulled her hood over her hair, eyes continuously scanning the forest. All seemed calm, but that was the trick. The deeper one wandered into the woods, the more danger one encountered. She shivered as she remembered previously fleeing in the darkness and plunging into the pit. This time, she had to be more careful.

Time passed, and Tempest moved on, ghosting through the forest. Hours passed, and sweat dampened her temples, despite the frigid temperature. Tempest huffed out, irritated. The damned kitsune had told her to meet him in the woods, but he hadn't said where. Her belly growled when early afternoon hit, and Pyre was still nowhere to be seen. She pulled some dried meat from her sack and gnawed on it. Where the hell was he? Why would he insist she meet him if he didn't intend on showing up?

Tempest sat down on a moss-covered rock with a disgruntled sigh.

More games.

She tossed a handful of dried nuts into her mouth and chewed. She could simply turn back, but that wouldn't really do any good. Destin wanted her to infiltrate the rebels. He expected her to disappear for some time. She smiled wryly and took a swig from her waterskin. She was in the Jester's domain now. No doubt, he'd find her eventually. She tipped her head back and eyed the faint light shining through the tops of the trees. If she could get high enough, then she could spot the river and follow that. Perhaps, she could discover the village where Aspen and Rina lived until Pyre decided to show his rotten mug.

The hairs along her arms rose, and Tempest stopped chewing. The woods were now silent. She released the daggers from her wrist sheaths and slowly pushed to her feet, her eyes and ears straining to discover a hint of what had spooked the birds and woodland creatures into silence. Was it a friend, foe, or the Jester?

She heard a subtle but distinct shift in the trees behind her. Tempest spun around, cocked her head to one side, and listened intently. Nothing. Her lips twitched. Whoever was watching her was not very good at remaining undetected.

"Show yourself," she demanded.

"You do not get to command me, dog," an annoyingly familiar voice growled, dripping with displeasure.

Lovely. Tempest's mood fell, and she straightened somewhat, daggers loosely in hand. "Brine." The wolf shifter stalked from the trees, finally making himself known. "Where is—"

"Too busy to deal with the likes of you," he interrupted, thrusting a small note toward her.

"What is this?" Tempest asked, frowning. She sheathed her daggers and eyed the prickly shifter.

"Read it. Or do they not teach your mongrel group how to?"

Tempest rolled her eyes and resisted the urge to punch Brine in the face. That wouldn't help. Brawling with the wolf wouldn't solve anything... Although, the satisfaction of hitting him *would* give her immense joy, she was sure.

He huffed and waved the note impatiently at her. Tempest

snatched the note from him and opened it. She eyed elegant, slanted handwriting scrawled across the paper.

Temp,

Brine needs your assistance in retrieving my stolen property. His bark is worse than his bite.

Fox

P.S. I lied. His bite hurts.

She snorted and arched a brow. How typical of the Jester.

Tempest lifted her gaze and stared pointedly at Brine. "Apparently, I am supposed to help you receive his property from a thief," she said.

The wolf's lips thinned, but he said nothing, merely nodding before turning tail and walking through the trees, in the direction of the coast. She sighed. Why in the blazes would Pyre team her up with Brine? The shifter had no love for her. Chances were Brine would be happy to take her out and leave her corpse behind for scavengers. She'd have to keep an eye on him. The idea of finding Rina's village still held appeal, but ultimately, the venture was pointless. While she did not want to dance on the Jester's puppet strings, there wasn't much of a choice. Perhaps, she'd gain more info tailing Brine anyhow.

She adjusted the sack on her shoulder and jogged to catch up with the moody shifter. "So, where are we going?"

He said nothing. For three bloody hours.

They broke through the forest edge and began winding their way north, up the coast, following the path that Tempest had originally taken. Annoyance pricked her. She'd wasted hours walking. *Hours.* She winced when her left foot slipped and a sharp piece of granite poked her ankle through the worn leather. "Is there an easier way of getting to wherever we're going?"

"Giving up already?"

For Dotae's sake. "No," she gritted out. "But I'm not a blasted mountain goat. This side hill and shale is killing my ankles." Her gaze moved to the steep drop-off. "One slip, and I'd be dead." She paused. "Unless that's what your goal is?"

Brine snorted. He glanced over his shoulder, amusement in his dark gaze, all the while still managing to avoid every divot and pointed rock. "That would be too easy." The shifter faced forward. "To answer your first question, we're heading to a northern port city." He paused. "Can't remember the name of it to save my life. I hate the sea."

"So, can't we cut across easier ground to—"

"Are you telling me, a wolf, how to best navigate the environment around me to reach a destination?" he growled.

Tempest bristled. "No, but if we keep heading this way, we'll hit the docks outside of Demrias. Don't you want to avoid the trading city?"

Brine barked out a laugh. "We can pass through the docks no problem. Just cover your hair. If we navigate *around* the city, our journey will take hours longer than it should, and we'll risk getting spotted by the perimeter guards. Now, shut up and walk, dog."

Insufferable bastard.

Well, he wasn't wrong about the shortcut, but she had enough bossy males in her life. It would be so easy to dig her heels in and fight him. But… it was clear that Brine was the Jester's right-hand man, which meant it was important for her to try to make nice with the grumpy shifter, even if he had no qualms about killing her. She watched the tall, lithe man lope gracefully ahead of her, moving so quickly she had to jog to keep up with him.

And the good times just kept rolling. Brine never slowed other than when they passed through the docks outside of Demrias—Tempest's nerves twisted her stomach this way and that the entire time they were there. The journey was relentlessly fast and uneventful, but eventually they passed by a village a few hours north of Demrias, sitting right on the edge of the coast.

Her stomach grumbled loudly. Winter's bite, she was hungry, and her legs ached. She needed to up her strength training. "Can we stop at the inn here?" she asked, noticing the tell-tale signs of cat ears and large, owlish eyes on a few of the villagers standing outside of said establishment. "It's a shifter village, so won't they—"

"Absolutely not," Brine cut in, fervently shaking his head.

"But—"

"Not all shifters are on our side. I thought even you were smart enough to know that. And keep your hair tucked away or you'll get us both killed."

Tempest ignored the jibe, though it took a lot of effort to do so, and double-checked her hood. Her hair was tucked away.

"Perhaps they simply want to go about their lives," she reasoned, giving the inn a final, wishful glance as they moved around the bitty village and even farther north. "Not everyone is a fighter, Brine."

"They are cowards," he said, spitting out the last word. "They are complacent. They think if they don't get involved then they won't get hurt? It's madness."

"Maybe protecting their own families is all they can do right now."

"The only way to protect their families is to fight with an organized, collective front."

Tempest considered his words. Brine wasn't wrong, though he wasn't completely right, either. "They're farmers. How do you expect them to fight? They've had no training."

Brine said nothing to continue the debate, so they soldiered onward in now-familiar silence as the sun's rays bled out of the sky and the dark clouds crept even closer.

Full darkness had descended by the time the two of them arrived at their destination. Tempest vaguely recognized the city, though. How did she know this place? She'd never been this far northwest before, other than when she'd been found as a child. Before her trial, Tempest had been too young to travel from city to city with her Hound brethren.

"Anything I should know?" she murmured.

"It's a place of corruption. Full of pirates." He slid a look her way. "Too violent for a pup."

She'd show him how much of a pup she was.

Tempest pulled her hood back and tucked her braid into the back of her shirt. She reached for her hood, but a huge hand wrapped around her wrist, nails digging into her skin. Hissing, she glared at Brine.

"What are—"

"Keep your damn hair hidden, fool!" he chastised, speaking in an undertone. "Don't be so stupid."

"I *am*," she growled, yanking her arm out of his grasp. She tugged her hood low over her eyes.

He grunted. "Keep your mouth shut and follow me."

Tempest bit back a retort. Brine clearly had more expertise in the area; if he was telling her to hide her hair, keeping quiet was likely wise. They descended into the small port city, winding through dark streets and empty marketplaces full of flickering lanterns. Metal bars covered the small windows of every home. Given the city's reputation for crime, Tempest was not surprised.

Her nose wrinkled as a mixture of the smell of sewage and mold assaulted her nostrils. The place stunk. It was even worse than the slums in Dotae. Her boots slurped as they slogged through the muddy streets, surrounded by dilapidated buildings. Green scum clung to every bit of stone and wood. She slipped and gagged when she caught herself against the side of a rundown apothecary, the green gunk squishing between her fingers.

Nasty.

She wiped her hands on her trousers and followed Brine. The quiet houses faded as taverns began to appear on almost every corner, spilling light, loud music, and raucous laughter into the streets. She tried not to stare when she spotted scantily clad women poised in front of a brothel. A nightwalker caught her eye and smiled.

"See something you like?" the woman called.

Tempest ducked her head and hurried after the wolf.

"I thought I told you to keep your head down?" Brine growled softly.

"I did," she muttered. "There are more brothels here than Dotae." She'd never seen so many half-naked women. Was this how all cities were? Her knowledge of Heimserya abruptly seemed small and insignificant. Why did women subject themselves to such things? Could they not find a proper occupation?

"I can hear you thinking and judging. Stop."

Tempest glared at the shifter's back. "I thought we were supposed to be quiet."

A grunt was all the answer she received.

Tempest shook herself from her thoughts and scanned the area around them. They settled into silence as they moved deeper into the city. The stench of rotten fish grew stronger, and Tempest shallowly breathed through only her mouth. Winter's bite, that was rank. She could taste it.

Brine let out a short laugh. "Stinks, doesn't it? Imagine what it smells like for *me*."

"I'd rather not, thanks," she wheezed, allowing the smallest of smiles to curl her lips—though it was hidden by her cowl. It was the closest the two of them had ever gotten to civil conversation.

They ghosted along the docks, ships bobbing restlessly in the harbor. Tempest eyed the black water. She didn't want to know what lurked beneath the surface. Brine paused next to one of the larger, more expensive-looking ships along the docks. She frowned. The ship looked out of place.

Brine spun and snatched a handful of her cloak, pulling her closer. She blinked up at him in surprise as he pressed even closer, his chest touching her own. What in the hell?

The wolf leaned closer and murmured, "Act as my bodyguard. Don't say a damned word unless I instruct you to. Can you do that?"

Tempest nodded, because it was the kind of plan she would have suggested. She had no idea who or what exactly they were dealing with. She eyed the ship. Whoever had stolen from the Jester was stupid, though. She knew that much.

Brine stalked up the gangway, and she followed suit, careful not to trip. She'd never been one for developing "sea legs," and when the water beneath her rolled and the gangway lurched, she cursed underneath her breath as she stumbled. Now was not the time for a swim. Straightening, she schooled her expression and stepped onto the ship, shadowing Brine as her stomach rolled.

Don't throw up. Don't throw up.

The shifter headed straight over to whom she assumed was the captain. His clothing was absolutely gaudy. Embroidered boots gave way to red velvet trousers. He'd foregone a shirt, only wearing a black leather vest and emerald green scarf. His tattooed arms were bare to the world, despite the freezing temperatures. Few men could do that. A shifter, then.

The wind blew the huge purple feather tucked into his hat right into his face, and Tempest's lips twitched.

"Damn hat." He yanked the garish hat from his head, revealing cat ears hiding among his artfully tousled brown hair.

She blinked. That's how she knew him—he was one of Pyre's shifters. Her lips curled. One who had chased after her alongside Brine and the rest of their friends, right into a speared pit.

Chesh. The name came unbiddenly to her.

The cat shifter did not send a single glance her way as he and Brine sat at a long table with a portly man and began playing cards, swigging from a bottle of rum and mindlessly gossiping. Tempest took her place a few paces behind the wolf, keeping her eyes open for trouble.

"How has trade been?" Brine asked, handing the bottle of rum over to the portly man. "I heard you've been dabbling in the sale of women these days?"

It was difficult, but she kept her expression blank.

"That's where all the money is, especially trading overseas."

The man laughed, his jowls jiggling. "Well, that and drugs, of course."

Tempest bristled. This was the kind of conversation she didn't want to be privy to. Her skin crawled. Human and drug trafficking. She stared hard at the back of Brine's head. With how straight-laced the wolf seemed, it surprised her that he was so calm about selling human beings.

"But I've been looking for something different these days," the merchant continued, a lavish smile on his lips. "Something... exotic." His eyes flashed to Tempest like he could see through her cloak and clothing. "I've heard word that the fabled little female Hound has been seen out of her cage. A real beauty, apparently."

"She's definitely a fiery one," Chesh said, sliding his own gaze over to Tempest in a way that made her spine tingle. What the hell? Her hand twitched toward her sword. "A real prize. But she's expensive."

The man raised an eyebrow. "Oh, I can do expensive. How much to hand her over?"

Tempest couldn't believe what she was hearing. She carefully pulled the daggers from her hips and glared at the back of Brine's head, willing him to turn and face her. Were they brokering a deal for her? Or was this part of the ruse? Had she been double-crossed?

Chesh lazily stretched and unwound the scarf he was wearing. Her breath froze as more markings were revealed. Tattoos ran across his chest, up his neck, and stopped beneath his chin. She spotted a crown with three stars across it just below his right ear. Tempest's blood ran cold.

The only time she'd ever seen such markings was when she studied the Hinterlands.

The bloody Hinterlands. And royalty, no less.

That wasn't good.

The Hinterlands and Heimserya had been enemies for generations. What was he doing here? Mimkia was killing their people, the Jester was organizing a rebellion, and now a Hinterland prince was in one of their ports? It was all wrong. Were Brine and Chesh working against the Jester? How did the creepy merchant fit into it all?

Whatever it was, she wasn't sticking around. No matter the outcome, it wasn't good for her. Tempest took two slow steps away from the table just as the portly man grinned outright.

"And where do you think you're going, Lady Hound?!" the merchant bellowed after her, moving with surprising speed for someone of his size around the table. "Stay a little while."

Time to go. She darted for the gangplank when guards materialized around her, blocking the path off the ship. Wicked hell.

"Get out of my way before I cut you down!" she snarled.

The sounds of swords sliding from scabbards echoed around her. The wind tugged at her cloak. She shook her head so the hood fell away, exposing her hair. She smiled nastily. Their stances told her everything she needed to know. They weren't well trained, and they looked human. She had years of experience fighting soldiers and city guards. They didn't stand a chance. And it did not take long for Tempest to disarm both men and leap across the gangway.

Her boots pounded along the dock as she sprinted back into the city, slipping and sliding in the mud. She veered toward the smellier part of town, gagging at the scent. It couldn't be helped. With shifters involved, they'd probably picked up her scent. Hopefully, the odor would mask her smell.

She darted into a dark alley and paused to catch her breath; her gaze locked on the entrance. Her pulse thundered in her ears. Had she escaped? She didn't think it was that simple.

"Why so quick to leave, Temp?" Chesh crooned into her ear, snaking a hand around Tempest's waist as if they were lovers.

Her instincts and training kicked in. She slammed an elbow into his gut before stomping on his instep. He hissed and released her. Tempest swung her leg out to knock him off his feet. He'd already stepped out of the way and hovered just out of reach. Chesh gave her a crooked smile that said *come and get me.* She'd do no such thing. Only a fool would go on the offense with someone so much bigger than themselves. Tempest wasn't a fool.

"I will *not* be sold to some sleazy smuggler. I'm not sure who you work for—"

"Hush, pet," Chesh replied, closing the distance between them. She slashed at him, and he paused, arching a brow at her. "No need to be so feisty."

Her top lip curled back, and she lifted her daggers higher. "I'm going to walk away, and you're going to let me. I don't know what you have going on right now, but I do know what those markings are for. Do your partners know who you are?"

He gave her a mischievous smile. "Fox was right. You are just delightful."

Tempest took a step toward the mouth of the alley at the same time Chesh *moved.* One moment, several paces separated them, and the next, he was only inches from her daggers. He calmly wrapped his hands around her wrists and gazed evenly down at her.

"Let's put the daggers down and speak like reasonable people, shall we?"

She lashed out, aiming to kick him in the shin, but he sidestepped. He squeezed her right wrist, slowly prying the dagger from her fingers.

Not happening.

Instead of pulling away, she jerked forward and viciously bit his forearm. Chesh grunted and put more pressure on her wrist. She cried out and released his arm as he forced her to drop the dagger. Tempest prepared for his counterattack and grunted as he yanked her close. She gasped when he did the exact opposite. A purr vibrated his chest, and he rubbed his face affectionately against her temple and cheek. She leaned back as far as she could and gaped at the shifter.

"What was that?" she barked, losing some of her fear and anger. What the bloody hell was going on?

Chesh laughed and leaned closer, brushing his nose against hers. "Just a friendly hello."

"Knock it off," she demanded as he rubbed his face against the top of her head.

"Just returning the favor, pet. You're the one who initiated it."

"Me?" she gasped.

"You bit me." His smile was slow. "This kitty likes to scratch."

Tempest's brow furrowed. "You attacked me. I was protecting myself."

"In my world, you just declared that you want me."

She gaped. "I don't think so! I thought you wanted to kill me or sell me off."

"Trust me, Temp," he said, once more using her nickname uninvited, "if I wanted you dead—if I ever meant you harm— then I would have killed you the first time I laid eyes on you."

Nothing made any damn sense. "Then what in the name of Dotae is going on? Why were you bartering my life with that man if—"

"You served as a distraction," Brine growled, appearing from the entrance to the alleyway with a box in his hands. "Something that you're actually very good at, it seems."

"A distraction?" she repeated. They'd scared years off her life. Her gaze moved back to the cat shifter holding her hostage. "I hope you have nine lives," she muttered. "Because I am going to kill you."

He winked at her. "It was all in good fun."

"That was not my idea of fun." She glanced pointedly at his hands. "Now, if you'd be so kind as to set me free?"

Chesh released a rumbling purr. "I could show you how I have fun…"

Tempest growled as her cheeks heated at his insinuation. "No, thank you."

Chesh sighed. "Your loss, pet." He let her go, and Tempest slashed at him half-heartedly with her left hand. "What fun you are," he said.

"I'll show you fun," she muttered, stooping to retrieve her discarded dagger from the mud. Her nose wrinkled as she cleaned the hilt with her cloak and slipped the weapon into the leather sheath at her right hip. She stood and pinned Brine with her gaze. "And what did you need a distraction for?"

He held up the plain box in his hands. "This." He glanced at Chesh and rolled his eyes. "Will you stop your antics? You're worse than Fox."

The shifter in question had crept closer to her, still purring. He gave her a mad grin and then moved a respectful distance away. He inclined his head politely, which only served to confuse Tempest beyond all reason. What was his deal? What sort of game was he playing? And why was a prince of the Hinterlands consorting with the Talagan rebels? Questions for another time.

She forced herself to concentrate on the matter at hand. "What's in the box?"

"None of your business," Brine replied, so quickly Tempest felt like swearing at him. What she didn't expect was for Chesh to take the box from Brine and pass it over to her.

"Thank you…" she murmured, running her fingers over the intricate wooden surface. It almost looked like a puzzle. She rotated the box, looking for a latch.

Chesh tsked and laid a hand over her own, halting her exploration. "You may carry it, but no opening it," he said. "You have to take this to our lovely Jester as is."

"Seriously?" she huffed.

"Yes, be a good girl and listen to your elders."

Tempest felt like screaming, but she tamped down her irritation. "You can't be much older than I."

"I'm an old soul."

"Positively decrepit," she said dryly. Tempest ignored his narrowed eyes and focused back on the glowering wolf. If they wouldn't let her open it, then she needed to gain as much information as possible. "Was this box in the smuggler's possession?"

"Indeed," Chesh answered. "He's been touting a deadly drug to Heimserya's neighboring countries claiming that it's protection against the disease that's affecting the country. Everyone is terrified by the news coming out of Heimserya, so people are buying this drug in droves."

Her stomach twisted at the notion. Now there was not just one killer drug on the market, but two.

"He was also stealing from the Jester," Brine added. He waved a hand toward the box. "We were collecting evidence to prove it. Now the Dark Court can rightfully eliminate him."

Eliminate. Lovely.

She ran the back of her arm over her face, then indicated behind her with her dagger. "So, where is blasted Fox, then?" she asked. "Where do I have to go to—"

"I'm taking you there, of course," Brine cut in, looking thoroughly unhappy. "Why would we *tell* you where he is, you stupid dog?"

And they were back to square one. "I'm too tired to deal with your insults, Brine." She'd walked for hours today, been falsely sold, and chased through a pirate city. Her body was done with the abuse.

"Good," he said, smiling viciously. "Then you won't put up a fight for the next few hours."

She baulked at the idea. "The next few hours? Can't we find somewhere to rest first?" She was hungry and needed a proper bath. She stank.

Brine merely laughed. "A wolf travels best at night, girlie. So, if you want to prove your worth, then you'll keep up with me without complaint."

Tempest didn't know if she wanted Brine's respect or not, but it became clear she was going to have to continue traveling with him on his terms, regardless.

Chesh sashayed up to her, and, quicker than lightning, licked the side of her face.

Tempest skittered backward and wiped at her cheek with her sleeve. "Disgusting!"

"It was nice seeing you again, pet. Stay safe."

She glared at the cat shifter as he disappeared into the darkness.

"Let's move. I'm tired of waiting on you already," Brine grumped.

The night was going to be *long.*

CHAPTER 11: TEMPEST

empest had a new appreciation for the notion of silence after three days of traveling with Brine. With every step, the Dread Mountains to the northeast grew larger—as foreboding as their name suggested—and, by the end of the third day, she was overwhelmed by the sheer size of them.

She shifted on her mount, and the horse nickered softly. "I know, I know. It's hard not to wiggle," she muttered. In the beginning, she'd been thankful that Brine had procured a horse for her. Her legs had turned to jelly, and she just couldn't keep up with the wolf's stamina—which he liked to complain about —even though she was in excellent shape. What she hadn't counted on was Brine acquiring a *shifter* horse. In fact, it was the damned one she'd ridden into the forest the first time she trespassed into the woods.

Swiftly. An unoriginal name to be sure.

Luckily, she'd been spared most of the awkwardness. Swiftly

didn't shift into human form, not even to greet them. Instead, he had snuffled through Tempest's bag until he found her stash of dried apple slices she had forgotten all about. They hadn't been on the best of terms last time they met, so Tempest was more than willing to sacrifice her apples if that meant he wouldn't buck her off and make the rest of her journey smooth.

She ran her hand along his glossy, midnight neck. He nickered softly, and she smiled. They'd become fast friends, and all it cost her was a few treats. Even though Swiftly was as silent as Brine, his quiet seemed more companionable and easygoing. The late afternoon sunshine slanted through the forest at the base of the Dread Mountains.

"You know, I like you better this way," she murmured to the horse, stroking his mane.

Swiftly whinnied, and she giggled.

Brine clucked his tongue, his expression one of utter distaste. "So easily won over, Swiftly. Do not forget who she is."

Sweet poison. This *again*.

"Considering how you all attacked me earlier this year, I doubt he does," Tempest fired back, though there was no genuine anger behind her retort.

She and Brine had formed an uneasy alliance during their three-day journey so far. While they could hardly be considered friends, nor even acquaintances, she no longer considered themselves strictly enemies. It had been tough, but she had kept up with his brutal, unforgiving pace without complaint and, in turn, Brine had limited his threats and insults.

It was progress… no matter how small it was.

She eyed Brine as he prowled through the trees, his ears perking every time he heard something she couldn't. "Why are you so on edge, Brine?" Tempest asked after a short while of observing the wolf shifter from her vantage point on Swiftly's back. The wolf's mannerisms were stressing her out. She forced herself to release her tight hold on the reins and muttered a quick apology to Swiftly.

The wolf froze and glanced back at her, his ears pricked up to attention. "Hush." He sniffed the air, turning from her to investigate the left side of the narrow path they were following. His gray eyes moved to her face, and his lips thinned. "There's something—someone—nearby. But I don't…" Brine trailed off, which only served to unnerve her.

She frowned and pulled her bow from her shoulder at a rumbling sound that set her teeth on edge. No, it wasn't a rumble… more like a bone-rattling roar. She scanned the trees around them, trying to find the source of the sound. Brine ran to a gap in the trees and glanced at the sky. Tempest urged Swiftly ahead and followed the wolf's gaze. She stiffened, and her heart began to race. *It couldn't be.*

"A dragon," she breathed, equally terrified and in awe. The dragon roared again and disappeared from sight. It was a bloody dragon. She wasn't prepared to take on a dragon. Her arrows would just bounce off its scales like a child's toy. "Have you ever—"

The whistle of an arrow passed her ear. Tempest's attention snapped from the sky to the forest, and she held her bow higher. Dragons didn't wield bows. People did. A dark smile curled her lips. She was ready for people.

Brine partly shifted, his claws lengthening from his fingertips. The dragon called again, and it was as if it was right above them. The sound rattled her teeth. She glanced at the wolf and spotted a shadowy figure just as it leapt from the trees.

"Get down, Brine!" Tempest yelled, firing her arrow at the

shadowy figure who was getting ready to impale the wolf shifter with his sword.

Brine ducked, and her arrow struck true. She didn't spare them much attention as they collapsed to their knees and then crashed to the forest floor.

Tempest released an embarrassing squeak when she swiveled, and another figure bore down on her. There wasn't enough time to ready another arrow. Swiftly sidestepped and then bucked, striking his back hooves against the assailant's chest. She winced at the sickening crack and tumbled over Swiftly's head. She groaned and rolled out of the way. That hurt.

"A warning next time," she wheezed.

Swiftly tossed his head and whinnied loudly.

"He needs to shift," Brine said, his words more of a growl.

Tempest stood just as the horse became a man. He snatched a dagger from her waist and threw it over her head. A dull thud sounded behind her, followed by a scream. She yanked her other dagger from her hip and handed it to the tall, lanky man with shaggy black hair. He flashed her a smile with very straight, square, beige teeth. She grinned back and let another arrow loose as Brine loped after one of their attackers.

Another dropped from the trees. And, so, it went on. She kept shooting until Swiftly cried out. Tempest spun on her heel and nocked another arrow just as another assailant pulled a dagger from the horse man's back before landing a blow to his head. Swiftly was unconscious when he hit the ground, his assailant following behind him, but in a more permanent sleep.

"Swiftly!" Tempest yelled, moving to his side. She touched her fingers to the base of his throat. He still had a pulse, but they would need to bandage his wound. Brine jogged back into the meadow a bloody mess. "Who are they?"

"Bandits," he grunted. "Three more. We can handle them!"

A surge of pride moved through her at the statement. She wiped the sweat from her eyes as a small, male bandit charged at her and maneuvered herself away from Swiftly. She danced around the bandit and used the tip of her bow to swipe his feet out from under him. He growled and rolled onto his belly to get up. Tempest darted in and slammed her bow into the back of his head twice. He slumped into the foliage. He didn't get up.

The dragon cried again so loudly that her ears rang. Her eyes widened. Wicked hell. It was right above them. The world seemed to slow as a gargantuan, emerald shape descended upon them, blocking the sun and causing Tempest to shiver.

"Fall back!" she yelled. It couldn't navigate through the trees.

Brine let out a snarl of surprise that made her blood curdle. Across the glen, he limped toward one of the two remaining assailants, a dagger lodged in his calf and another protruding from his left shoulder blade.

Tempest's eyes watered as leaves and debris filled the air as the dragon tried to land. They were all going to die.

The dragon crushed several trees as it finally landed. It was as if they were twigs. Tempest faltered, and took a step away from the fight, then another and another. A wise soldier knew when to retreat. Now was the time. She took another step then halted, her fingers clenching around the bow.

"No!" she cried, shaking her head, ashamed. Brine needed her help. She left no one behind. Swiftly was defenseless, but Brine's condition was deteriorating; if she didn't stay to help, both of them *would* die. And they didn't deserve it. They were not the Jester.

She turned on her heel and sprinted back into the fray. Screaming, she caught the female bandit's attention. The woman smiled, revealing rotting, yellowed teeth as she swung her short sword and raced to meet Tempest. Tempest dropped her bow and pulled her sword from the scabbard. The woman swung, and Tempest dropped to her knees, skidding over the wet plants beneath the woman's guard and slicing the bandit's Achilles tendon. The woman howled and dropped to the ground.

Tempest launched to her feet and kept going. Brine faced her, and his eyes widened just as her cloak snagged on something. She choked as the metal clasp dug into her throat. She spun, lifting her sword.

And everything just stopped.

She couldn't even breathe as she came face-to-muzzle with the dragon.

The beast puffed out a metallic breath, blowing the hood from her head. This was how she died. Her periwinkle hair blew across her eyes, but she never took her gaze from the beast. She held up her sword, at a loss for what else to do. Running wasn't an option. Her sword could not pierce its hide. A hysterical laugh built up in her chest. Oh, how the bards would sing about the female lion slayer who was eaten by a dragon.

The beast didn't attack. She tucked her chin and glared at it. "What are you waiting for?" she screamed. Not her finest moment, taunting a dragon, but she didn't want to draw this out further than need be. Already, her legs were beginning to shake.

The beast huffed and stretched its sinuous neck until the edge of Tempest's sword was but an inch from its snout. She'd never seen something more terrifying or glorious. "You're beautiful," she whispered.

"Step aside, maiden," it—*he*—said, in a slithering voice that Tempest felt slide down her entire body. She jerked. Had the dragon just spoken? "Let me claim my prey."

Tempest staunchly refused, shaking her head and holding her sword a little firmer, her hands slick with sweat. The creature had *spoken*. Words. Human words. She blinked. The only conscious ones left in the glen were Brine and herself.

She swallowed hard. "We have felled most of the team, it seems. Let us be."

The dragon chuckled; a rumble that started deep in his chest and caused the forest floor to vibrate beneath her boots. "You are a brave one. Or foolish. Likely both." He tilted his huge, reptilian head to the side, regarding Tempest intently with his terrifying eyes. "Such remarkable hair. Quite beautiful. Unique. Rare. I like rare things."

Get in line. She kept those thoughts to herself. "We meant no trespass on your territory."

"So I am sure, and yet you are here," the dragon crooned. "You must pay a toll for stealing my prey. What payment can you offer me, lovely?"

Tempest faltered for a moment. All she had of any value was her Hound ring. While she didn't want to rid herself of it, it would be useless to her if she was dead. She held her hand out without taking her eyes off the monster in front of her, the silver ring dull in the fading light.

If the dragon had eyebrows, they would have risen. It was clear he wasn't impressed. "You can do better than that, I think."

"I—" Tempest began, frowning. She didn't own anything else. A lock of periwinkle hair crossed her face in the breeze.

She fingered the lock and then eyed the dragon. He seemed pretty enamored with her wild mane. "My hair?"

The shift in the dragon's attitude changed immediately; his stance relaxed, and the stiff lips around his teeth lifted. She blanched. *He's trying to smile.* But it was the most terrifying thing she'd ever beheld. *He is intrigued.* Although scared out of her wits, she managed to slap a smile on her face.

"If my hair is enough, take it," she continued, "only swear to me that you will not harm us if I pay your price."

The dragon huffed a breath. "I pledge not to attack you or your party. Satisfied?"

Tempest nodded, though she didn't lower her sword. Then, in a flash of sunlight upon wicked teeth, the dragon disappeared to be replaced by a man. She took a step backward and blinked slowly. "What the bloody hell?" she muttered under her breath.

He was massive—bigger even than Madrid and Briggs. He smiled, revealing wicked-looking canines, and brushed wavy, dark-green hair from his face, his eyes twinkling. She didn't even have the decency to blush at his nudity. She was too damn scared. However, the faint pattern of scales along his pale skin intrigued her.

Curiosity killed the cat...

She studied the strange, terrifying man in front of her and slashed at him when he lunged for her. Tempest gasped when he grabbed the blade of her sword and yanked it out of her hand, tossing it aside as if it were a child's toy. Her finger moved to the blade at her thigh as he yanked her into his arms. She pressed the blade beneath the dragon's crotch, expecting him to flinch away.

He didn't.

Instead, the green-haired dragon shifter grinned a smile full of fangs and lowered his head toward Tempest's ear.

"I do enjoy a fiery female," he whispered. "It has been quite some time since a member of your species has intrigued me enough for me to change form."

"Take my hair and leave us be," Tempest said, ignoring his compliment. She could not lose her nerve—not now.

"Hmm," the man said. "As you wish."

She expected him to chop it all off, to leave her with nothing. But when he raised a talon to her head, he cut just one lock of hair from beneath her right ear.

Tempest arched a brow. "That's it?"

"For now." He smiled again, displaying all his frightening teeth. "Come home with me, lovely. I can assure you my lair is more than comfortable for a human. I have many a shiny, pretty things to entice a woman."

"I think you'll find such things do not appeal to me," Tempest said, keeping her voice soft and even, despite the fact her insides were shaking. "I am not so easily won over. Please release me." She pressed her blade a little tighter against his crotch to emphasize her point.

The man shook his head in apparent dismay, though he chuckled. "I have no doubt of that. But you would be well-cared for. You would want and desire for nothing."

"And what would I be to *you*?" she countered, humoring the strange creature for a moment.

"My treasure. My plaything."

Tempest curled her lip in disgust. "I am no man's plaything."

"And I am no *man*."

With deft movements, he pulled the blade away from between his legs, grabbing Tempest's wrist and pulling it to his lips. He kissed the delicate skin there, surprisingly gently, though the kiss still hurt her.

It burned.

She managed to keep her expression bland and not flinch as the unsettling sensation trickled up her arm. When the dragon let her go, she brought her wrist up to inspect it, but there was nothing there. It was smooth and unblemished as it had been before.

"What was that?" she asked.

"Just a little something to remember me by," the shifter said. He eyed her once more before releasing her and turning his back to her, his body already beginning to morph. "I will see you soon, my lovely." He said the words with certainty.

"I hope not," she muttered when he fully transformed. Tempest covered her eyes with her arm as he leapt into the air, once again stirring up debris. She gaped at his rising form. Did that just happen?

Woodenly, she looked at her wrist, to Swiftly, and then to Brine who lay face-first in the meadow.

Just what in the hell had happened?

CHAPTER 12: TEMPEST

empest shivered and wrapped her cloak tighter around her body, the bare skin of her arms breaking out in goosebumps. Winter's bite, it was bloody cold. She eyed the remains of her shirt that she'd used to wrap Swiftly's and Brine's wounds. There wasn't enough left to even save the garment. At least she had her corset, so she wasn't completely bare.

The shifters were in bad shape, but not terribly so that she'd have to leave them in the forest. Or so she hoped. Tempest swiveled to face Brine and placed the back of her hand against his forehead. He was burning up already. That wasn't a good sign.

"Brine," she said. "How far are we away from Pyre?"

He groaned and gazed up at her through bloodshot eyes. "Few hours."

Her lips thinned, and she eyed both men. Stars, she hoped

they both could walk. She wouldn't be able to carry them herself. "Can you walk?"

"Havvvvve to," Brine slurred.

"Swiftly?" she murmured.

The horse man cracked an eye. "I can walk. Been hurt worse before."

"Brine's calf is injured. I need you to help me with him if you can bear it."

Swiftly smiled his horsey smile. "We have to. Help me up."

With many curses and grunts, Tempest managed to get both men on their feet with Brine between them. They began their journey once again. It was a miserable struggle. Tempest panted as they left the dark pine trees that lined the base of the mountains to painfully climb through a deep, narrow valley, its walls the precipitous sides of two neighboring mountains covered in early winter snow.

And you thought you'd be cold.

She huffed out an exhausted laugh. Her body was dripping with sweat, more so from the heat Brine was putting out than from the climb, although her thighs and calves burned. She had no clue how the wolf was keeping up.

Their footsteps upon the stony ground echoed all around, slapping and reverberating off the sides of the mountains until the noise drowned everything out around them. The sound pushed heavily on her ears. From the corner of her eye, Brine winced, his ears lying flat against his skull. She was tempted to ask how much farther when the wolf stumbled and leaned more weight on her. Tempest grunted and dug deep down for more strength, not daring to speak and add to the overwhelming racket around them.

The sun had fully set, and the moon had risen in the sky,

lighting their way. Thank Dotae for the small miracles. If the moon hadn't been out in all its glory, there was no way she could have made this hike in full darkness.

Brine caught the tip of his boot and stumbled once again. Tempest braced her legs and wrapped her arm tighter around his back. He hissed and jerked away from her touch. Liquid ran down her fingers from his back. She'd grabbed his wound.

"Sorry," she whispered as softly as she could.

The wind whistled above, a haunting melody that caused every deep shadow to look like a monster. She inhaled slowly and tried to calm herself. Even in Brine's state, he wouldn't want a creature bearing down on them. And where were they going? There was nothing in the Dread Mountains but danger and death. Once again, her question sat on the tip of her tongue, but she swallowed it back. Neither shifter would tell her. Might as well save her breath.

They pressed onward, and their pace slackened. Swiftly careened back and forth, and Tempest could hardly stand, yet they continued on.

Count each step. One foot in front of the other. You can do this. You have to do this, or you will all die.

Somewhere around the count of one-hundred-and-fifty, she registered the sound of footsteps. Footsteps that weren't theirs. Couldn't they catch a break? Brine's head lifted, and his ears stood at full attention. One twitched—a tell-tale sign that somebody else was around. If he'd noticed them at the same time as she had, then the wolf was in worse shape than she'd thought.

Shifters? She brushed the thought aside. They were too loud for shifters.

"I need to set you down," she whispered to Brine. "I can't fight and balance you."

His grip around her waist tightened. "No. Keep going."

Her lips thinned. At this pace, their pursuers would catch up to them in no time. But, still, they soldiered on through the valley at a snail's pace. She kept throwing glances over her shoulder. Still no one in sight yet. That was promising at least, but it didn't last.

Several minutes later, the sounds of their pursuers' footsteps had become more and more apparent. Tempest glanced behind them and spotted shadows gaining on them. Enough was enough. It was time to stand and fight.

"No more," she huffed. They couldn't outrun them.

She manhandled Brine to the side of the ravine, then pulled her bow from her shoulder and nocked an arrow. Hunting in the dark. Ridiculous. The first shadow drew closer at an alarming speed, and her lip curled.

They were shifters. Damn it.

Tempest inhaled and released her arrow with a soft exhale. It went wide and slammed into stone. Hell. Quickly, she whipped another arrow from her quiver when shifters appeared all around them.

An ambush.

Shale rained down from behind her, and she spun just as a lion leapt from an impossibly thin shelf of rock above Tempest's head. She released the arrow and it pierced the beast in the shoulder. Her mouth bobbed as he shifted mid-drop and landed in a crouch, golden hair ruffled in the breeze.

Hands tried to grab her, but she whipped her bow around, keeping them back. Weight slammed into her from the side, and she found herself staring into the pale eyes of the lion shifter. He slapped a medicinal-smelling cloth over her mouth.

"That hurt," he snapped. "You could have killed me."

Tempest wiggled and fought harder, involuntarily taking in a breath. Her muscles twitched, and then her eyelids fluttered closed, sending her plummeting into darkness.

Tempest opened her eyes slowly, her head aching.

She hurt too much to be dead, so that was something. Slowly, she glanced around the room. It was a luxurious room, just as expensively furnished as the cave she had woken in last time.

The Jester.

She'd know his gaudy taste anywhere. Why had he felt the need to knock her out? He could have just thrown a bag over her head and called it good. Staging an ambush and the drugging? That had the Jester written all over it.

Tempest rubbed her eyes and willed herself to be more alert. Whatever they'd drugged her with hadn't completely left her system. Her basic bodily functions were moving too slowly. She could have woken up somewhere worse. At least it wasn't a prison.

Some cages are gilded.

The fact that he had now moved her twice while she was unconscious made her ill at ease. A person was at their most vulnerable while they slept. She stretched her muscles. Everything seemed to be okay. Other than being exhausted and bruised, she was whole, which was a bloody miracle in and of itself. She slowly sat up and inspected the room a little more closely.

The bed was large—as large as King Destin's. A soft bedspread lay over her legs, embroidered with woodland creatures. She ran her fingers along the decoration, pausing when her fingertips brushed over a fox. Tempest averted her gaze from the golden eyes of the kitsune stitched upon it. She'd been much too interested in foxes of late. It was unhealthy.

Tempest eyed the empty fireplace. She'd assumed they were underground somewhere beneath the mountains. How did they ventilate the fire? Wouldn't the smoke escaping give up the location of this place? Thoughts for another day. A shiver worked through her. How she wished there was an actual fire burning in the hearth. She was freezing.

Beside the hearth, however, was a familiar mountain of a man sleeping on a rocking chair, bringing back memories of the shifter village and the cottage she'd spent weeks recovering in.

Briggs.

Scooting to the edge of the mattress, she swung her legs off the bed in order to hug her friend. She'd missed the healer. Tempest stiffened as she realized how scantily she was dressed. Her cheeks burned, and she used the covers to hide her figure. Who had undressed her? She scoured the room for something suitable to wear, but all that was available was a long, silken nightgown lying on the end of the bed. When she reached out to rub the fabric between her fingers, it was like water.

A stupid grin crossed her face, and Tempest stamped down her joy.

Beautiful, but impractical. The garment wouldn't keep her warm at all.

It's your underclothes or the nightgown.

There wasn't much of a choice.

Tempest spared no time in slipping it over her head and sighed when the fabric whispered over her skin. It was the softest thing she'd ever worn. She stood and hissed as her toes touched cold stone. Her skin pebbled, and she yanked the blanket off the bed and wrapped it around her shoulders before padding across the floor to a patchwork rug in green-and-gold thread near the hearth.

"Briggs," she whispered.

His dark eyes flashed open, and he immediately grinned. "I was wondering when you would wake up," he said.

"You were the one sleeping."

His smile widened as he stood. "I was just waiting for you." He pulled her into a crushing hug. For the first time since she'd left the capital, she felt comfortable and safe.

"It's good to see you, too, Briggs," she wheezed against his chest. After a few seconds, she pushed out of his arms and smoothed down the skirt of her borrowed nightgown. "How long have I been out?"

"Long enough," he paused and then added, "Pyre will be with you soon."

No, the dark prince would grace her with his presence now.

She shook her head. "No, not soon. Now. Take me to him *now*. I've jumped through all these hoops—I nearly died on the road and got sold off to a smuggler—just to follow his stupid orders. He will see me now, or he will not see me at all."

Briggs pulled a face. "He won't like this."

She was counting on it.

"I will disappear and cause more mischief," Tempest said, smiling slightly. "You know I will."

He sighed. "There's no stopping you. Might as well save myself the trouble. Your satchel is on the floor." He chuckled. "Plus, Pyre hasn't been needled in a while. Follow me."

Tempest grabbed her satchel, which lay by the base of the bed, and followed Briggs out of her room. He led her through a network of arching hallways made of dark, imposing stone. The place seemed grander than King Destin's palace, though it lacked the same polish. It was rougher; Tempest could tell that the place was carved from the literal mountains themselves. But that only served to make her like the place. There was something wild and beautiful about the stone walls and the cold wind that blew through the corridors whenever they turned a corner.

The only drawback was that the stone beneath her bare feet was bitter and freezing, and the tingle of pain in her toes reminded her that she had not arrived at this strange place by herself. "How are Brine and Swiftly?" she asked, keeping her voice small and quiet in case it echoed off the walls as it had done outside.

"Recovering," he said, smiling reassuringly. "It'll take more than that to knock them down. And their injuries were nothing a good dose of mimkia couldn't solve."

She flinched at the mention of the drug.

Essential for medicine, yet deadly.

"How strange it is," Briggs murmured, reading Tempest's mind, "that the very thing that has been causing us so much strife can just as easily save our lives. Don't you think, Temp?"

She nodded and pulled her blanket closer, the tail end of it dragging like a train behind her. The rest of their wandering was done in silence as they traversed the labyrinth of hallways. The lanterns flickered eerily as Briggs brought her through a doorway, into a dark, shadowy corner at the rear of a cavernous room.

It was bigger than even the ballroom in Dotae. Nothing she'd ever seen compared in size. Near the end of the room, a group of people sat in luxurious chairs.

She surveyed the gathering with curious eyes. At the front, presiding over the rest of the group on a carved, stone plinth, was a man with white hair and skin the color of milk. *Or moonlight.* Even from her position at the back of the room, Tempest could see that his eyes were a piercing shade of blue. Tempest supposed he was beautiful, but there was an ethereal quality to him that she found unsettling instead of alluring.

Who was he?

Forcing herself to turn her attention to the rest of the group, she noted that there was a giant of a man sitting on the floor. He was immense. A giant from Kopal. Another man sat beside him with broad shoulders and scales imprinted on his skin. She blanched, knowing immediately what he was. A dragon.

The woman beside the dragon shifter chuckled and waved her hand, her skin a strange aqua, almost an iridescent quality to it that seemed to move like water itself. Beside this woman was Nyx, and, behind them all, a further group of shifters that Tempest did not know. Who were these people? Criminals? Rebels? Allies?

The white-haired man cleared his throat, pulling Tempest's gaze back to him. "Destin has sent his sons as ambassadors to your nation," he said to the giant. "Clearly, it's a ploy of some sort. I would not be surprised if they are bringing in purified mimkia or other dangerous substances to your kingdom."

Tempest grew rigid. The man was speaking about well-kept secrets, and he was speaking about it to a room full of shifters.

"Who is he?" she asked Briggs.

He bent low to talk directly into her ear. "That's the Jester's right-hand man, Mal."

"I thought Brine was his second?"

A flash of something Tempest couldn't quite understand crossed Briggs's face. "That's what a lot of people think," he said. "Brine is more like... his man on the ground, as it were. Mal is Pyre's political partner."

Political partner. She didn't like the sound of that.

Anyone who was conspiring to gain power was bound to be corrupt. And she didn't like Mal's smile. It was too perfect. His words were smooth. *Too* smooth. Even she was inclined to believe what he said was the truth even though she knew it was based on mere conjecture.

He's good.

She knew there was something more to the king's plan of sending off his sons than a mere ambassadorship. But she doubted very much it was to make an enemy of the giant kingdom. Heimserya did not have enough allies to fight both Talagan insurgents *and* the giants, especially when the Hinterlands were already an antagonistic nation. They needed allies. Who better than the Kopal brutes?

"You will have to do something about the princes," Mal continued, "but, for now, it is best for your people to simply observe them. I am sure they will make a mistake, eventually. The boys are fools."

She drew closer, Briggs at her side. They drifted closer as the giant drank up every word Mal said.

He wasn't wrong. The princes were idiots, but she did not like the tone in which Mal spoke about the boys. It felt cruel, though he painted it as a joke that everyone laughed at. He continued to address the crowd, spinning lies around kernels of truth—often information Tempest herself had passed onto Pyre —and Tempest's initial dislike for the man grew, along with disgust. He sold lies as truth.

Just like Destin.

Mal cast his pale eyes across the entire room. "And now, I suppose, we should turn our heads to a happier topic of conversation: The masquerade." A murmur of excitement buzzed across the room. "It is but a few weeks away, and I sincerely hope to see every faction there. Earlier today, I even managed to make last-minute negotiations with the merfolk to attend. This will be an exciting event for all of us!"

Tempest's mind went to the beautiful invitation in her satchel—the one decorated with a silvery mask. Why didn't Pyre just tell her outright? Why all the secrecy?

Another few minutes of discussion later and the folk in the room began to filter out through the gigantic double doors. Even in the shadows, she and Briggs stood out. Tempest supposed between the long, silken night gown, the blanket, and her periwinkle hair, they were hard to miss. Most of the group just stared but said nothing as they passed her by.

The woman that undulated like waves and seemed to have skin made of water sauntered toward Tempest, her hips swaying like ocean waves. Tempest blinked slowly as she realized that the woman's skin was blue beneath its iridescence. She was gorgeous, and she smiled, exposing a mouthful of tiny, pointed teeth, which sent a shiver down Tempest's spine.

"What lovely hair you have," the woman hummed.

"Leave her alone, Salvae," Mal said, appearing behind the woman on disturbingly silent feet. He looked the siren up and down with the slightest hint of disgust. Salvae hissed and tossed her light-green hair before storming from the room. Mal followed after without so much as a glance in Tempest's way.

Rude and strange.

She tipped her head back and stared up at Briggs. "Where in the world is Pyre?"

"Oh," a familiar voice chuckled from the doorway, "did you miss me that much, Temp?"

CHAPTER 13: TEMPEST

empest's lips curled. The devil finally showed himself.

She resisted the urge to look at him as she tried to get her temper under control.

Getting angry won't solve anything. Take a deep breath. Dima's voice echoed through her mind.

Tempest inhaled slowly and swallowed down her annoyance. She swiveled to face the doorway as the Jester made his entrance, arms wide and laughing, like they were the best of friends. Briggs tapped her on the shoulder twice before moving toward the door where Nyx waited.

They were leaving her alone with the knave. Dotae save her.

Pyre grinned, a vulpine fang making an appearance. She wrinkled her nose as he stopped, just a little too close for comfort.

"Do you like our lovely home, Tempest?" he asked.

"Mmhmmm," she hummed, not able to speak past her irritation that she couldn't rid herself of.

Pyre tugged at his velvet waistcoat and cocked his head, seemingly waiting for her to continue. He wasn't getting anything more. It was uncanny how different he looked to when they'd first met. Gone was his pine-green cloak and plain but well-made clothes he had worn during their time in the forest. Now, he was opulently dressed—even more so than when Tempest had been taken to his bizarre cave room. He could rival any prince with the lush velvets and rich silks he adorned himself with.

This wasn't Pyre. It was the Jester.

She glanced away and swallowed. She hated the outfit, but, more so, she hated how *good* he looked.

He held his arms out once again and walked toward her, as if he meant to hug her. Like hell. Her rage combusted, and she found herself dropping the blanket and meeting him head on, not with a hug but with her fist. She punched him squarely in the face. Her knuckles screamed, and she shook out her hand as Pyre immediately grabbed his nose and tilted his head backward, a growl beginning in the back of his throat as blood dripped between his fingers.

"That's for keeping me in the dark and not upholding your word!" Tempest shouted, still shaking her throbbing hand. Her anger had made her punch sloppy. She was lucky she hadn't broken any bones. Satisfaction slid through her. Messy, it may have been, but successful, she was.

The fox shot her a narrow-eyed glare. "You may have broken my nose."

She snorted. "I'm sure I'm not the first female to ever punch you in the face. Plus, you deserve it, and you know it."

"Just what are you talking about?" he asked, annoyance in his tone. "I think you ruined one of my favorite shirts. This is the second time, you know. You're making this a habit."

"You were supposed to meet me in the forest!" she replied, shocked by Pyre's sheer audacity to act as if he had no idea what she meant. "But then you never showed and forced me off onto your cranky wolf subordinate."

"Brine is lovely," he retorted. "One of my best."

Tempest ignored his comment, knowing full-well the Jester discerned how much Brine disliked her. Just another game. "And then I was almost sold off on a ship to some old deviant who, I believe, deals in slaves and drugs. Not only that, but he thought it wise to steal from the Jester. Who does that?"

"No one was really going to sell—"

"I'm not done," Tempest continued, cutting Pyre off. She knew if she gave him even an inch of leeway, he would take over the conversation and she would not get the answers she needed. "What's the deal with Chesh?" she demanded. "The bloody Hinterlands are the stuff of nightmares. They're our *enemies*, and yet you have one of their royals in your pocket? Just what in the blazes are you up to?!"

The Jester took a moment to pull a handkerchief from his pocket and mopped his face with it. Her breath sawed in and out of her lungs as he touched the bridge of his nose gingerly. Stars, she *hoped* it was broken. He deserved to have at least one blemish. The kitsune was too good-looking.

She stiffened.

You do not think he's handsome.

It wasn't the first time she'd lied to herself.

"It's not broken." He sighed. "How did you know about Chesh?"

"Though you believe me ignorant, I'm not. I've had one of the best educations Heimserya can offer. I speak four languages fluently and have extensively studied the neighboring kingdoms and our enemies. Why would you think I would not understand the tattoos on Chesh's body were indicative of the highborn lines of his culture? Hinterland markings are distinctive. They document major life events on their skin. The symbols on his neck and arms were a dead giveaway." She held a finger up. "And I don't understand why he was flaunting them on the ship. Does the crazy cat have a death wish?"

"Speaking of said cat… You two were very close."

She blinked. "What does that mean?"

"Even with a bloody nose I can smell his scent all over you." Pyre gave her a mocking smile and then wiped the rest of the blood off his face. "Did you take some time out of your busy schedule to *play* with Chesh?"

"Excuse me?" Tempest gaped at him and crossed her arms over her chest, feeling self-conscious at his insinuation. "There was no time for any sort of *playing*… Plus, I'm not that sort of girl, anyhow." She scoffed. "As if I'd risk my reputation and future by carelessly taking up with him."

"Because he's an unworthy shifter?"

"No, because I refuse to give something I consider precious to someone I barely know. I may have been raised with men, but they taught me to know my worth, and I know I'm worth more than some tumble in a stinking alley." Several moments of silence passed between them. She hadn't meant to give him that much information.

"Are you done?" he asked, picking at his nails.

His question only riled her up again. She wasn't near done. "The journey was *hell* to get here, Pyre," she spat. "Did Brine tell you we were ambushed in the forest? A bloody dragon appeared! I didn't even know those existed anymore. And then —" she held her hands in the air "—he *shifted*. It was a lucky thing that I had something he wanted, or he would have slaughtered us all for whatever perceived slight he imagined between us."

Pyre stiffened. "Did you barter with him?"

His tone of voice had her stomach quivering. "I did what I had to. You should be thankful. If it weren't for me, your men would be dead."

Pyre's eyes sharpened. "What did you give him?"

"None of your business," she replied, careful to avoid touching her hair beneath her ear where a lock of it was missing. It was only hair, so why didn't she want to tell him? Tempest shook her head and turned the conversation back on the kitsune. "And what are you doing dealing with damn dragons, anyway?" She stabbed a finger at the door. "There was one here not even five minutes ago!"

He shrugged. "It seems as if you had a full day, Temp." The glint in his eyes changed, and he scanned her from head to toe and back again. She crossed her arms, feeling like he could see right through her nightgown. Why had she dropped her blanket? "Going by the way you're shivering, I'd say you're in need of a warm drink in front of the fire."

It truly was freezing standing barefoot on the cold stone. The cavernous room was drafty. For a moment, she considered saying no, but practicality won out over her insatiable desire to make Pyre as miserable as she was. She nodded slowly and rubbed the bare skin of her arms. The chill seemed to go as deep as her bones.

"Then, let's go to my study," he replied, a pleased smile

lifting his lips. "I have some tea brewing in there, and it's a hell of a lot warmer than in here. Come, follow me."

Pyre started for the door, his boots echoing on the etched stone floor. She darted back to her filched blanket, shook it out, and then wrapped it around her shoulders. Quickly, she snatched her bag from the ground and followed him through the huge double doors. He led her down a series of winding corridors lined with columns until they reached a very ordinary-sized, wooden door. The kitsune opened the door and indicated for Tempest to enter first. She sighed at the wave of heat that welcomed her. Tempest hummed in relief as her toes sank into a plush rug. She wasted no time tossing her bag next to a cushioned armchair near the fire and then collapsing into it. It was so nice to be off her feet after days of traveling. Her brows slashed together as she inspected the room closer.

"This room looks as if it was taken straight out of your cottage in the forest," she mused, noting the paintings on the wall, the old wooden desk, and chipped kettle sitting in the fire, releasing a little steam from the spout. The place felt homey. Nothing like the cave, her lavish temporary chamber, or the cavernous meeting hall they'd just come from.

"That was the point," he replied. Pyre knelt beside the fire to remove the kettle. "Even one such as I needs his home comforts... even during a rebellion."

One such as I. She pursed her lips and stared at her lap. It was little moments like this that she forgot what he was, *who* he was. It would be her downfall if she wasn't careful. He was the Jester, not her Pyre.

He's not your anything.

"Temp?"

She lifted her head, and he flashed her a grin.

"What's on your mind?" he asked, pouring a cup of tea.

"Nothing that would interest you," she murmured.

"Everything you do interests me."

Her heart stuttered. *He's playing you. Proceed with caution.* She nodded at the teacup. "I hope that's for you. Tea won't cut it this time. You have any fire whiskey?" She didn't drink spirits that often, but whiskey was the only thing that would chase the chill from her bones. Then, she'd have some tea.

Pyre chuckled and set the kettle back on its stand before moving from the fire to a glass-fronted cabinet behind the desk. He set the teacup on the wooden desk and removed a small bottle of amber liquid from the cabinet. "Anything for my Lady Hound."

"Do *not* call me that," Tempest warned. "You know I hate it." It reminded her of Destin, someone she wanted nothing to do with.

An emotion flashed through Pyre's eyes, but it was gone too quickly for her to discern. She wasn't the only one hiding things.

With deft hands, he poured two fingers of fire whiskey into a glass and then another with less. He picked up both glasses and moved to her side, holding the one with more spirits out to her. She took it carefully from him, her fingers brushing his. Something electric passed between them, but she ignored it. Tempest swirled her whiskey while Pyre sat in the armchair opposite her. She eyed his drink. If he was aiming to get her drunk, it wouldn't happen. She was more careful than that. Plus, she had too many secrets that could come spilling out if she wasn't cautious.

He raised his glass. "To surviving brigands, smugglers, and dragons, then."

The smallest of smiles curled Tempest's lips despite herself. She *had* survived all three, and, at least for a little while, she could rest and recover, but she didn't raise her glass.

He frowned. "Not celebrating?"

She shrugged and took a small sip. "Seems wrong to tempt fate."

"Fate?" he murmured. "Doesn't exist."

"Agreed, but let's be careful, shall we? No need to be disrespectful to the powers that be."

Pyre smirked. "Don't you know who I am? I'm the Jester. I *am* the powers that be."

CHAPTER 14: PYRE

*T*empest's scent was killing him.

Every breath he inhaled made the primal side of himself roll beneath his skin. He was simultaneously drawn closer to her and repelled at the same time. The intoxicating smell of pine needles, mint, and female made his mouth water, but it was the scent of the dragon and Chesh that sent him almost to the edge of a frenzied madness he could barely suppress. The fingers of his left hand drummed along the arm of the chair as he tried to breathe only through his mouth. Why had he thought it would be a good idea to be in such close quarters with her?

Because she's never affected you this way before.

He scowled and glared at the fireplace. What was his problem? His control was legendary.

And then there was the way she looked…

Pyre glanced at Tempest from the corner of his eye. Her hair was a wild, wavy mess around her face and tumbled down her back. The blanket she'd been using as a cloak had slipped off her right shoulder, revealing pale, creamy skin. Skin he wanted to lick and bite.

He grunted and took another sip of the fire whiskey, savoring the burn. Tempest shifted in her chair, the blanket slipping farther, so he got a better look at her form beneath the silken nightgown. It was modest and covered more than most of the dresses women wore to court, and yet... It clung to every curve of her, exaggerating the lines of her body in such a way that it almost felt indecent. Pyre was struck by his desire to toss the young woman over his shoulder, take her to some white-columned temple, and worship her in every way he could think of.

And she had no clue.

Women were his favorite creatures roaming the world. He'd spent years in their company and had come to know when a woman was truly unaware of her beauty. Tempest was clueless. He pursed his lips and appreciated the way the fire illuminated her luxurious, periwinkle hair, turning it into seemingly magical flames. Her uncles should be ashamed of themselves for not taking more care of their most prized possession. They'd allowed her to enter the Jester's lair, and she was a lamb among wolves.

She brushed a wayward lock from her face and gazed at the fire, oblivious to his staring.

Or she's pointedly ignoring you.

It was most likely the latter. He knew she rarely missed anything. Despite this, he wanted to touch her. Wanted to bury his nose in her hair and drink her in, run his lips along her graceful throat.

Resist the urge. Just behave yourself. She's the enemy.

He squeezed the glass in his right hand and forced himself to stop dwelling on things that could never happen. Plus, he needed to deal with the proverbial storm cloud hanging over her. She was angry with him and rightfully so, which was the best way for him to keep her at arm's length. He had to keep the Hound on her toes—wondering what his next move would be—and she could not get closer to him. Things couldn't change between them. It was risky giving her more knowledge than necessary. Tempest was unpredictable.

The incident where she embraced him at the cottage still haunted him. One moment had changed him. What would happen if he allowed her even closer?

She tasted of salvation, but the female would destroy him and everything he'd built.

Pyre downed the rest of the whiskey in one long draught, eyeing Tempest carefully as she watched the flames in the hearth. He smirked when she set the glass aside, leaving spirits in the glass. She was a suspicious one and had caught on to his game. He'd hoped to loosen her up, but she wasn't taking the bait. Smart girl.

He glanced down at his own glass and gazed longingly into the empty bottom, wishing there was more. The stuff was delicious, but he wasn't dumb enough to imbibe. He'd been drunk exactly once in his lifetime and would never go that far again. He liked control, and too many spirits stole any semblance of that. It wasn't worth it.

"Tea?" he asked softly, pushing out of his chair and holding his hand out for Tempest's glass.

"I suppose," she said without looking at him.

Stubborn woman. After the bloody nose and tongue-lashing

she'd given him, the female had gone oddly silent, not saying more than three words to him at a time. He didn't like it. Not one bit.

Pyre placed their cups on his desk and moved back to the hearth, busying himself with pouring tea into two cups painted with gold leaf and a bright-cerulean blue dye. He added a spoonful of honey to his own cup. As a child, they were too poor to have sweets. Now that he could afford them, he realized he liked sweet things. His gaze darted to Tempest.

And spicy things.

He huffed out a breath and gestured to the honey pot.

She shook her head. "I don't like it sweet. I'm surprised that *you* do."

"Not sure what that is supposed to mean." He shrugged and then winked at her, which caused the prickly female to scowl. "There is a lot you do not know about me."

He held out her cup of tea, and she took it from him, this time pointedly not touching his fingers. Pyre hid his smile. So, she felt it too. When they touched, it lit him up. He straightened and moved back to his chair and sat. They drank in silence, sipping at the scalding tea far slower than the spirits.

Her scent swirled around him, and he grimaced at the metallic scent of dragon bleeding through her own pleasant scent. It set his teeth on edge. He could tolerate Chesh's trespass. The Hinterland mischief-maker was always messing with him, but the dragon was something else. His scent marking was blatantly disrespectful of the scents Tempest already carried.

The silence stretched on.

He couldn't handle it anymore.

"I'm sorry about your journey," he said. "It wasn't supposed to be like that." Them being attacked, at least.

Tempest's gaze moved from the fire and met his. Her lovely eyes were troubled and stormy. "Who were those people? The ones in the forest and the ones who brought us here?"

A pause. His soldiers. "I think you know who they are."

Her lips thinned against the rim of her teacup. "I imagine you're gathering allies. But who *are* they? It's one thing for me to know you and Nyx and Briggs and Brine. It's another entirely for you to expect me to work alongside brigands and murderers."

Pyre did not reply. It was war. War wasn't pretty. It was dark, gritty, and deadly. There wasn't room for valiant heroes, only men and women who got the job done. Destin needed to be removed from the throne at all costs. He shrugged, knowing anything else he said would only anger her.

Instead, he redirected the conversation. "Did you manage to retrieve anything from the smuggler?"

She froze and then nodded slowly. "I did."

"Do you have it?" he asked, amused that she'd let him change the subject so easily.

Tempest released her blanket, and he swallowed as she bent over to riffle through her bag. He cursed underneath his breath as her nightgown gaped, and he was rewarded with a glimpse of more flawless skin. Pyre dropped his gaze to her feet, feeling like a complete rogue. He'd never been ashamed to look at a woman before. Why now?

She fumbled through her satchel, and, after a few moments, pulled out a familiar wooden box. "This," she said, unceremoniously thrusting it at Pyre. "I hope me almost being sold off was worth it."

"Oh, it is." He pulled the box from her fingers and brushed his right hand across the smooth surface. Pyre ran his fingers along all the joints and edges. It hadn't been tampered with. He flicked a glance at the female and then back to the box. She hadn't tried to open it. How unexpected.

"What is it?"

"Something special." He didn't elaborate further.

The Hound huffed and pulled the damned blanket closer, hiding her from his gaze. "When am I leaving this place?"

The frankness of her question caused him to laugh. "So eager to leave, aren't you? You're under orders from Destin to infiltrate my rebels, are you not?"

She slumped her shoulders and returned her gaze to the fire. His lips twitched at the grumpy expression on her face. Her lips pursed, and she schooled her expression, her feelings masked from him. His hands clenched on the box. He didn't like Tempest hiding from him.

Look at me.

"Those are my instructions from my sovereign," she murmured. "Which you are not. I do not belong to you, nor do I work for you. I'm tired of being ordered around with no explanation."

His face softened. He knew exactly how Tempest felt, yet there was nothing to be done for it. They were both in an impossible situation. Uneasy allies.

"Stay here for a while, Temp. Make yourself at home here. Feel free to explore the place and go wherever you like. You're not a prisoner here, but in the next few weeks, I'll need your help if you're willing to give it."

"Doing what?"

"Any number of things."

"I'll not kill for you," she said resolutely.

"I haven't asked you to," he responded.

Tempest snorted. "It's only a matter of time. I know what your type are like."

"My type?" he asked, a little bit annoyed.

She faced him fully and stared him down. "The power-hungry type. I stare at one every day I'm summoned in the palace."

Rage, hot and fast, exploded in his gut. He leaned out of his chair, his lip curling and a growl rumbling in his chest. "I am *nothing* like him."

The stupid female didn't even have the brains to blanch. He was a hair's breadth away from shifting. She arched a brow and leaned forward so they were breathing the same air.

"Prove it."

He blinked slowly, and, despite the rage churning just below the surface, Pyre smiled. "I like challenges." He glanced at her mouth as her lips twitched. "I need you to come with me to a ball."

"You mean a masquerade?" she drawled.

She missed nothing.

He gave her one of his charming smiles. "A party is just what everyone needs right now," Pyre explained. "We need to reduce the tension and ensure continued goodwill between the factions as much as possible. We *must* keep up a united front against Destin." And it made for the perfect cover for what he had planned that night.

Tempest teetered her head back and forth, and then pointed at the box in Pyre's hands. "What's in the box?"

She wasn't letting it go. He hid his grin, and, with deft fingers, made quick work of the puzzle that protected the contents from the wrong hands. He lifted the lid and pulled out the delicate mask he'd had commissioned. A wolf.

"Are you serious?" she exclaimed, affronted. "I risked my life for some trinket? Why was Chesh so adamant that I not open it? It's a bloody mask, for Dotae's sake!"

"Ah, Temp, it was not the mask that was important," Pyre replied, shaking his head good-naturedly. He held up the box for Tempest to inspect, pointing out a mechanism on the latch. "If you had tampered with it—tried to open it without knowing the precise solution to the puzzle—the box would have released a poison that would have killed you within four hours."

She stiffened. "So, all of this was—"

"A test of your trustworthiness," Pyre said. Tempest began trembling as he set the box on the floor and leaned back in his chair. "Be mad at me all you want; I had to do it. And I have no qualms about telling you how *happy* I am that you passed." He was relieved, in fact.

"You are *unbelievable*," the Hound hissed. She sucked in a breath and stood.

Here it comes.

A knock upon the door stilled her.

He glanced at the door as Nyx glided into the room, followed by Briggs, who paused in the doorway.

"Out of my chair," his sister demanded.

"My lady," he said sarcastically, standing. Nyx flopped into his chair. "Make yourself at home." He let out a huff of indignation, then moved over to the doorway where Briggs hovered.

"Tempest," Nyx said warmly. "It is great to see you. You were not hurt on the road, were you?"

She shook her head. "Brine and Swiftly weren't so fortunate, though."

Nyx laughed lightly. "They will be fine. I've tended to their wounds myself. How have you been doing?"

"Oh, same old, same old. Trying not to get caught for being a traitor and being hanged. The usual."

Pyre rolled his eyes and left the two females in his study. Briggs followed him and closed the door behind them. Pyre moved down the hallway, his friend shadowing every step.

"Any word of anyone following Tempest here?"

Briggs bent low to reply. "Brine kept everyone off their trail. It's clear Destin sent other Hounds after Tempest. Presumably to infiltrate your court."

Pyre let out an arrogant grunt. "They could try, for sure. Oh, they could try."

They would fail. He'd make sure of it.

CHAPTER 15: TEMPEST

empest was ashamed to admit that it was too easy to fall into her new routine. Time flew by as days turned to weeks. She'd always been a creature of habit, after all; her entire life with the Hounds had been strictly regimented. A good routine made her feel grounded.

She spent much of each morning training. In the afternoons, Nyx always had something to occupy her time, followed by a friendly sparring session. The female shifter was *fast*. Tempest had more bruises from their matches than she'd acquired in a long time, but it was worth it. She'd become faster out of necessity. It also kept her too exhausted and preoccupied to think of much else.

When dinner rolled around, it was a lesson in endurance. Tempest had always been an outsider, but her uncles had made sure to make her feel at home. The den of deceit—the name she'd given the Jester's mountain castle—was not kind to strangers. Each evening, it was made abundantly clear that she was not *one* of them. Normally, baleful glances and malicious whispers didn't bother her. She'd dealt with them her whole life at the king's court, but this was different. In the king's court, Tempest was an oddity. Here, she was the enemy.

She'd taken to covering her hair with a hood because it attracted too much attention and marked her for what she was: a Hound. Tempest wanted to dye it, but Nyx wouldn't hear of it. Though Nyx didn't say *why*, Tempest had more than a sneaking suspicion that it had something to do with the Jester wanting to show off the traitorous Hound at his side. Every crook and degenerate from leagues away who'd come to stay in the mountains seemed to want to look upon the Jester's *trophy*. It rankled her, but she shoved it down. She had a job to do, and information wouldn't be gained if she kept to herself or allowed the suspicious lot to push her out. And they were right to be wary of her. When she discovered all the parts of the truth, she was coming for them. At least, the ones who were the worst of the criminals.

Tempest pulled the linen from her cracked knuckles and dropped to the sparring mat, the lantern light flickering. She rolled her neck and savored the quiet. Nyx hadn't been the only one she'd been training with. Tempest would be the first to admit, it was brutal. It made sparring with the Hounds seem like mere warm-up sessions by comparison. Everyone wanted a go at the Hound. There was a lot of bad blood between the Hounds and those of Talagan descent.

During the first two weeks, she thought she might die, but she was too stubborn to give up. No matter how hard she fought against Pyre or Mal or Brine, Tempest lost four out of five rounds. Luck only granted her a win. It wasn't skill; it was sheer willpower not to lose and chance, no matter how much they beat her. Tempest *always* got up, even when they told her to stay down. Nothing was ever gained by admitting defeat, or so Maxim said.

Maxim.

Her heart clenched, and she leaned her head against the cold, stone wall, closing her eyes against the traitorous tears that fought to escape. She missed her family. And while she thrived on confrontation, Tempest longed for a safe place just to be herself, to feel like she mattered. Like she had worth. The shifters made her feel like a child all over again—the pitiful female novice taken in by grown men, who indulged their amusement by giving her a chance to fight them. Her fingers curled into fists.

Stop feeling sorry for yourself. You're not a child. Take what they dole out and learn from it.

She was getting better, or so Brine told her.

A small smile lifted her lips. That was an unexpected turn of events.

Apparently, their journey had bonded them. Brine's temperament and attitude had changed toward her since their arrival at the den of deceit. No longer was the wolf shifter directly hostile or snippy just for the sake of it. Well, he was still as prickly and gruff as ever, but he wasn't outright mean anymore. He'd become decidedly neutral, and in turn, he'd become one of her favorite sparring partners. She had studied his aggressive, direct form of attacking, and had then quickly learned how to battle against it. Their matches always left her heaving and covered in sweat, but in a satisfied way. What was even more satisfying was when she'd surprise the wolf, and he'd give an itty-bitty smile. It was like winning a bag full of gold.

Battling Mal, on the other hand, was another matter entirely.

From the very beginning, she had not wanted to fight him at all. She'd seen him in the ring with massive shifters, and he was ruthless. He took down every single man, no matter how far he had to go. He'd almost killed two men and didn't even blink an eye. In addition to his disturbing actions and his need to win, he hated her. Tempest had no clue what she'd done to gain such malice or attention from the man, but it was a problem, especially when he challenged her in the ring. Her uncles had taught her to be wise and humble. She knew she couldn't beat him. But Mal had insisted, goaded, and embarrassed her until she had no choice but to accept his challenge.

Damn her pride.

In battle, he was just as arrogant as Pyre, but far more devious and cutthroat. He didn't pull his punches. The moment her guard dropped even the slightest always meant pain.

Now, Tempest lifted her shirt and stared at the purple bruise spanning her navel. Just today he'd jammed the hilt of a dagger into her stomach so forcefully that she'd puked and then wheezed for five minutes. She dropped her shirt and shook her head. Dima would call her an idiot for going back for more. Tempest huffed. Even if it killed her, she would best the pompous deviant one way or another.

And then there was Pyre...

His fighting style intrigued her. He was just as playful in fighting as he was in everyday life, but make no mistake, he was just as deadly as Mal when he wanted to be. She wiped a hand down her face. From their very first match, she'd been intrigued, and though she was loath to admit it, Tempest enjoyed their sessions more than she should. Pyre was constantly in motion. It seemed as if his feet never touched the floor. Even so, he seemingly found it more interesting to dodge her attacks than attempt to land any of his own.

It was an intricate dance.

And intimate.

She swallowed and tamped down the butterflies that tried to take flight in her belly. It was easy to become enamored with the man one sparred with. Emotions and adrenaline were up. Chemistry was understandable, but if she let any feelings develop... that was too dangerous. She couldn't get wrapped up in the Jester. Any attraction would get her in trouble eventually. While he strived to only show her the playful, fun parts of his personality, she'd always experienced the darker parts. They were deal-breakers. It was important to keep those in mind.

She looked at the door and willed herself to get up. It was late. For a normal household, people would be asleep, but not here. The Dark Court came alive once the sun set. Which worked well for her. While the degenerates were drinking and causing mischief and mayhem, she was exploring the strange mountain palace mostly without disruption. She'd gotten into a few scrapes with loudmouthed, randy lay-abouts on more than one occasion when exploring the place, though the fighting never came to much. A dagger lodged between their thighs was all it took to send most of her would-be opponents running off like frightened children. Her lips twitched. It even scared dragons off.

Pyre had given her permission to explore every nook and cranny of the place. But despite this, she was convinced that *something* was hidden in its depths that she wasn't supposed to find. But she hadn't found anything—yet. It was only a matter of time.

With a groan, Tempest hauled herself from the floor. Her whole body ached, and she longed for bed. She snatched the bloody linens from the floor and tossed them into the bin on her way out of the sparring room. Chills rippled down her arms as she entered one of the draughty hallways. The palace was so cold. There weren't enough fires to warm the place. The lanterns cast writhing shadows against the stone walls, and she frowned as she moved down the hallway. It was much too dark for her taste.

She wandered down staircases and corridors, memorizing them as she went. Even though her thighs protested the stairs, she was determined to find the dungeons. Surely, they were on the lowest floors, but who knew? The Jester was eccentric. Maybe he liked to toss his prisoners from the ramparts?

Tempest sighed as the air warmed. She liked this part of the journey. The air was warmer here, though more suffocating. It was like breathing water, but she preferred it to the draughts on the upper floors. The haunting breeze whispered secrets and betrayals in her ear. She ran her right hand along the wall of the spiraling staircase. There was so much to learn. Information was key when she dealt with Destin. He wasn't an idiot. She needed something that would appease him. While training was fulfilling, she hadn't gained any more information... Her lips thinned. The annoying kitsune was keeping her out of the loop.

You're not here to look pretty. Dig deeper.

The scuff of a boot against stone caught her attention. Tempest paused. Just a drunk knave or something more insidious? The footsteps quicken. Winter's bite, she didn't have time for this. She took two stairs at a time and ducked into the first corridor she came across. Fighting on stairs was just stupid. She sprinted into the darkened hallway twenty paces and then turned to face the stairway, pulling daggers from her wrist sheaths. Her breath sawed in and out of her chest. Tempest scowled at the doorway when two shifters burst into the hallway. She didn't have time for this. Her body ached, and she didn't want to fight anyone. Why couldn't they leave her alone?

They paused. Her pulse leapt. Not just shifters. One was a giant. The enormous man took a slow step closer, a weak light playing over his face. There wasn't any kindness there, only malice.

"Would you like to play?" the giant asked softly, menace blanketing his tone. Her jaw clenched. Whatever happened next would hurt.

"Yes, she wants to play," the slithering voice of the shifter said as he emerged from the shadows behind the giant. She fought a chill as a forked tongue flicked from his mouth. A reptilian shifter. The only question... was he venomous? She couldn't allow him close enough to find out.

The giant grinned and pulled a broadsword from his sheath with an evil hiss. Wicked hell, a broadsword? Really. He raised his heavy sword and charged. She dodged beneath his guard and popped to her feet, just in time to parry an attack from the shifter. He was fast. She sliced at his arms, and he bared his teeth in a hiss.

Damn. A snake, not a lizard.

She spun away and grunted as she met the giant's second attack. Her teeth clacked together from the strike that rattled her very bones. Her spine cracked against the stone wall, and she cried out as pain ricocheted through her system. She wouldn't last long if she kept taking hits like that. She needed to fight smarter.

Tempest bared her teeth and ducked away, slashing at the giant's abdomen.

"Stupid little wench!" the giant growled.

Tempest panted, keeping both men in her sight. Her legs wobbled. She shouldn't have trained so hard today.

Dig deeper. You're not weak.

Her fingers clenched her daggers. She hadn't broken for Mal, the Jester, or King Destin. She would not break now, especially to such unsavory brigands. If she gave them the slightest bit of weakness, they'd tear her limb from limb.

"So, boys, are you just going to stand there all day, or can we crack on?"

Her words did the trick. It riled both men, and they attacked.

She fell into a dance of sorts, defending herself. Her arms were shaking, and sweat slicked her body to the point that the hilts of her daggers slipped in her palms. She needed to get out of there. The snake man darted forward, and she feinted backward, her left foot slipping, twisting her ankle.

Heat and pain exploded around her foot. She hissed and shifted her weight just as the giant slammed his fist into her left shoulder. Tempest crashed painfully to her knees. The reptile shifter sliced her leg. Tears sprung to her eyes, and she cried out. The wound was deep. The giant lifted his huge foot, and only years of training saved her life. She rolled out of the way and stumbled to her feet. She lurched toward the staircase. Maybe she could just roll down them.

A hysterical laugh bubbled in the back of her throat. She was dead.

So much for standing strong.

Blood poured down her leg in waves of red; throbbing

agony crashed into her over and over again. She limped to the stairs and glanced over her shoulder. The giant and shifter weren't attacking. They just stood in the flickering light like specters.

The giant nodded at her, his fathomless gaze locked on her. He chuckled. "Remember this. You might eat with us, train with us, but you're not one of us. Your weakness and arrogance will get you killed."

She swallowed and stumbled onto the staircase. As quickly as she could, she dragged herself up the stairs, pain and blood loss making her dizzy. Her whole body trembled as mocking laughter echoed up the stone staircase. She paused to make a tourniquet for her leg from her soiled shirt before continuing her death climb. She passed no one.

By the time she reached the level her room was on, she crawled along the floor, her leg dragging behind her. *Just a bit farther.* The hallway spun, and she barely clung to consciousness. She almost cried when she spotted her door along with the most unwelcomed visitor lazing on it like a petulant lord without a care in the world.

Mal.

Tempest struggled to her feet and tried to act like she wasn't hurt, but it was useless. And completely dumb. Anyone could see she was a bloody mess, between the odd set of her shoulder, her bloody leg, and her twisted ankle. Mal scanned her from head to toe in one fell swoop of his icy gaze. He said nothing.

She clung to the wall and lifted her chin. "Go on," Tempest challenged him, shaking on the spot with her effort to stay standing. "Make fun of me. Call me weak. Call me a coward for running away—"

Mal did none of those things.

One moment he was leaning on her door, and the next she was in his arms and they were moving into her bedroom. She flinched as he kicked the door shut behind them and stormed across her room, his frigid expression revealing nothing. He gently sat her on the chaise lounge near the fire and wordlessly moved across the room. He rummaged through the large wardrobe opposite her bed. He returned with a box full of bandages and healing supplies, his steps stiff. Stars, she hurt. All she wanted was her bed.

Mal motioned for Tempest to lower her camisole from her shoulder, which she reluctantly did.

"What are you doing?"

With a vicious pull of her arm, he reset her dislocated shoulder. She screamed before she could stop herself and then slumped into the chair, her body trembling with discomfort. Her head lulled, and her eyelids seemed just too heavy to keep open. Mal lowered himself to his knees, and she blinked slowly as he grabbed her ruined trousers and ripped them off of her.

"Strong," she muttered, her tongue feeling clumsy in her mouth. And indecent.

"Shapeshifter," he muttered.

Tears squeezed out of her eyes, and she panted as he began to clean the cut on her leg. Sweet poison, that hurt. He opened a pot of salve and the familiar, cloying smell of mimkia filled Tempest's nostrils. She gritted her teeth as Mal began applying the drug to first her leg wound, then her shoulder, and finally her ankle.

It was nothing like when her uncles cared for her. Mal was efficient, but cold—begrudgingly helping her. Tempest resisted the urge to outright cry when the mimkia burned her skin, but she bore through it. In a few moments, she knew there would be no pain at all. Hopefully, tomorrow she'd be healed enough to walk. Thank the winter for miracle drugs.

Tempest dipped her chin and blinked slowly at Mal. He ignored her and inspected her ankle. He clucked his tongue as he gently moved it this way and that to check if it was broken.

"Careless," he muttered.

She glared at him. If she'd been careless, she would have been dead five levels down in an empty corridor. *Bastard.* As if this were her fault.

Apparently satisfied with the state of her ankle, he carefully bandaged it up before gracefully rising to tower above her. Everything he did was like an exercise in control. She'd not seen him express any emotion other than disdain and snobbery since she'd arrived. But despite that, there was something about his strong, silent presence that made her feel small and protected, as odd as it was.

"Who caused all this pain?" Mal asked bluntly, his voice cutting through her like a winter breeze.

There was something about the way he asked the question that bespoke death and pain. Her lips thinned, and she glanced at the fire. She didn't know who exactly attacked her, but she could describe them. Was it worth it, though? Her assailants had caused pain, but they hadn't killed her or attempted to rape her. That was more than she could say for some of her other fights since arriving at the mountain palace. If she gave the men up, it could result in losing the trust of the shifters she'd worked so hard to gain.

Don't protect the guilty.

She closed her eyes and inhaled deeply. Were they truly guilty? Or were they just acting on prejudices, just as she had done at one time? Tempest didn't know, and only time would tell.

Tempest kept her mouth shut and met Mal's icy gaze. She'd stay silent. For now. He cocked his head and studied her. She expected a biting comment or a threat. Instead, he smiled.

Her whole body stiffened, and her heart began to pound. It was a charming smile—or should have been charming—but she saw right through it. It was the kind of smile that signaled death was standing before you.

She shivered and opened her mouth to protest, but before she said one word—to protest or lie or anything else that she could think of—Mal left the room.

Tempest wavered, her eyelids lowering as she stared at the door.

What had she done?

CHAPTER 16: TEMPEST

"...empest. Tempest? *Tempest!*"

She shook herself and turned from her breakfast, her gaze blurry. Stars, she ached, and her head was killing her. To say she'd slept poorly the night before would be an understatement. Tempest blinked repeatedly and was greeted by Briggs's worried face. "I'm fine," she mumbled.

He crossed his arms and lifted one brow. "You look like death."

"Thanks," she mumbled, pushing her eggs around on her plate. Even drugged up, she could feel the stares of those around her.

"No training today, okay?" Briggs murmured, gently laying a huge hand on her back. "I want to examine your wounds."

Tempest nodded. She didn't care what he did as long as he let her go back to bed.

"You need to rest until those wounds heal. Do you understand me?"

She nodded again, feeling queasy.

"Don't just nod like a bird; use your words, lass. Don't forget that I know you. You push yourself too hard."

For once, she agreed with him. Tempest pushed her plate away, her silverware clattering against the clay plate. "I swear I shall not train today." She smiled warmly and bumped Briggs's shoulder with her own. "I need a walk, and then it's back to bed for me."

He raised an incredulous eyebrow, then pointed at Tempest's bandaged ankle. "How far are you going on that leg, do you think?"

Pesky bear.

"As far as I can manage," she insisted. "And besides, the mimkia is doing its job. Another day, and my ankle will be good as new." Or so she hoped. Being cooped up in her room sounded a miserable option. Her gaze swept the room, noting the glances and blatant stares being thrown her way. When would it stop? Were they staring like normal, or was it because they knew what had happened the night before? She dropped her chin and stared at the table, tracing her finger along the woodgrain. Did they know she ran from a fight?

"I need to get out of here," she said, pushing to her feet. Even standing and with Briggs sitting, they were eye to eye. He gave her a worried look, which she ignored. She'd be fine. "Feel free to visit me when you have time." Tempest kissed his dusky cheek and then hobbled toward the door. It wasn't until she'd made it down the hallway, that she realized what she'd done. Briggs wasn't family and yet she'd treated him like one of her uncles. It just came naturally.

This place is messing with your head. You're letting your guard down.

Tempest growled and soldiered on, determined to take a walk through the draughty hallways. Hallways that were still dark. The mountain palace seemed to be a place of eternal night. With no windows nearby to let in light, it was always dark. At first, it had disoriented her, but she'd grown used to it.

She paused her mindless wandering and huffed out a weak laugh when she realized she had accidentally made her way to the training hall. Even broken and battered, she couldn't keep away. Tempest leaned against the wall and eyed the door. While she couldn't spar, there was no harm in watching people train. If she was lucky, she'd work out a few new tricks by observing the others.

Tempest pulled the door open and stepped inside. Her skin prickled, and she froze when she took in the scene. In the middle of the sparring ring were the two males who had attacked her the evening before. They were strapped to the floor, bleeding. Her stomach rolled at the stench of coppery blood. Despite herself, she trembled as she caught sight of the man in charge of the beating.

Mal.

His back was to her, and he held a wicked-looking whip, while a large group of shifters stood silently by, watching. The giant yelled when Mal brought the whip down over his face and then his back which was a meaty mess. Mal turned slightly, exposing his profile. He smiled, *smiled*. It was as if he *liked* doling out the pain.

Bile burned the back of her throat, and Tempest held a hand over her mouth. Stars, she might be sick. While she did want justice for being attacked, she didn't want it like this. This, she wanted no part of.

Mal raised his whip to strike the reptilian shifter, and she lurched away from the door before she could fully process her actions, putting far more strain on her ankle than was wise. She limped in front of the shifter, raising an arm just as the whip came down. White-hot agony burst across her forearm and wrapped around her wrist. Heat pressed at the back of her eyes, but she managed to stay silent against the pain.

A dangerous, oppressive silence swelled in the room, only broken by the panting giant and her pulse beating in her ears. Tempest dragged her gaze around the room as fat drops of scarlet liquid dripped from her arm to the floor. She made note of everyone who had happily allowed such a display of torture to occur. She lingered on Nyx, and her lips curled at the woman who didn't look ashamed in the least.

Barbarians. Animals.

Blood slipped down her arm, and, yet, no one said a word. No one moved.

She turned her attention back to the ring master. Tempest unleased all her disgust, hatred, and judgement she could muster in her expression. Five heartbeats passed, and she couldn't look at his impassive face one second longer. She used her left hand to slowly and carefully remove the whip from her flesh. The end fell to the floor in a wet splatter. Tempest turned her back to Mal and knelt on the floor, her fingers working at the first knot that held down the snake man. He moaned as she tugged harder on the knot.

"I'm sorry," she whispered.

"Stop," Mal commanded from behind her, his voice cutting through the air like a knife.

Not on his life. The men had been punished enough. She ignored him and finished untying the last of the knots around the snake man's wrists.

"I'm going to help you up," she murmured as she helped him into a sitting position. He glanced at her from his swollen eyes before his gaze dropped to his hands, shame clear in his expression.

She scooted toward the ropes around his ankles, then she registered footsteps approaching. Although painful, Tempest spun and unsheathed the blades from her hips, keeping them aimed at Mal as he drew closer. He paused and regarded her with pale, soulless eyes that betrayed nothing.

"Stay back," she growled.

"They deserved their punishment," he said simply. Not an ounce of emotion.

"Do you always torture your own men? Your allies?" She barked in laughter. "What a leader you are." Her lips twitched in victory as his jaw began to tick. It was his only tell. The icy lord did indeed feel something from time to time. He was furious. It only spurred her on further to prod him. "You're as bad as Destin, do you know that? Did you do this of your own accord, or was this sanctioned by Pyre?" she spat.

Mal refused to answer.

Tempest shook her head, disgusted, before turning her attention to Nyx. She stared the woman down until a slight shift in her shoulders told Tempest that Nyx was uncomfortable.

"Their actions were against me, and their punishment has been served," Tempest said severely. "Care for these men."

Nyx blithely moved into the training ring and untied the

giant as Tempest limped toward the door without another look at anyone.

"I'm disgusted with you all." Tempest shoved the door open and stormed into the hall, though her gait was more of an aggravated limp.

Tempest swung around a corner, her own door coming into sight. She'd almost reached her room when the sound of light footsteps crept up behind her, and a hand grabbed at her arm, the scent of sage and pine invading her senses. Pyre.

She shook him off and yanked open her bedroom door. "Get away from me, Pyre!" Rage boiled in her gut. There was no way she could deal with the kitsune without stabbing him. She swung around, intending to lock him out, but he sneaked in and slammed the door behind him, sparks igniting in his eyes.

"Oh, that's rich," she snarled. "You don't get to be mad." Tempest stabbed her finger toward the door. "Get out!"

"You had no right to interfere. Mal said—"

"Don't you dare!" she hissed, moving toward her chair by the fire. She had to sit down, or her ankle would give out. Tempest plopped down on the arm of the chair and glared at the Jester. "I can't believe you. Do you have any idea what your *right-hand man* was up to? Or did you sanction it?"

Pyre's golden eyes glittered dangerously. He paced to the end of her bed, around her chair, and back to the door, circling the room like a caged tiger. "Of course I knew. Do you think anything in this place happens without my say so?"

Trembles ran up her arms. "How could you?" she cried, flinging her uninjured arm out. "How can you hurt people under your command? Are you so heartless and depraved, Pyre? Do you enjoy their pain like young, damned henchman Mal?"

"It is because I *have* a damned heart that I do it!" he fired back, rushing toward the chair.

He reached for her arm again, but Tempest pulled away. Winter's bite, her arm hurt, but at least it had stopped bleeding.

"Explain how that works," she sneered. "Tell me how having a heart justifies torturing two men half to death."

"Because they touched you."

His words were so fierce that it robbed the breath from her lungs. She couldn't believe what she heard. Her eyes narrowed. "Excuse me?"

"You heard me the first time," he replied, fox ears flat against his skull. Pyre growled, flashing his long incisors. "They touched you. They hurt you. Nobody is allowed to touch what's *mine.*"

Mine. The word echoed through her mind. She didn't belong to anyone, let alone the Jester.

She held up a finger. "First of all, I am not *yours.*"

"You're under my protection, are you not?"

"I don't need it," she gritted out.

"Is that so?" he purred. Pyre moved in closer.

Something in his expression had her heart racing. She clumsily stood and put the chair between them. The kitsune laughed softly and brushed a finger over the top of her hand. Her jaw clenched, and she skittered around the chair as he slowly stalked her. He ran his burnished fingers along the top of the wingback chair, a smirk playing about his mouth.

"So fiery, and yet, so delicate," the kitsune whispered.

Tempest bristled. She was not delicate. Pyre blurred, and she inhaled sharply as he pressed her against the back of the chair. She hardly dared to breathe. His fingers skimmed her neck and cheeks softly, emotion flickering through his eyes too quickly for her to discern. He was like fire. One moment, warm and comforting, the next, so hot she'd been burned.

"Such fragile skin," he whispered, tracing Tempest's cheekbone. She pulled her blade from her hip, the soft hiss filling the air, but he didn't move away and neither did she.

"I am not as fragile as you think," Tempest said, her voice just as quiet as Pyre's whisper had been.

His finger drifted to her throat, and he lightly caressed her. "I keep coming back to you," he murmured. He leaned closer, his breath whispering over her forehead. The throb of his pulse picked up speed at the base of his throat, and she licked her lips. He watched the movement, and a thrill raced through her.

You're a fool. Fight. Do something. Don't you dare give in.

He smiled—a genuine, gentle smile, rather than a mischievous grin or a sarcastic, knowing smirk—and then his mouth drifted closer. Lips brushed against lips, and as Tempest took a breath, he stole hers.

Pyre pressed closer, his mouth opening over hers, tasting her, a soft flicking of his tongue over her mouth. *Wicked hell.* Her eyes snapped open, and she felt the press of his chest against her palms, her blade sandwiched between her right hand and his chest as she held him at bay. But it was all an illusion. If the Jester wanted to take more, he could, but the kitsune didn't.

Her fingers flexed against his torso, and she gasped as the muscles of his chest contracted beneath her palms. An odd sound rose in her throat. A damn sigh. She was kissing him, allowing him to kiss her.

As though he sensed her distance, Pyre drew back, his amber eyes scanning her face. His brows slashed together before his eyes narrowed. He caught her face in his hands, and then his mouth swooped down over hers. It was a claiming. The first full sweep of his tongue was a shock, and she tensed as he pressed her harder into the chair, his lips hungrily devouring her own.

Too much. Too far. He had to stop.

You're losing yourself.

CHAPTER 17: TEMPEST

Tempest broke the kiss and slapped him. Her palm stung when she pulled it away, revealing that Pyre's cheek was angry and red. Tempest glared at him, even though she was angrier at herself than anything. He'd played her, and she'd fallen right into his hands.

"How dare you—"

"How dare I?" he cut in heatedly. "Don't act like I'm the villain here."

Tempest's palm tingled. Stars, she wanted to slap him again. "You're the one who pinned *me*. I didn't ask for your unwanted attentions."

"Unwanted attentions?"

His arrogance sluffed away, and his lovely eyes went blank as he stared at her. Her pulse pounded as he remained silent. She had expected him to be reproachful or sarcastic or laugh at her 'over-reaction.' Him doing nothing at all was a hundred times worse. Slowly, Pyre held up his hands and then turned tail. She gaped at his back as he yanked open the door and slammed it so hard the paintings on the walls rattled. Stunned, Tempest was frozen to the spot. She could still taste him on her lips. Her anger gathered along with adrenaline. How dare he storm away like that!

"This is *your* fault!" she screamed at her door. Any normal human being couldn't have heard her, but she was betting the Jester's ears picked up her bellows. "Your fault..." she yelled again, limping over to her bed. She fell backward and slumped against the pillows as the adrenaline left her system just as quickly as it had appeared. Her arm stung like hell. Tempest lifted it up and stared at the raw flesh where Mal's whip had cut it. That was going to need some mimkia, otherwise it would take weeks to heal. But part of her didn't want to go near the drug ever again. Her shoulder, leg, and ankle would be fully healed over the next day or so because of the plant, as if the injuries had never been inflicted in the first place.

Like she'd never been attacked. Like the shifters hadn't attacked her.

More and more, it felt as if her actions were tiny in the face of everything happening. If she did nothing, then things, of course, could only get worse, but when she actually *did* something to bring about change, it seemed as if that made her situation worse.

"Damn you, Pyre," she whispered, turning onto her side and clutching her aching arm to her chest. It took her far too long to realize the wetness on her face meant that she was crying.

For three days, Tempest avoided Pyre like the plague, though it wasn't difficult. The kitsune had scarcely been around in the first place. She huffed. So much for a partnership. She'd been there for weeks and done nothing of consequence. If only she could get rid of Mal so easily. He'd been a thorn in her side since she'd challenged him in front of all the shifters. His presence only served to further distance herself from Pyre. The fact that Pyre had such an amoral person working for him as his right-hand man only lent further credit to her suspicion that the Pyre she met months before no longer existed, if he had existed at all, even then. The worst part was that she missed that man—the fun, playful fox with sparkling eyes and a wicked sense of humor.

Tempest explored the second floor, thankfully without a chaperone. While she loved Briggs and didn't mine Brine, she was tired of being watched. She just wanted to be free to roam without being studied. She was jittery, but that was on the account of going nowhere near the training hall in days. Boredom did not suit her. Walking was not cutting it but at least no one bothered her. Persons of questionable reputation kept to their shadowy alcoves and doors. No one dared touch her, though she did receive a fair number of glares, scowls, and mutterings.

"As if it was *my* fault, damn criminals," Tempest bit out as a woman glared at her so hard she thought her hair would light on fire. She had not given her attackers up, and she was the one to save their lives. It was bloody unfair.

Life is unfair. Aleks's voice echoed through her mind.

She smiled and wandered farther through the upper levels which were considerably more opulent. Tempest snuck through a gaudy, expansive ballroom, an attached kitchen of-sorts, and a handful of stupidly large bedrooms which she learned were currently unoccupied. With the masquerade fast approaching, she reasoned that most, if not all, of the bedrooms were reserved for important guests—heads of factions, brigands, smugglers, and the lot. If only she could be a fly on the wall. Tempest would bet her daggers that the rooms had secrets just like their owner.

She scowled at the mere thought of the Jester and stalked down a smaller corridor on her left, then another. Her mind wandered, and, by the time she got a good look around, she had no idea where she was. Damn. That was sloppy.

"Come on, Temp," she muttered, tossing her head from side to side, trying to figure out where she was. The second floor was larger than she'd expected. She crept down the corridor as silently as was feasible. No need to alert anyone she was here.

Two voices speaking softly pulled her attention to an open doorway on her left. She slunk closer and paused, leaning against the wall.

"It will be okay," a familiar female voice said. *Nyx.*

"I don't think so," Mal's chilly voice answered.

Tempest's nose wrinkled. She hated that bastard. She pushed from the wall and moved to pass the doorway, catching a glimpse of Nyx smiling softly in a warmly-lit room. It screamed of intimacy. No need to bother them.

"No need to run away, Tempest, though that is what you're good at, is it not?" Mal called.

Freezing, she turned on her heel and strode into the room. If he was going to toss out insults, he'd better be prepared for the consequences. Mal crossed his arms over his chest and cocked his head to one side, white hair flashing in the firelight as he looked down his nose at Tempest with arrogant, ice-blue eyes.

"Nyx, it's nice to see you," she said softly, pointedly ignoring Mal.

"And the coward shows her face," he muttered.

Tempest stiffened. "You think someone who stands up for what they believe in is a coward?" she fired back, closing the distance between them. He wouldn't win this battle. What he'd done was wrong.

"Is that what you were doing when you protected the scum who attacked you?" Mal asked, a bark of laughter escaping him. "What kind of person does not want to see justice performed on those who harmed them? They were not innocents. You protected the guilty."

Tempest stabbed a finger against his chest. "And who appointed you as judge, jury, and executioner?" She hid her smile as his jaw began to tick in agitation. She was getting to him.

"I'm beholden to no one, little Hound. The Dark Court is my playground."

"Don't let the Jester hear you say that. I'm sure he has a stringent punishment for those who challenge his position." She cocked her hip and smirked. "I was the one who was attacked, and, by your own rules, I should have been the one to serve justice to those who wronged me. Why did you take it into your own hands? Were you just so bloodthirsty that you shunned real justice? Because that's what it looked like from where I was standing. You're nothing but a washed-up version of Destin."

Mal's eyes flashed, and he lunged for her arm, but she was expecting it. Tempest deftly moved out of the way and swung her leg out to sweep his feet out from underneath him. Mal jumped over her leg then snapped a kick toward her stomach. She dodged the kick, her blood singing.

"Tempest—" Nyx began, moving toward the two of them, but Mal put out a hand to stop her, his gaze not leaving Tempest.

"Leave this to us, Nyx," he snarled. "It's long overdue." He grinned at Tempest, all gleaming teeth and wicked intent. She found herself matching his almost-snarl rather than being intimidated by it.

"It seems we can finally agree on one thing."

"It was bound to happen." He waved a hand at her. "Then let's see you do your worst, *Lady Hound*. Or are you all show?"

The insult riled her. She knew he was baiting her, but she couldn't help it. Tempest went on the offense and threw a straightforward throat punch. He blocked with a solidly muscled forearm, and she swept under his guard to land a punch to his ribs. He spun and grabbed her around the waist, like a lover's embrace, and lifted her off her feet. If he got her onto the floor, she'd lose. Mal was just too big.

Tempest jabbed her elbow into his stomach, and his grip loosened. She ducked out of his arms and put space between them. He began to circle her, but never reached for his knives, so neither did she. He smiled and then attacked. Several minutes passed with their brutal to-and-fro, neither of them giving an inch as their skin grew slick with sweat and their breaths came in heaves and stolen gasps. She scowled at him. He was the most vicious sparring partner she'd ever had. He clearly wouldn't have any compunctions about tossing her around; yet, he hadn't done so.

"You're going easy on me," she spat, brushing her blue hair out of her face.

He shrugged. "I didn't want you to feel as weak and powerless as you are."

Hell, no.

Tempest yelled and attacked. It wasn't sparring anymore. It was her against him. He'd challenged her ideals and her worth. She got in one good uppercut before he gained the upper hand and toppled her to the ground, straddling her hips to keep her in place while his hands pinned her wrists.

His white hair hung around his face, giving them a curtain as he lowered his lips to her ear. His breath tickled her skin as he growled, "Are you done yet?"

"Not even close," she breathed. He pulled back, just far enough so her gaze could focus properly on his blue eyes. If he was going to use all his strengths, so was she. For the first time in her life, Tempest played dirty.

She kissed him.

She clenched her gut, preparing for the man to loosen his hold and jerk away from her. Instead, Mal did the exact opposite; he tightened his fingers around Tempest's wrists. She gasped, her mouth giving him the opening he was looking for. A shudder went through his massive frame that blanketed hers. His hard body melted into hers, and he kissed her like a desperate man, passion threatening to drown her.

Tempest turned her face to the side, gasping into his snowy hair as she tried to remember what the hell she was doing. Mal grabbed a fistful of her hair and pulled softly. She arched her neck, and his heated mouth moved feverishly down her skin.

He moved back to her lips, leaving a trail of licks and nips. The kisses deepened, and his tongue rasped over her teeth. Mal kissed her like he needed her to breathe. His lips easily pressed against hers, molding their mouths against one another. It was a desperate claiming.

One that was oddly familiar.

Tempest froze.

She turned her face away from Mal's, breaking the kiss as the cogs of her brain turned wildly. *It can't be.*

He twisted his fingers through her hair and began planting gentle but desperate kisses down her neck once again. It wasn't just that his lips had felt familiar.

They were exactly *the same.*

Tempest began to shake uncontrollably—from anger, from disbelief. Mal lifted his head, icy eyes warm for the first time. His love-drunk expression faded, and a frown formed between his brows.

It couldn't be true.

Using his temporary distraction to her advantage, she wriggled free, leapt to her feet, and ran a shaking hand through her hair. How had she not seen it before? Out of the corner of her eye, she noticed that Nyx had disappeared. Her gaze darted back to the man in question who stood and brushed out the wrinkles in his clothing like he'd not been minutes away from tumbling her.

"You deceitful liar!" she whispered.

Mal's frown deepened. "What's wrong with you now?"

"Don't talk down to me like that! Just stop pretending! I'm so sick of the games. Aren't you exhausted from all the lies?" She was.

In an instant, Mal's entire demeanor cooled, until his expression was as icy as his eyes. "Calm down, Tempest. You're imagining—"

"Don't you *dare* say that to me!" She took a step backward toward the door. "I'm done being the butt of your jokes." Another step. "I'm done." To her embarrassment, heat filled her eyes. Oh god, she was going to cry. "You're the most despicable man I've—"

"I'm quite tired of this," Mal bit out, grabbing Tempest and throwing her over his shoulder.

"Let me go!" she demanded, slamming her fists into Mal's back. But he didn't respond. He jogged swiftly through a series of twisting corridors until he reached a black, wooden door, kicked it open, and then shut behind them. It was completely dark. He jostled her around and somehow lit a lantern without letting her go.

"Put me down," she said flatly. He didn't. Tempest twisted and writhed until she slithered out of his grasp, landing heavily on her knees. Pain ran down her shins, but it was better than being manhandled by the double-crossing psychopath.

Mal cursed and bent to help her up, but she kicked him in the chest and pulled out her knives instead.

"What the bloody hell?" he snarled.

"I should have seen the signs," she gasped, chest heaving. "I've been so stupid. You've been lying to me all this time!"

Mal rolled his eyes. "Why so mad, my lady? You were the one who kissed me. It seems as if your love life is getting a little busy. You're going to have to pick a man… me, Pyre *and* King Destin seem like a bit much."

Tempest saw nothing but red. She lunged for Mal, every cell in her body intent on forcing the truth out of him.

There weren't three men.

There were only two.

Destin and the Jester.

CHAPTER 18: TEMPEST

When Mal met her attack, Tempest angrily grappled with him.

"Just shift!" she yelled. "I know who you are, so damn well *shift!*"

"I don't know what you're talking about!" He gnashed his teeth together, as he tried to pin her. He grabbed at her arm with claw-tipped fingers, the razor edges slashing across her upper arm. She recoiled, and his blue eyes widened. He took a step in her direction. "Tempest, I'm sorry. Let—"

"Don't touch me," she uttered, wanting to cry as she cradled her arm. Blood seeped from the wound into her shirt, staining it crimson. "You just can't help it, can you? Everything you touch, you ruin." His jaw flexed, and he looked away. *That's right. Feel ashamed.* "I'm so sick of the lies. You asked *me* to help *you*, not the other way around. Just—stop lying," she begged.

"Stop it. Be honest with me for *once*. I've earned that much by now."

He pursed his lips and opened his mouth before closing it. That was a first. The question was if he was debating telling her the truth or was currently thinking up another lie? He rubbed the back of his neck and sighed, a very unlike Mal thing to do. Goosebumps ran down her arm as Mal's face contorted, and he groaned, his whole body rippling. She'd never seen a shapeshifter fulling shift in front of her. She clung to the post at the end of her bed as Mal dropped to the floor—white hair deepening to a red wine.

He slowly lifted his head, and Pyre's amber eyes locked on her.

Heart racing, she was rooted to the spot. Even if she'd wanted to run, there was nowhere to go. The kitsune stood, his lips pressed firmly together.

"Ta da," he muttered.

Tempest gasped and rubbed at her eyes, struggling to accept what she'd witnessed. "I—you—" she stuttered. She took a deep breath, her emotions all over the place. Feelings could be sort through later. "I've never heard of a shapeshifter having two human forms." It was the stuff of myths.

Pyre's fox ears twitched, and a cocky smile flitted across his face. "It is not a common ability. But it is not impossible, either; I am proof. It takes lots of practice and a will of iron. Plus, you have to be able to deal with the pain."

"The pain?" she murmured.

"Our cells literally reform the foundation of our body. Don't you think that would be painful?"

Tempest nodded slowly. It wasn't something she'd really thought about. He brushed his hair from his face, the stark, white highlight in the front of his hair pulling her attention. She'd always assumed that it was a fashion statement, another ostentatious quirk of the Jester. But the clue to who he was had been in front of her the entire time.

Her stupidity knew no bounds.

"So which persona is the *real* you?" She rubbed her right temple. "Pyre the fox—the man I met in the woods who is gentle to children and loves his people? Or Mal—a hateful white-haired demon who savagely tortures his own men in the name of *justice*... and enjoys it and who deals in death, drugs, slaves, poisons, and weapons?" Tempest eyed Pyre carefully, looking for any sign of remorse from him. When he didn't flinch, she continued, "You told me that *the Jester* was just a name, a mantle taken up by one person after another to keep up the ruse that the figure is immortal—someone to be forever feared—but it seems as if you've taken your position as the dark leader of the underworld far too close to heart."

"No person is all good or all bad, Temp," Pyre said tiredly, running a hand through his sweat-soaked red hair to push it away from his face.

But Tempest did not believe that one bit. "That's a load of rubbish. That's the kind of thing a bad person tells themselves to justify falling even deeper into evil. That's the kind of thing you tell yourself to deal with how far from *good* you really are."

"Oh, get off your high horse," he shot back, ire dripping from his voice. He pointed a finger at her chest. "You've lied, killed, and stolen, same as me. The only difference is that yours was sanctioned by real evil. Stop thinking you're better just because you believe *your* justifications are better than mine. War is ugly, Tempest. Sometimes you have to do ugly things to change the future for the innocent. And if you can't accept that then you'll never get anywhere; you'll remain stuck to one spot, too terrified to dirty your hands to save those who need saving. And they will die, and then at whose feet will their deaths lie?"

He was not wrong. That was how the world operated.

A single tear escaped Tempest's left eye before she could blink it away. She hated that a sliver of her agreed with Pyre. She had seen how despicable Destin acted behind the scenes—how he had no qualms about putting his own people in the line of fire in order to garner false sympathy and support for his illegal wars. If the side of evil was willing to do anything for its cause, what hope did she have of defeating it, if she always played by the rules?

You don't have to play by anyone's rules but your own.

"That's not how the world should be," she said resolutely. "If good people keep performing evil acts in the name of righteousness, then somewhere down the line, they will become the people they fought so hard to overthrow. Are you willing to become as vile as the king?" Tempest eyed him, thinking of the hell Mal had given her over the last several weeks. Her heart clenched, and she swallowed. From the beginning, she'd known he wasn't her friend. "Or are you already worse?"

Pyre snarled and prowled closer, looming over her. An intimidation tactic. Too bad she saw right though him. Tempest tipped her head back and glared up at the ferocious male. His fiery, golden eyes that spat sparks, his sharpened canines, and his animalistic features didn't frighten her.

"You don't know what you're talking about!"

"You wouldn't know right from wrong if it slapped you in the face," she argued.

"And you know nothing of war, sacrifice, or loss. You're just playing the part of a soldier."

That burrowed under her skin. She chuckled and stepped into his space. "I suppose you're so well-versed. You can't be all that much older than me, Pyre—"

"Age has nothing to do with it, you ignorant girl," he shot back, inches from Tempest's face. "As Talagans, we learned very early on about the reality of our situation in Heimserya. For generations we have been oppressed—made to feel like second-class citizens—or even worse: slaves. We have suffered for what we are, for our natural-born talents and abilities. We've borne hate and suspicion when none of it was warranted. We have *died* for what we are. Can you say the same?" He eyed her with disgust. "You know nothing of suffering."

"Because you know me so well?"

"You've been pampered among the Hounds, and you know it."

But she'd lost everything before the Hounds took her in. "I'm lucky to have my uncles, a roof over my head, and food in my belly. It could have gone very differently for me if they—" Tempest froze mid-sentence. She had been about to tell Pyre her own story of her mother's death. How Tempest still heard her mother's screams night after night. How her silence was so, so much worse than the screaming.

He doesn't deserve your honesty and truth.

Glancing away, she stared at the door while she got her emotions under control. The Jester hadn't earned her confidence. He was not entitled to her secrets or the pain that plagued her night and day. They were *hers*, and hers alone to carry. Allowing him to have any more information would be a mistake. Who knew what he'd do with it, or if he'd try to twist her into something she no longer recognized? She was no man's weapon.

Lie. You're the king's weapon.

"What are you going to do once Destin is removed from the throne?" she asked softly. She gazed up at him. "That is the ultimate goal, isn't it?"

"Removing him is the goal."

He didn't answer her question. "Who do you plan to place on the throne?" She cocked her head. "You?"

Pyre barked out a humorless laugh. "Me, rule? Don't be ridiculous. I don't want to get anywhere close to that throne."

"That's a relief to hear. No one would support you on the throne."

"Because I'm a Talagan?" he challenged.

"No, because you've already caused too much unrest." She ran her finger along the woodgrain of the bedpost. "If you don't have plans to rule, what will happen to the kingdom once you've wreaked havoc upon our realm and upended the royal family, what then?"

Silence.

She lifted her chin and arched a brow, daring him to answer her. He didn't. His chin jutted out and his jaw clenched, but his lips stayed firmly sealed.

Unbelievable.

Tempest chuckled and backed away from him. She turned to grab her sack.

"What are you doing?"

"What I should have done weeks ago." There wasn't much to pack, but it was time to go back to the capital. She tossed a shirt into her bag and shot a glare at Pyre. "I should have known not to get mixed up with you. You only deal in disarray and disorder. You'll break open the kingdom and leave it to die."

"And you think you could do better?"

"I don't know," she said, snatching her bow from beneath the bed. "But I know I'm not so morally corrupt that I can't see the truth in front of me." Tempest hauled her bag over her shoulder and moved to the wardrobe, where she pulled out her black cloak from the brightly colored silk dresses. She tucked it under her arm and headed toward the exit. She wrenched open the door. Pausing in the doorway, she stared at the kitsune with disappointment. "I expected more from you. Although, I don't know why."

Tempest turned on her heel and stalked down the hallway.

"You should check in with that traitorous king of yours. He no doubt misses you," Pyre's voice called.

"Well ahead of you!" Tempest tossed over her shoulder. "Don't contact me. I'll come to you if need be."

She was done with the Dark Court and Pyre's many lying faces. Dotae might have been a nest of snakes, but it was a nest Tempest was familiar with. She had to escape the mountains before she became just as twisted and broken as Pyre himself was.

CHAPTER 19: TEMPEST

Snow.

Tempest stuck her tongue out to catch a few flurries as she slogged her way to the barracks, snow crunching beneath her boots. Her cloak trailed behind her, creating a path. Although heavy-hearted, she smiled as snowflakes bussed her lashes and left cool kisses on her cheeks. The first skiff of snow was always magical, but the first real snowstorm was her favorite. It covered all the ugly filth of the city and transformed the capital into something from a fairy story, every home looking like it belonged in a sleepy village.

Relief surged through her as she spotted the barracks. She skirted the training ring, her pace picking up as she reached the door. Bawdy laughter rumbled from inside, bringing a smile to her lips. Maxim. No one had a laugh like his. Reaching for the door, she paused and inhaled deeply. For the last several days, she'd gone over and over her story so she wouldn't make any mistakes. Guilt pricked her. It was wrong to lie to the men who raised her.

You're not any better than the Jester.

Her breath fogged in a mini cloud in front of her face before dissipating. She'd had a lot of time to think on her journey home. Not all of her thoughts were of good things.

Just open the damn door, Tempest.

"My lady?"

Tempest froze and slowly turned toward the feminine voice. A palace servant garbed in a drab gray cloak and a sensible working dress shuffled closer. Tempest almost screamed in frustration. The king was calling for her already? She hadn't even had a moment to unpack. Plus, how the bloody hell did he know she was in town? Someone must've been watching her. She'd snuck in through the slums. No one should have known about her arrival.

Sloppy, that's what it was.

"King Destin requests your presence at—"

"Yes, I shall meet him within the hour," Tempest interrupted, a wooden smile on her face even though she wanted to punch something. It was not the servant's fault that she was in a bad mood. People were not emotional punching bags. She swallowed down her bitterness and forced her tone toward something more polite. "I just need some time to bathe and change my clothes."

The servant bobbed her head and quickly retreated, her hurried footsteps a sharp staccato. Tempest rolled her neck and opened the door, warm light spilling out onto the snow. A wave of heat hit her as she stepped inside, knocked the snow off her boots, and closed the door behind her. The laughter cut short, and she turned to face the room. The

Hounds and trainees all stared her. She gave a little wave and smiled.

"I'm back."

Dima stood slowly from his bunk, followed by Maxim.

"You're home," Dima said with no inflection. That wasn't a good sign. He was angry.

She shouldered off her backpack and set her bow gently against the wall, before unclasping her cloak and hanging it on a hook near the door. "Finally," Tempest said lightly. "Seems like forever since I've been home."

"You better get over here right now and hug me, girlie, before I lose my temper," Maxim rumbled. Her shoulders sagged. He'd never lost his temper once with her growing up.

Maxim held his arms out, and she walked right into them. He squeezed her tightly against his chest and laid his head on the top of hers. For the first time in ages, she felt safe. *Loved.* "You have to stop leaving like that."

Tempest nodded, her nose rubbing against his flannel shirt. "I'll work on it."

"You better," Maxim muttered. "My poor ticker can't handle the stress."

He pulled back and released her to Dima. Her quiet uncle clasped both her cheeks and slowly studied her. "Who hurt you?"

"No one," she said, her voice not wavering. You had to care about someone for them to hurt you. *Lying to your uncles and yourself. A slippery slope.*

His eyes narrowed. "You know I interrogate people for a living?"

She held his gaze resolutely. If she wavered one bit, he'd never let this go. "It was a long journey. I'm tired."

Dima nodded and pulled her into a hug. "I'm letting this go for now," he murmured, voice low in her ear. She forced herself to stay relaxed, even as her pulse picked up. "But we will come back to this."

"It's nothing," Tempest argued.

He learned back and ducked to catch her eye. "It's not nothing. I can see the pain in your eyes." His gaze hardened. "I will find out the truth."

She chuckled and maneuvered herself out of his arms. "The truth is that I'm in need of a bath." Tempest waved a hand at the bathing chamber. "Is it empty?"

"Go ahead," Maxim said.

She nodded and strode toward the door next to the massive fireplace, whispering hellos to her fellow Hounds. She slipped into the bathing chamber and closed the door, leaning her back against the wood frame. Dima wasn't going to leave it. She pushed away from the door and began stripping off her clothes. The brazier in the corner gave her enough light to slip into the pool in the middle of the room. Heat enveloped her as she sank into the water. Thank all that be for hot springs. Placing her arms on the edge of the pool, she pillowed her cheek on her forearms and closed her eyes. Nothing felt as good as this, but still, she couldn't fully relax.

Time was ticking away, and the king expected her. How had her life become so tangled? From either direction, she had a sovereign trying to manipulate her. Well, if one could call Pyre —the Jester, Mal, whoever he was—a ruler. He seemed to think he controlled everyone around him. It still rankled her that she hadn't seen the signs sooner. There were similarities if one looked close enough. But how was she to know? Shifters weren't supposed to have two human forms. It was unheard of —a legend, a myth.

Tempest pushed away from the side of the pool and grabbed the scented oil from the southern side, steam rising around her. It had been a gift from Maxim one year. She uncorked the bottle and poured a generous amount of soap into her hands and lathered her hair and scalp. Even in the Jester's den of deceit, his tubs hadn't compared to this. She moaned and then dunked her head, rinsing her wild locks.

Rising from the water, she fingered a wet strand of hair. Unbidden, a memory floated to the forefront of her mind. Mal's hands threaded through her hair, insistently pulling her closer, his mouth slashing over hers, eyes heavy with desire, challenging her to give in. Tempest shuddered and then slapped a hand against the water. She had to stop this nonsense.

You feel nothing for him. You were lost in the moment. Heated emotions can lead to such things. It meant nothing. He means nothing to you.

Pyre was the Jester. He wasn't a good man. She moved toward the stairs that led out of the pool. That was an understatement. 'Not a good man' was a shady slumlord, loan shark, or a merchant who hit his wife. The Jester was another kind of man entirely; he was the other side of the coin to King Destin. Corrupt, ruthless, and driven. *Passionate.* She ignored the last one as she climbed the stairs, water droplets dripping from her skin.

Tempest grabbed a towel and dried her face before running it over the rest of her body. She paused, blankly staring at the roaring fire. If Pyre was simply the same as King Destin, what did that make her? She had been willingly working with Pyre.

Just how much of his evil behavior was she supposed to tolerate in the name of the people?

Protect the innocent. Deal with everything later.

She couldn't change Pyre any more than he could change her. *Is working with the Jester and the Dark Court the only way you can make a difference?* Stars, she didn't know. "Stop thinking about it. There is nothing you can do about it now," she muttered to herself, wrapping the towel around her body to hide her important bits. Her abdomen cramped, and she winced as it began to ache.

Of all the times to begin her moontime. Life just wasn't fair.

She rolled her neck and exited the bathing chamber. Someone whistled, and she gestured rudely, before disappearing behind her dressing screen. Tempest eyed the limited dresses she had and then her leather breeches. Her upper lip curled. If the king wanted her to come immediately, he'd get her as she came. She wasn't going to dress up for him. Quickly, she gathered her clothing along with some toiletries for her moontime and stalked back into the bathing chamber.

Wet skin and leather were a bloody nightmare. Dressing took much longer than normal. She yanked the brush through her wet hair and plaited it, before moving back into the barracks. Maxim lounged on his bed next to her.

"I sent for some food."

"Thank you," she murmured, dropping onto her bed. Tempest tugged on some socks. "I'll tuck in when I get back."

"Get back?" he asked.

"I've been summoned."

"I see." Maxim eyed her up and down. "You're wearing that?"

"What's wrong with this? It's my nicest outfit."

"It's not very courtly."

"Well, he demanded me to come now so this is what he gets." She snatched a bottle of vanilla oil from the shelf next to her bed and dabbed it on her wrists and at the base of her throat. "Does that make you happy?"

"Lower your voice," Dima admonished, moving to the end of her bed. He crossed his arms and stared her down. "You need to be careful."

He had no idea. She smiled grimly. "Believe me, I am."

"Tell us what has happened over the last few weeks, lass," Maxim said. "We know that you've been sent on missions for the king, but that's the extent of it."

"Ask Madrid." She wouldn't breathe a word of any of it. Plus, there was a chance that her uncles were part of the mimkia ring. Winter's bite, she hated doubting them. Tempest tied her wrist sheaths on.

"We have. He's said nothing," Dima bit out. "You shouldn't be out there on your own. You may have won your trials, but you're still a novice. Dealing with traitors to the realm is very different than training in the ring."

"Tell me something I don't know."

"We're not trying to antagonize you, lass," Maxim said.

"I have faced nothing I could not handle," she interrupted, trying her best to make the smile on her face somewhat genuine. She strapped her last dagger into place at her hip. "And on the subject of the king... I will be late, if I don't leave now. And you and I both know it's unwise to keep the king waiting." She shoved her feet into her boots. "I'll be back soon."

Tempest squeezed Dima's arm once as she passed him, before moving to the door and tossing her cloak over her shoulders. She pulled open the door and tugged up the hood of her cloak, her wet hair chilly against her skin.

To the lion's den we go.

Reaching the king's chambers happened far too quickly. What disturbed her the most was that she hadn't seen another living soul. Usually, a servant escorted her, but not this time. Something wasn't right. Her heart picked up speed, thumping against her chest. She stared at the heavy wooden doors that served as the entrance to the king's chambers and took a few seconds to steady her breathing. Destin was only a man. She was a trained assassin. If he tried anything, she'd kill him. Plain and simple. True, she'd have to flee for her life, but she could always live in the Fire Isles as a pirate. The weather was supposed to be delightful.

You'd never run away.

She knocked on the door, her nerves on edge. A second of silence. Two. And then—

"Come in," a deep voice called.

Well, here goes nothing.

Gathering all the willpower she could muster, Tempest opened the door. His chamber was exactly as she remembered it. She moved into the room and managed not to flinch as the heavy doors slammed behind her. The king stood by the stained-glass window at the back of his chambers, his signature tumbler of fire whiskey dangling negligently between his fingers.

"Your Majesty," Tempest said, bowing politely, her stomach twisting. "It has been a while."

She straightened and locked eyes with Destin. Wicked hell, he was handsome for a psychopath.

"Don't just stand by the door." He crooked a finger at her. "It has indeed been a while," he said, his tone playful and yet edgy.

Not a good combination. "Too long. I have missed your radiant presence around the palace, Tempest."

Tempest had the sense to look abashed. A small smile flittered across her face. "You flatter me, King Destin."

He chuckled and shook his head like she was the most amusing creature in the world. What a crock.

"This is exactly what I missed," he said. "How have you been these past few weeks, my Lady Hound? The rebels haven't been giving you too much trouble, I hope?"

"It was nothing I could not handle," she said, repeating the same line she'd fed to Maxim and Dima. "If you wish me to debrief you on the matter now, I'm happy to oblige."

"Oh, no, no, no," the king said quickly, laughing again. "That's what I love about you. Always right to the point, and yet, such business can wait."

That was new. She frowned, her nerves ratcheting up a notch. "Then why, may I ask, am I here?" If he didn't want to know about the rebels, then that meant it was personal. She was very thankful she'd worn her trousers and not a dress.

The king approached her, his steps prowling. He reached for her hands and took them in his own.

Oh, bloody hell, this wasn't good.

His thumb ran over the top of her right hand. "All I have been able to think about is our encounter before you left." He licked his lips, and her stomach dropped. "So, I have a question for you, Tempest. An offer, if you will."

"Whatever do you mean, Your Majesty?" Tempest asked, feeling lightheaded.

Destin leaned in closer until his lips were but an inch from hers, his golden gaze smoldering. "Marry me."

Oh, no.

CHAPTER 20: TEMPEST

Tempest blinked repeatedly, mouth gaping as she stared wordlessly at the king. He raised an eyebrow at her. She couldn't have heard him right.

"Something the matter, my lady?" he asked.

Sweet poison, he was serious. She pushed through her shock. The weeks she'd spent surrounded by liars and thieves weren't for nothing. Tempest curtseyed, the movement awkward as she was wearing trousers. "I am honored, sire, truly. But I... am wary about accepting such an offer, wonderful though it may be."

"Oh?" Destin drawled.

Oh stars, how was she supposed to turn him down without him ripping everything dear from her? Scorned kings were not known for their mercy. "See, I am afraid that I will be criticized as a Hound for being romantically involved with the king," she began. "You must see how it looks, Your Majesty. The first female Hound, with only a few months of missions under her belt and already on the war council, now engaged to the king? It may be... unsavory for your reputation, and I would never want to bring reproach to the Crown." She bowed her head lower, staring at the decorative rug beneath her boots.

"There's no need for that, my dear."

She squeezed her eyes shut and arranged what she considered a proper smile onto her face. *Please, please, let him not see right through me.* Tempest opened her eyes and straightened. "I've striven to be completely honest with you." *A bold-faced lie.* "I would be a liar if I didn't tell you that it would also damage my credit as one of your faithful Hounds. I live my life to serve you, my liege."

The king's face softened, and he nodded in apparent understanding. "Of course," he said. "I was so excited to ask for your hand in marriage that I had not considered how this might affect you." He reached out and brushed a finger along the apple of her cheek. "I must admit, it's been a long time since I've taken into account the wishes of someone other than my councilors."

I bet.

He dropped his hand and ran it along her arm. Goosebumps rose in the wake of his touch. A small smile lifted his lips. "As the king, I'm awarded certain privileges. Women are usually one of them."

She almost scowled but managed to hold her mask in place. Women weren't possessions to be given and collected.

Destin stepped closer and fingered the loose strand of hair near her temple. "I don't tell you this to make you jealous or angry. I want honesty between us. I'm not a young man who flits from woman to woman, not knowing their worth." He smiled, and chills ran down her spine. His expression was predatory. "I know what I have within my grasp, and I won't let you go easily, dearest."

Terror choked her as she tried to get a decent breath. He was above all scrutiny, and he knew it. The king could do whatever he wanted without reprimand.

"You look pale," he murmured.

"I have pale skin," she whispered. Wicked hell, dots flashed across her sight. She couldn't faint here. *Breathe.*

Destin chuckled and ran the backs of his fingers down her cheek. "I'm sorry to have put you in such a position," he continued and then took both of her hands in his own. "Take your time considering my proposal. Take all the time you need... though I hope that won't be too long. But you're worth waiting for, so I will happily deal with my own impatience if that makes you feel better about the engagement."

Tempest nodded, her head stuffy. "You are too gracious, Your Majesty," she said, the words tasting like ash on her tongue. "Thank you for taking my concerns into consideration." She paused, then gently extricated her hands from Destin's. "I do not wish to be ungrateful, my lord, but it has been a long journey."

"Of course!" Destin murmured. "There goes my impatience again. You only just returned to Dotae, did you not? You must be exhausted."

Ha. As if he did not know exactly when she arrived. More games. Deadly ones.

She smiled gratefully, letting her shoulders slump and her very *real* fatigue peek through. "Very much so. I shall consider your proposal. Good evening."

He leaned close, and she stiffened when he pressed a

lingering kiss to her hair, his breath heating her temple. "Good night, dearest. I'll see you soon."

She pulled back. Her steps were wooden as she exited the king's chamber. The palace passed by in a blur. The winter night bit at her cheeks and ears as she wandered toward the barracks, his words replaying over and over in her mind. What was the bloody king thinking? Marriage to her? She entered the barracks and found most of the Hounds were sleeping. Except for one.

Maxim lifted his head from his pillow and pointed to the tray at the end of her bed. "There's some stew and bread."

Tempest shook her head. If she ate now, she'd just throw up. Her fingers shook as she tugged the cloak from her shoulders.

"What is it, lass?" Maxim asked, sitting up.

She shook her head. How was she supposed to explain what just happened? She climbed into bed and yanked her covers over her shoulders.

Her uncle watched her with worried eyes. "Did he hurt you?" His words were hushed.

"No," she whispered.

"I'm worried."

"So am I." Tempest closed her eyes, her body trembling. Sleep would be a long time coming.

"Pay attention, Tempest!" Madrid yelled, whacking her on the back with the edge of his wooden sword. The third hit that morning. "You need to focus. Get your head out of the clouds. You would be dead three times over."

Wincing away from Madrid's blow, she straightened her

back and shook out her shoulders. Her performance was embarrassingly poor. She took a swig from her waterskin and wiped her mouth with the back of her hand. It was not often she had an opportunity to fight against the head of the Hounds, even in training. That she was squandering it because she had a million-and-one things to think about was decidedly un-Tempest-like.

No excuses. Work harder.

She bowed her head apologetically to Madrid. "Sorry," she mumbled and sketched a quick bow before exiting the ring, aware of the curious looks being tossed her way. Could she go nowhere without making a damn spectacle of herself?

Tempest grabbed her cloak from the barracks, the sweat cooling on her skin. She needed time to think. To be alone. Dima and Maxim had been whispering all morning, and it was only a matter of time before they cornered her.

She lifted her hood over her hair and skulked down the busy streets. Dotae was not the kind of city where you could ever truly be alone. There was always someone watching you, someone gossiping about you, or some underhanded deal being conducted in the back of an alley that you were never supposed to stumble upon. So long as she kept her thoughts inside her head then nobody could use them against her.

The Jester could shift into an entirely different person. What was to say there wasn't someone who could read minds?

Shivering at the uncomfortable thought, she scanned the buildings around her before choosing a promising one. It was just high enough to get her out of the fray. Tempest climbed up a brick wall before swinging her legs up and beneath her as she reached the snowy roof. She hid behind a chimney to remain unseen. She brushed the snow from the roof tiles and sat, the chill from the pottery seeping through her layers. She adjusted her cloak until she was almost warm and comfortable.

Almost.

It wasn't the bite from the winter morning that made her uncomfortable. It was all the secrets she was carrying. Too many secrets.

One of them is going to get you killed. The king would want an answer soon.

Tempest tucked her hands under her armpits and studied the cloudy sky, weak winter sunlight breaking through in beams here and there over the colossal city.

She hunched forward and leaned her forehead against her knees. Days prior, she had been wondering if there was any way she could make a difference to the fraught situation between Heimserya and Talaga without having to debase herself by aligning with the Jester and the Dark Court. Here was a solution laid neatly at her feet.

She could be queen.

Queen of Heimserya. A position that afforded her some protection if she challenged Destin. A way to bring about change for their kingdom.

The Jester's plan involved the removal of the king from power, but that was where his plan stopped. He had nobody arranged to ascend the throne once his anarchy brought the kingdom to its knees, which spelled only more trouble and left Heimserya vulnerable to their enemies. She lifted her head and glanced toward the south ports, in the direction of the Hinterlands. There were monarchs just as bad, if not worse, who ruled. Which meant that creating a balance of power with the existing kingdom was perhaps exactly what was needed.

You're just a forest girl.

"No," she whispered. "I'm the first female Hound. I could do it if I chose to." Living as the king's consort would not be an easy choice, but when had she ever taken the easy route? The question that bothered her the most was *why* he'd offered her marriage. Tempest didn't come from a highborn family, nor was she from one with money. Her reputation as a respectable female was nonexistent, thanks to living with men and being raised by them. Hell, her trousers and smart mouth had made more than one lady of the court swoon in shock.

He wants you because of the Hounds.

A warrior queen.

Her lips thinned. She may be young, but she wasn't stupid. In the game of kings and jesters, she was considered a pawn.

You could be so much more.

Tempest looked at the palms of her hands. She'd have to be crafty, and, still, it boded well for her if she married Destin. There'd been rumors of how his previous wife died. She didn't doubt for one second that the man could commit murder. If she accepted his offer, her life would never be safe.

It isn't now.

From the moment she had been born, death had marked her. Life as a Hound was a gamble each time she exited the barracks. She sighed and wrapped her arms around her knees, pillowing her cheek on them.

You'll have to bed the monster.

Her stomach rolled. The idea of his bloodstained hands running over her body made her sick. *What's more important? A bit of bed sport or the thousands dying because of his tyranny?*

One lone tear squeezed out the corner of her eye. While she'd never imagined herself married, she hadn't imagined her life like this. She closed her eyes and breathed deeply. Once she left this roof, everything would change. There would be no escaping the decision she made.

As queen, you will need allies.

The Hounds would be her greatest weapon. She was one of them. They wouldn't forget that. And the Talagans... There were many of them she liked. Some of them she trusted—even Brine, who had wanted her dead in the beginning but had forged a respectful alliance with her through training. Was it so radical to believe that some of them might align themselves with her if she became queen? They were the allies Tempest needed. Ones who could move about and do her bidding beneath the king's notice.

It was a risk, of course. A huge risk. It wasn't just Tempest's life on the line if she went through with this. She couldn't stand idle while innocents suffered and died. If the Jester and Destin planned to use her, she'd let them, all the while seizing power for herself.

"Please, let me make wise decisions," she murmured, her soft prayer swept away in the breeze. Gentle snowflakes began to drift from the sky, and she stood, her gaze drifting to the palace in the distance. "You started this, but I'll finish it."

Tempest entered the grand doors to the palace, feeling simultaneously numb and raw with nerves. She brushed the snow from her hair and cloak.

"My lady." A female servant bobbed a quick curtsey.

"I'm here to see the king," Tempest said.

"This way. He's been expecting you."

Ice filled her veins, and she squeezed her fingers into fists to battle back the fear. He was just a man. One that she was going to manipulate to get what she wanted. They rounded a corner, and the servant came to an abrupt halt, as the man himself prowled down the corridor toward them. The servant bowed and back away.

Tempest's heart hammered in her chest, but she lifted her chin. Fear didn't freeze her—it sparked the fight in her.

King Destin looked at her questioningly. "Is something the matter, Tempest?"

"Yes. Yes, I accept your proposal. I will marry you," Tempest said, the words tumbling out of her mouth, sounding nothing like herself.

It was done. She'd sealed her fate.

CHAPTER 21: KING DESTIN

"*A*h, I can always rely on you for a *satisfying* evening. Lady Grey."

He took a long draught of fire whiskey and eyed the decanter with the remaining amber spirits glinting from the light in the fireplace. He reclined on his chair, stretching his toes toward the flames, and sighed contentedly. "Really, there's nothing better than a few hours with a good woman to put me at ease."

He glanced back at his bed, where a long-limbed beauty with disheveled hair smiled sleepily at him. Her hair was naturally blonde, but Destin had insisted on her dyeing it blue for the occasion. Whenever he ran his fingers through it, he'd imagined it belonged to Tempest, his future queen and bedmate. The image never failed to inspire passion. The fiery Hound was soon to be his.

"Anything to appease my king," the woman said, shifting on the bed until she was sitting with her back against half a dozen silken pillows.

Destin laughed. That was true. Almost every woman in Dotae would do anything to appease him. But Tempest... She was his crown jewel.

She had taken his order to do *anything* she needed to do to reintegrate herself into the Talagan rebel group without a word of complaint. Though she was proud and confident and powerful, and the idea of sleeping with shifter scum was something she was clearly loathe to do, she'd accepted her king's mission.

A woman determined to do her duty even if it killed her. A rarity among the breed.

His lip curled at the thought of her bedding a Talagan male. He knew it was unlikely that she would have slept with any of the rebels; that he had told her to use such means *if necessary* meant she would no doubt have been more determined than ever to complete the mission *without* resorting to such tactics. Destin was pleased that he knew how to manipulate his Lady Hound into doing his bidding.

Including into marrying him.

Her reaction to his proposal was telling enough.

He could see how conflicted Tempest had been about his offer of marriage. How she was terrified of him but just as equally intrigued. How she could see the advantages the position of queen would give her, while at the same time wondering if those advantages were worth it. Tempest was intelligent, capable, and calculating.

Which made the idea of breaking her all the more irresistible.

"Appease your king indeed," Destin replied, slowly standing from his chair to make his way to the bed. "But it is, unfortunately, the last time you will please me in such a way. Soon I will be married to my little Hound."

The woman pouted, her lush bottom lip quivering.

It occurred to Destin that he had not bothered to learn her name, though this was the fourth time he'd bedded her. *Tiana, perhaps, or maybe Britta.*

"I thought you took women to bed during your last marriage, Your Majesty," she said, shifting over on the bed to make room for Destin. He sat down beside her. His bedmate batted her lashes and ran a finger up his arm. "I'm always willing to serve the Crown. If you're tired of me, I'm sure I can become more creative to keep you satisfied."

"Ah, but my Lady Hound is different," he said, which was true. "It would pain me to sleep with another in her stead once we are married. I understand she believes in morality."

"Ironic since she lives with men, no?" the woman crooned.

"I need her to be undeniably on my side for what's to come, and sacrifices must be made, my beauty." Destin lightly pushed on her shoulder.

She stretched out on his bed, a seductive smile on her lips. "What's to come?" she purred.

His mouth split into a wide grin. "Why, war, of course." He touched the tip of her nose with his fingertip, then ran it down over her lips, chin, and neck until it rested on the pulse at the hollow between her collarbones. "We will stamp out all resistance, and then, we will take the Fire Isles."

"I—I assume it is for the good of the kingdom," she replied, though her voice was uncertain. Destin moved his fingers to her shoulder and then her back, before sweeping back over her collarbone until his touch rested on the hollow at the bottom her neck once again.

Such fragile skin. Such a pitiful creature. Weak.

"Oh, it is for the good of some of us, all right," he said, his grin turning feral. His fingers curled around the woman's neck. She squirmed, her smile dimming. Leaning closer, he brushed his lips along her cheek and across her lips. He squeezed his fingers, and she gasped, the sound music to his ears. "You know the difference between you and a queen? It's all in the fight. Queens are vicious and rare, you, however—" He lifted his head to stare down into her panicked gaze. "You are expendable, easy to break."

"Y-Your Majesty!" she choked. "I c-can't breathe."

He gave her a tender smile. "I know. My spies have told me you're not careful with information. You were warned, love."

"I shall remain silent, I swear!" she wheezed.

"Silent, you shall be," he murmured, admiring the way her face changed color, "though not through any choice of your own."

He watched with sickening glee as the woman clawed at his hands, fruitlessly fighting for a life she was no longer in control of. God, it was a heady feeling, holding another's life in his hands. After a minute or two, however, her attempts lost their strength, and her mouth grew slack. A few seconds later, there was nothing left in her pretty blue eyes but glassy, empty nothingness.

"Thank you for the satisfying evening," he murmured, releasing the woman's neck and getting up from the bed. "You took the edge off."

He shook out his robe and returned to his fire whiskey

without a second glance at the dead body he had left in his wake. He had more pressing matters to think about.

Like how to conquer his new queen.

CHAPTER 22: TEMPEST

empest spent several days largely keeping to herself. Mostly, she slept; the last few weeks had been physically, mentally, and emotionally exhausting. Not to mention all the injuries she'd sustained. Her arm had now completely healed, though the snake-like pattern from Mal's whip on her arm had not faded. It looked as if it was going to scar—something that bothered her. Life involved scars— serving as a Hound ensured it. But a visual reminder of Pyre on her skin wasn't something she wanted. It was bad enough she had the memory of it, let alone having to look at it.

Tempest snuck across the icy roofs of the slums, her feet slipping here and there. Thoughts of her engagement and of the Jester had driven her from the barracks. The announcement hadn't been made yet, but she could already feel the noose tightening around her neck. While thoughts of Pyre inspired rage and hurt, she needed his allies—the good ones—which meant she could not cut all her ties with the Jester just yet. She had to hold out a little longer, and then she could pretend she had never met the twisted man, forever.

She dropped to the street and ghosted around the corners, looking out for anyone causing mischief. Maybe a good old-fashioned fist fight would calm her. Something snagged her cloak, and she paused, spotting a small child no older than eight years old.

She bent low and cocked her head. "What is it, sweetheart?" she asked the boy, a gentle smile on her face. Children knew her in this area.

The young one eyed her and then lifted Tempest's hood. His eyes examined her hair. "I have a message for you."

Tempest stilled. "Oh?"

"A dance with masks on the eve of the next full moon," the boy said, a frown of concentration creasing his brow. "Your presence is required."

It was difficult, but the smile on her face remained firmly in place, though she no longer meant it. She ruffled the boy's hair. "Who told you to say that to me?"

"Jeb did. He hangs around the docks. Someone else told him, though, and someone else before them." The wee one shrugged.

Disgust filled her. Of course, that's how Pyre had decided to contact her. Even after how she'd left everything, he still had the gall to command her back to the Dark Court, to expect her to play his good little Hound while he paraded her among his followers.

The little boy shifted on his feet, his boots a little too worn to be warm. Riffling through her pockets, she pulled out two silver coins and handed them to the boy. His eyes grew wide, and his mouth gaped, revealing his missing front two teeth.

"For… me?" he asked, entirely uncertain, his gaze flicking from her to the coins and back again.

"Of course!" she replied, ruffling his hair again. "You delivered the message perfectly. Now, put those away, and don't brag about them. That's a sure way to lose them."

"Promise!"

"You have somewhere warm to sleep tonight?" she asked, standing.

He nodded. "Yeah. Old Harry lets me sleep in the back of his bakery."

"Then off with you. It's too late to be out."

"Of course," the boy called as he scampered off, clearly delighted with the coins. "Thank you, pretty lady!"

"I'm not a—" Tempest began, but then stopped. Of all the people who considered her a lady when she was not one, the children were the only ones she could tolerate doing so. After all, technically she *was* a lady to them—she was an adult. They did not say it to make fun or demean her. It was genuine. It was rare that she met anyone who was genuine these days.

She kicked at an empty glass bottle before turning tail and heading back to the barracks. The next full moon was in under a week. It had taken her and Brine and Swiftly four days—that she was actually conscious for—to reach the mountain palace. It would take less time if she went there directly, although the snow would slow her down somewhat.

In truth, she did not want to go to the masquerade, especially not after the message she had just received. It was a summons through and through. Another order from Pyre that he obviously expected Tempest to follow. Her jaw flexed. It was painfully clear that he never meant for her to be his equal.

You have no choice but to attend.

For her plan to succeed, she had to gain his allies. The masquerade was the right place to convince as many of them as possible to follow her instead. It was her best shot.

She reached the barracks and entered. Immediately, she frowned. The energy in the room was off. Some of the Hounds were sleeping, but the others weren't speaking or looking in her direction. On edge, she slowly moved through the silent room. Her lips thinned as her gaze rested on her bed.

A gilded box sat atop her pillow, an elaborately handwritten note lying beside it. The Jester? But he wouldn't be so bold, would he? Then again, she wouldn't put anything past him.

Tempest picked up the note and read it, intrigued.

To my future queen,

May these tokens of my regard for you find you well.

Yours, Destin

Her shoulders stiffened. The Hounds were known as gossips, and she was sure they'd already seen the note. Her fingers tightened on the card. Destin had done this on purpose. She'd wanted the announcement postponed. He was already playing games.

"I suppose I should have known," she muttered, putting down the note to open the golden box. Inside were a wide array of heavy, glittering gems and beautifully crafted necklaces, bracelets, and earrings. A small fortune. Although, she had never been one for feminine decorations, they did have their appeal. How many families could she feed with this?

She smiled, blatantly ignoring her nosy fellow Hounds as they eyed the loot in her palms. What they saw was a woman happy with the gift she'd received. Satisfaction wormed its way into her belly. Unwittingly, Destin had given her exactly what she needed. Those she couldn't woo to her cause at the masquerade, she could bribe, and the king had given her the means to do it.

"So, are you going to explain that note?" Dima asked, casually sitting at the end of her bed.

She ignored her uncle and carefully packed away the box of jewels in her bag and then retrieved several sets of clothing from her trunk, along with a few weapons.

"Lass, this is serious," Maxim rumbled.

She shoved her clothes into the bag and paused, lifting her head to meet his serious gaze. "I know."

"I don't think you do," Dima muttered. "You're playing a game you know nothing about."

"I'm doing my best."

"Your best is going to get you killed," Dima said.

Tempest glared at Dima. "I didn't ask for this."

"Never said you did, lass," Maxim cut in. "But why have you not come to us?"

She scrubbed away the frown on her face and tried to keep her voice level. "And you think you could help me? He's the king, and we are his Hounds. We are *bound*. We made an oath."

"Not in this," Dima said lowly. "You do not have to accept him. This is your choice."

"There's no choice."

"There is," Dima whispered. "All you have to do is say the word."

She glanced incredulously between her two uncles. "And what? You'll spirit me away?"

"If that is what you wish," Maxim answered gravely.

"Enough. I would never put either of you in danger." She swallowed. "I love you, but it is already done."

Dima hissed and stood, his expression going eerily blank.

Tempest reached for him, her hand grasping his fingers.

"I will need you in the times ahead."

He nodded curtly, squeezing her fingers once, before exiting the barracks. She stared after him and then moved her attention back to Maxim.

He crossed his arms and eyed her bag. "Going somewhere?"

"Orders." Not exactly truthful. She strapped on her weapons and placed the rest in her bag. She moved around her bed and hugged Maxim. "If anyone asks, I'm on an assignment."

"You're playing a dangerous game, lass."

She pulled back and smiled weakly at him. "Yes, the one you all taught me. Trust my training. I'll be back soon." Tempest stooped to collect her bow and quiver from beneath the bed, then strode from the barracks, very aware of all the eyes on her. The king would have news of her departure within half an hour. She needed to move.

Leaving Dotae through the slums was a simple matter. No one liked to travel at night, especially with a storm brewing. Flurries fluttered around her, but not so heavily that she couldn't make her way north. She managed to borrow a horse from a village just outside of Dotae, but her journey wasn't as quick as she would have liked it to be. Nonetheless, she pressed onward.

The weather held for several days, just snowing enough to be annoying, but not cumbersome. But her luck eventually ran out. By the time Tempest made it to a tiny village at the base of the Dread Mountains, the small winter storms had grown into a blizzard. Passing through the mountains themselves was an impossible feat until the squalls cleared.

She slipped from her exhausted horse and handed the reins to a stable boy wrapped in layer upon layer of wool. Her butt was numb and needlelike pain ran up and down her legs. Tempest stumbled toward the brightly-lit inn and pushed open the door, wind blasting over her and snow pelting her. Warmth surrounded Tempest immediately, and she slammed the door closed. Her bag slipped from her shoulder, and she sagged against the wooden door.

"That cold, huh?" a female voice asked.

"You don't know the half of it," Tempest groaned. She brushed snow from her cloak before joining the only other patron at the bar and was met with a pale face and the long, braided brown hair of a girl around the same age as herself— perhaps younger. Her eyes were as brown as her hair, and there were no defining features that set her apart from any other average girl from Heimserya.

Plain. Just a normal girl.

She smiled at the stranger and nodded at the innkeeper. "Some spiced cider and a room, please." That would heat up her insides. Whiskey would be better, but every time she caught a whiff of the stuff all she could think of was the king.

"I didn't think it would be so bad," Tempest admitted. The girl motioned for her to sit by her, so she obliged, her butt complaining at the continued abuse. "I didn't expect my journey to be so difficult."

"You should always expect snow by the mountains," the girl replied. "The weather here is nobody's friend."

That was the damned truth. "Noted." Tempest held her hand out. "I'm Juniper."

The girl smiled, the corners of her small mouth just barely lifting up. "Thorn. I'm a treasure hunter… of sorts."

A treasure hunter. Fascinating.

The innkeeper bustled into the kitchen, shouting at

someone. Thorn eyed her and then tugged Tempest's hood lower. "I'd keep your hair covered, *Juniper*, if I were you."

Tempest held the girl's gaze and tucked a stray lock of hair beneath her hat completely before lowering her hood. "Thank you."

"We females must stick together." Thorn grinned.

Tempest studied her new acquaintance. Although plain, there was something about Thorn's face that was captivating. A softness was present alongside a sharpness. A life borne of difficult times and perseverance. That was something she was more than familiar with—the kind of sharpness borne through years of needing to defend oneself.

Perhaps I have found a spirit sister.

She grimaced when the roar of a dragon blew through the tavern upon the wind. "You're in the right place for treasure," Tempest said. The noise had followed her for the last half a day through the snow; clearly, the creatures lived in the mountains.

"Oh, I have no doubt about that," Thorn replied. She finished the goblet of wine in front of her in a few, large gulps, then jumped from her stool. "I am afraid I must retire for the evening, Juniper. It has been a long day, and tomorrow will be even longer, I fear. I hope you rest well tonight... though the dragons may have something to say about that."

The two of them shared a knowing smile before Thorn headed upstairs to the rooms above the tavern. The innkeeper returned with Tempest's cider and a key to her room. She paid and then slogged up the stairs to her chamber. It was small, but nicely furnished, and warm, most importantly. She locked the door and moved the dresser in front of it. One could never be too careful.

Tempest shook out her cloak and placed it near the fire to

dry before kicking off her boots and crawling into bed. Exhaustion rode her hard, but the roaring outside kept her from falling asleep. Did they never stop?

She tossed and turned beneath the thick blankets she had piled on top of her. As the night wore on, the roaring of the dragons grew more insistent, the wind and snow swirling and merging with the sound until it was all she could hear.

"How in the bloody hell am I supposed to sleep when dragons are screaming in my ear?" she groaned, after several fruitless attempts at burying her head beneath her pillow. She glanced at the shuttered window, making out the snow plastered against the warped glass through the cracks. How was she supposed to make it back to the den of deceit? While she hadn't wanted to initially be there, now being there was tantamount to her plan. Her lips twitched and delirious laughter spilled from them. She'd even started to look forward to showing up at the masquerade with nothing appropriate to wear, just to needle the Jester.

But, at this rate, she was never going to get there in time. The masquerade was in three days; with all the snow around and no Brine to help her navigate the unfamiliar terrain, there was a slim-to-none chance of reaching the palace of the Dark Court in time.

Another dragon cried.

"Oh, shut up," she hissed, flinging her pillow at the window as another scream cut through the air. Tempest froze, an idea striking her. A bizarre idea.

An insane idea.

She slid from the bed and shoved her feet into her boots before striding over to the far wall. Tempest shoved open the window and unbolted the shutters. The wind whipped them open, and she was greeted with a face-full of snow.

Here goes nothing.

Tempest began to sing at the top of her lungs. Her voice wasn't the best, though she was sure that didn't matter. Either way, she could at least carry a tune. A fairy tale filled her head—one of the stories she remembered her mother telling her as she tucked her into bed.

Sing a song to lure a dragon, her mum had said. *They will come without fail.*

Nothing. Maybe she needed to get on the roof.

Quickly, she gathered her possessions and struggled along the slippery sill until she could gain enough purchase to climb onto the roof. This was crazy. Pulling the hood of her cloak tightly around her face, and blinking back flurries of snow, she began singing again, the wind snatching away her song.

Her eyes stung as she desperately searched the dark for a dragon. Nothing. She took one step forward and belted out another verse. Midsentence, she choked, taken aback when a dragon *did* appear in front of her—sapphire blue and about half the size of the dragon she'd met before. It beat its heavy wings, watching her with deep-blue, crystal-clear eyes.

Tempest thrust out her arm, pulling off her glove to reveal the spot on her wrist where the dragon shifter had kissed her, hoping the beast could smell the other dragon on her skin. Then she pulled down her hood and pointed to where he'd taken a lock of her hair. Not the best form of communication, but it would do. Hopefully. Shifters were all about scent, surely the dragon would scent its brethren upon her.

The beast didn't blink or move or acknowledge in any way that it had understood her.

Perhaps not all dragons can change shape.

Fear tried to creep forward, but she battled it back. She'd be no one's dinner tonight. Abruptly, the dragon screeched and then whirled, flying away. Damn. Her temper flared.

"Thanks for nothing, you oversized snake!" she screamed, collecting her bag and preparing to climb back down to her room. "Maybe we'll all get some bloody sleep if you'd shut the hell up!"

"That's a pretty powerful curse to throw at a dragon," a cultured, powerful voice murmured. She flinched, both daggers in her hands, as she turned to face the newcomer.

And there he was—the dragon she'd met weeks ago.

"Have you decided to take me up on my offer, lovely?" he asked. His voice did not shiver in the cold, nor did his body, though his chest and arms were bare to the inhospitable weather.

Tempest shook her head. "I am here for something else."

"Oh?" A flash of interest crossed his reptilian eyes. "And what would that be, exactly?"

"I need to get to the Dark Court in the mountains. I imagine a dragon as powerful as yourself knows exactly where that is," she simpered. Honeyed words went a long way with males in general.

"Flattery will get you nowhere, lass," he replied, sounding put-out. "I am not some common beast of burden."

"I never said I considered you as such," she soothed, before pulling out a huge sapphire pendant from the box King Destin had gifted her. She proffered it to him. "You said you like treasures."

A slow, greedy grin crossed the man's face. "That I do, girl with the lovely hair. Very well. I shall take you to the Dark Court. Have you ever flown before?"

Tempest's lips quirked into a smile. "I can't say I have."

"Then prepare yourself for a thrilling ride." He drew closer, a wicked grin on his face. "Be careful. I'm told that once you get a taste for dragons, it's hard to give up."

She placed the necklace in his hand and cocked her head. "I'm sure I will be just fine."

"We shall see," he murmured.

CHAPTER 23: TEMPEST

"*O*h, sweet Dotae!" Tempest cursed as the dragon swerved to miss a razor-sharp edge of a jutting shelf of rock. She clung to his neck with desperate, freezing hands. Every inch of Tempest's body was numb. One wrong move, and she'd fall to her death.

The dragon roared merrily. "We are almost there, lovely! You have done well so far. It's thrilling, is it not?"

"If you call almost dying half a dozen times thrilling, then yes!" Tempest screamed, burying her face against his smooth, emerald scales. Her hair whipped behind her in the wind, snapping and twisting with every turn the dragon took; it would take hours to untangle the knots it had surely gained.

Her hair should have been the last thing on her mind. It was funny how the mind latched onto inconsequential things when in a life or death situation.

It'll be a miracle if you make it to the Dark Court alive.

"Do you not risk dying every time you fight for your king... or Jester?" the dragon asked, throwing a sly look back at Tempest when she thrust up her face in shock. "Oh, come now," he chastised, in his hissing dragon voice. "Did you take me to be ignorant, Tempest of the Madrid line? I know exactly who and *what* you are."

Tempest did not reply. She had been foolish to assume the dragon shifter would not have found out who she was; the mere fact that she had periwinkle hair and had been heading into the mountains several weeks ago with two shifters was telling enough. Not to mention, she wasn't fond of getting any more snow plastered to her teeth.

She slid forward as the beast tilted downward, beginning the descent. Tempest clung tighter to him and focused on taking one breath at a time. Her body jerked as they touched ground. Lifting her head, she squinted through the storm, just making out a smooth stone platform that jutted out from the side of the mountain.

"Careful getting off," the dragon said.

She slid to the ground, her legs jarring as she landed—they were barely able to take the weight after the daredevil journey. Tempest lifted her head and eyed what looked to be balconies built into alcoves to protect them from the weather. Many of them were lit with lanterns, torches, and strings of lights, which fluttered and blinked in the snow.

There were floors with windows? Not just eternal darkness?
That kitsune bastard kept you in the dark.

Tempest angrily tried and failed to smooth her wild, tangled hair away from her face.

"Thank you for allowing me to fly with you," she said, when she had finally caught her breath enough to speak.

The dragon had shifted back into a broad-shouldered man with scale-imprinted skin and had crept silently to her side. He smiled with his strange teeth.

"I thank you for the sapphire," he replied, stroking the pendant where it hung from a chain around his neck. There were several other heavy, ornate necklaces already there, along with a much plainer, silver chain upon which a lock of lilac hair had been wrapped around.

That's not creepy at all.

She shrugged. Each to their own.

Tempest returned the dragon's smile before shaking out the insuppressible shiver that had been torturing her limbs the entire journey. The cold had chilled her to the very bone.

"Shall we head in?" she asked, indicating to the ornate iron door that separated the balcony from the inside of the palace.

The dragon man moved forward, barefoot in the snow. Tempest shivered as he opened the door and held an arm out. She entered, muttering a thank you before turning to face the room.

She froze.

A hundred pairs of eyes were on them. They had walked straight into the masquerade hall, which was full of servants and shifters busily preparing it for the ball.

Tempest stiffened further as she found the Jester in his Mal persona, standing in the middle of the room like the eye of the blizzard itself. He examined her and then stalked toward them.

Be strong.

A huge hand rested at the base of her spine. "Chin up, lovely," the dragon murmured.

Tempest raised her chin, a little unnerved that the dragon could read her so well.

Mal all but ignored Tempest, barely giving her a second glance before bowing deeply to the dragon. *Charming as ever.*

"Damien," Mal announced, clasping hands with the man as they shared a wicked smile. "King of the dragons. It is so good to see you."

Tempest froze. The king of—what? She'd been bartering with the *king of the dragons?*

Damien glanced at Tempest out of the corner of his eye, a smirk playing around his mouth. "You ought to be careful about letting your treasures wander around, you know," he murmured softly to Mal. "Otherwise anybody could steal them."

"I'm not a *treasure.*" Tempest scowled, all goodwill toward Damien thoroughly dissipating.

"Hush, lovely. All women are treasures... especially the interesting ones."

"Tempest, go rest," Mal ordered, once more without looking at her. "Damien, might I offer you lodgings? We were not expecting you so early, but a room has already been prepared for—"

"Oh, no," the dragon king replied with a shake of his head, his hand curling around her hip. Tempest knew Mal didn't miss the gesture, going by his icy gaze. "I shall return on the morrow. I still have previous business to attend to. This one simply distracted me enough to delay said business." Damien smiled warmly and dragged his hand along her waist until he caught hold of Tempest's wrist, bending low to place a kiss on the delicate skin there. As with the first time only weeks ago, a searing burn flared up Tempest's arm from his lips, threatening to engulf her very being. Damien locked his venomously green eyes on hers. "You're welcome for the ride."

"I—I already thanked you!" she bit out, pulling her wrist from his grasp. "And paid *handsomely* for the service." Damien merely laughed, a sound so infectious that even Tempest's lips began to curl into a smile. The devilish dragon. "I'll see you soon, my lord."

"You shall, lovely."

An embarrassing blush heated her cheeks as she turned on her heel and strode from the huge chamber. She barely made it out of the hall before Mal caught up with her, firmly wiping any semblance of a smile from her face.

Both his eyes and voice were tight as he asked, "How do you always manage to get caught up in such trouble?"

Tempest ignored him.

When, finally, she descended the stairs and found her room, she barely suppressed a sigh of relief. She was tired and sore and irritated; all she wanted to do was sleep. She pushed open the door and squeaked. A couple lay intertwined with one another on the bed. She promptly shut the door again. Her face flushed scarlet. That was unexpected.

"You've been assigned a new room," Mal said from behind her, almost lazily. "If you'd acknowledged my presence, I'd have warned you about the room swap and saved you the embarrassment of seeing what you just saw. If you follow me, I can take you there."

The last thing she wanted to do was follow him, but if it meant reaching a bed upon which she could collapse, and a fire that could warm her soul, then she'd do just about anything.

Wordlessly, she trailed after him and much to her chagrin, he took her back *up* the stairs until they reached a set of handsomely carved, mahogany doors. With the turn of a gilded handle indented with amber, he let her inside.

She gaped in awe. It was one of the most beautiful rooms she had ever seen. A balcony took up much of one wall, protected from the bitter outside with a solid sheet of semi-opaque stone. Lights twinkled out of focus behind the stone, transforming it into something quite magical. The hearth to her left was almost as large as the balcony, a gargantuan fire burning merrily within it. But the flames weren't orange; they were purple and blue and icy and blinding white. "What sort of witchery is this?" she demanded.

Mal rolled his eyes. "It's nothing but a parlor trick. When you burn certain oils, they change the color of the flames."

"Nyx?" she asked, eyeing the painted white columns of the room—as well as the sizeable four-poster bed—in the colors of the northern sky. Her attention moved back to the curious flames. Pyre's sister was gifted when it came to concocting potions and elixirs

"You know us so well?" Mal asked. She didn't answer. "It's a nice room, isn't it?"

"I'm not going to speak to you in this form," she said through gritted teeth, for there was no way she was going to admit to being enamored with the room to such a despicable man. She threw a glare at him and noticed, in the process, that Mal was staring at her wrist.

Where the king of the dragons had kissed her.

"He marked you. *Again*," he said, without inflection or emotion, though Tempest knew enough about Mal—Pyre—to tell that he was gravely unhappy.

Good. Let him be.

"Damien helped me," she said, knowing it was nowhere near close to a good enough explanation. "Now shift or get the hell out."

With a clench of his jaw, Mal shifted, groaning as his other human form emerged before Tempest's very eyes. It greatly unsettled her, seeing a man turn into another man entirely. It reminded her that she did not know which form was truly the Jester.

Do you even want to know? Does it matter?

"Are you happy now?" he bit out tersely.

She let out a short, humorless laugh. "Not in the least."

His golden eyes dolefully scanned Tempest's entire frame as she threw off her sodden, frozen cloak and shook out her bird-nest hair.

Eventually, he said, "Get some rest. You look like death." He began to exit the room, then turned and added, "Try not to let anyone else mark you, if you can help it."

Tempest threw a dagger at the door in response, but he'd closed it before it could reach him. It lodged in the wood with a thud. How many times would they go round after round?

"You cannot tell me what to do," she muttered, wincing as she stripped off her clothes. "I can do what I like."

But on the matter of men marking her as *theirs,* Tempest had to admit they were on the same page.

No more markings. She belonged to no one.

Yet.

CHAPTER 24: TEMPEST

"...*T*empest. Hey, Tempest. *Dog!*"

Tempest barely ducked in time to avoid the wooden cup Brine threw at her head. She hadn't even noticed the man sit down at the same table as her.

She grimaced and ran a hand down her face. "I'm sorry, Brine. I didn't sleep well."

"I can see that," he muttered, taking another cup of hot tea from a servant as they passed them by. "Has anyone told you that you look like death?"

It was early—*too* early to be up after her many days of hard travel and flight through the snowy mountains—but she had not been able to stay in bed after a restless night of tossing and turning.

"Someone may have said that to me, yes," she replied, feeling hot. "Do I really look that bad?"

"You have shadows under your eyes so big they look like

bruises." Brine frowned at her. "Did you come into any trouble on the way here?"

"Why, Brine, are you concerned about me?" Tempest asked with amusement.

The wolf shifter bristled. "After the ambush last time, I was expecting you to end up dead, traveling on your own. I was disappointed to discover you flew in, instead. Upon the back of the dragon king, I heard. Are you insane?"

Brine's 'disappointment' was very much a front and both of them knew it. His animosity and distrust toward her had long since abated. She laid her head on the table and gazed at the wolf. He was fiercely loyal. If she could convince him to work with her instead of the Jester…

He would never leave Pyre.

It was a rotten realization. He'd have been an amazing ally to have.

"That dragon king was the one who ambushed us, you know," she mumbled to Brine as if she hadn't just spent the past few seconds silently deliberating mutiny. She narrowed her eyes, her cheek squished against the table. "*Did* you know that, Brine?"

"Obviously not at the time." He scowled, his jaw working. "And even if the dragon king *is* one of the Jester's allies, he is strong enough to attack us without fear of reprimand. After the deal you made with him last time, I fully expected him to come after you again… though I guess he *did*, in a fashion."

"I called him for aid, actually," Tempest said, absentmindedly curling a lock of hair around her finger. Before dawn, when she'd finally admitted to herself that she'd get no sleep, she had crept to the baths and soaked and oiled her hair until it was easier to detangle it. Now it was soft, lustrous, and smooth once more, flashing in the light of the torches like a lilac flame.

Sweet poison, she didn't feel very good. Her head ached, and she was bloody hot.

Brine seemed to pale at her statement, but still set down his teacup with far more care than she expected. "Be careful, dog. Truly, be careful. You are playing with politics you do not understand."

Tempest knew he genuinely meant well, but the comment irked her nonetheless. She pushed her chair away from the table and stood up, smoothing down her shirt and leather trousers as she did so. "I understand far more than people think, Brine. Now, if you'll excuse me."

The room swam, and she stumbled. Strong arms wrapped around her. Brine's gray eyes stared down at her with concern. She blinked as he placed the back of his hand against her cheek.

"You're warm."

She brushed his hand away and wiggled out of his embrace. "I'm fine."

"You're not."

Tempest waved him away and weaved toward the exit, too prideful to admit that he was right. She felt like death. Brine and herself were two sides of the same coin. It was probably why she never hated Brine, even when he had hated her. They both hated to admit weakness.

She sighed and traipsed down the corridor. Her conversation with the wolf had reminded her that she had to tell the Jester about her engagement to King Destin. The news would no doubt reach his ears soon. It was better if it came from her. She needed to explain what she planned. *A traitor is still a traitor, and that is what he shall see you as.*

If only she could find him.

"Where are you, stupid fox?" she muttered, first checking the training hall, then the meeting chamber, and finally the masquerade hall. No kitsune. In a last-ditch attempt to find him, she headed toward his study. The door was cracked open, and Nyx's and Pyre's voices filtered through the door.

Her heart picked up, and sweat slicked the back of her neck. She stood outside the door, her fist raised to knock upon the wood. After their failed interaction last night, there was no telling how he would react to her.

Stop being a coward.

She steeled herself and knocked on the door three times.

"Come in, Tempest!" Nyx called out, unnerving Tempest to no end. Damn shifter's sense of smell.

Somewhat hesitantly, she opened the door and entered. She halted in her tracks. Acres of russet skin was on display. Pyre stood in the middle of the room, shirtless, while his sister used a length of tape to take his measurements.

Nyx flashed a smile at Tempest. "Last-minute costume alternations," she explained. "*Somebody* has lost a little weight since his jacket was made and insists upon the garment being adjusted."

Pyre shrugged, entirely nonchalant. "Things have been stressful, what can I say? You don't look like you slept well, Temp."

But Tempest barely heard him. Her eyes were glued to his back: it was covered in scars which looked suspiciously like those received from the lash of a whip. Her arm seemed to burn. She had a scar that looked exactly like it.

"Now I *know* you haven't slept well." Pyre laughed. "You are not normally so forward with your admiration of my body.

"I'm not staring." She broke her gaze from his scars and shot him a rude gesture that she'd seen Maxim use.

"Naughty." He grinned over his shoulder. "What, too tired for banter?"

Her lips pursed. His easy flirtations weren't what she expected. They were definitely at odds with their last few interactions. What was his game here? Was he trying to mess with her head? Because it was damn well working. "I... don't feel good."

"Oh?" His brows slashed together.

"It's nothing." She meandered farther into the room. "You're in a good mood?"

"There's no reason not to be," Pyre replied.

"All done," Nyx chimed.

He picked up a plain cotton shirt from the chair near the fire and slid it over his broad shoulders—shoulders that Tempest was desperately trying not to notice. What was her problem? She'd grown up with men—seen naked males of all sorts and sizes—and yet somehow the kitsune affected her. *Figures.*

"The masquerade is coming up; all the factions are coming... and I have my Hound by my side. Or has that changed?" He paused, arching a brow. "Have you betrayed me in your time away?

She scowled, even as her pulse sped up. "I haven't made plans to unleash the Hounds on you, Pyre. *Yet.*"

He laughed easily at her threat, waving a negligent hand. As if Tempest herself was insignificant. Did he have any idea what would happen to him if she unleased Madrid upon his mountain palace? If she made another deal with Damien, he had the ability to lead all the Hounds in.

Pyre frowned and sauntered up to her. Tempest backed up,

pressing against the wall as he invaded her space and leaned into her, inhaling heavily near her temple. "You're not well."

She wedged her hands between their bodies, her fingers meeting warm skin. Her stomach flipped, and Tempest shoved him away. "Stop with the sniffing."

"Nyx," Pyre barked. "She's not well."

"I'm fine," she argued. "It's just been a few long days."

The kitsune scowled, buttoning his shirt. "So why were you looking for me?" He ran his hands through his hair, pushing the deep wine-colored strands from his face. He flashed a grin Tempest's way. "I gather it wasn't to appreciate my good looks?"

"It doesn't matter," Tempest said, edging toward the door. "I think I'm going to take your advice and get some more sleep." Slipping from the room, her shoulders sagged, and she staggered down the hallway. Gone were any lingering obligations she felt to tell Pyre about her engagement to King Destin.

Let him find out like everyone else—as secondhand news. Let him discover just what insignificant feels like.

She squinted, her body aching.

"Shhhh... Go back to sleep," Briggs rumbled.

"What?" she whispered through parched lips.

"You've been running a fever," Pyre's familiar voice answered. She turned her head slightly. The kitsune sat on her bed, running his fingers through her sweaty hair. Tempest pressed her cheek against his cool hand.

"So hot."

"I know, love," he crooned. "Briggs and Nyx made you a tincture to help, but I need you to drink it."

Anything to get the pounding in her head to go away. Briggs handed Pyre a cup, and she sighed when he slipped his cool hand beneath her neck, cradling her head. He held the draught to her lips.

"It's nasty, but you need to drink it," Briggs admonished.

Tempest gulped the concoction and gagged. Her eyes watered, and her stomach rebelled. She was so damn hot. Kicking at the covers, she sighed when cold air hit her bare skin. A growl sounded, and the blankets once again covered her flushed body.

"No," she moaned. "Too hot."

"I know, love. I know. But you don't want to show Briggs your naked body, do you?"

"Don't care," she moaned.

"I do," Pyre murmured, once again stroking her cheek. "This is what happens when you make deals with dragons and ride them."

His words became gibberish, and her world dulled until there was nothing but darkness.

CHAPTER 25: PYRE

*T*empest moaned, her pale skin flushed pink. He stared down at her, wondering what in the blazes was he doing here? Nyx and Briggs were more than capable to care for the female Hound. Yet, he couldn't leave the bed.

"I can hear you worrying from here," Briggs muttered from his chair beside the bed. "She's *fine*. It's just a cold."

Pyre nodded and then rested his fingers on the pulse beating at the base of her throat, counting her heartbeats. For such a ferocious creature, his Hound looked awfully pitiful at the moment.

"Humans are so weak," he murmured, eyeing the blue veins standing out starkly beneath Temp's skin.

Briggs snorted. "Don't let her hear you say that. We'll never hear the end of it."

Pyre cracked a smile that felt a little too stiff. "True." The moment of mirth passed. "She should never have been on *that* dragon." Every time he thought of Damien's smug smile, Pyre's hackles rose. Even now he could smell the dragon's scent on Tempest.

"You're being unreasonable."

Pyre arched a brow at the healer. "How so?"

"Damien provided her safe transportation." The big man crossed his arms and rocked in his chair. "Would you have rather had her trying to traipse through the storms outside? Shifters die in weather like this all the time. What do you think it would have done to our girl?"

A valid point.

Temp thrashed and the sheet slipped, catching on the tip of her breast. His jaw clenched at all the flushed snowy skin on display. Pyre growled and yanked the linen up passed her shoulders and tucked it around her body. Maybe that would keep her from trying to flash the other male in the room.

"When are we going to talk about it?" Briggs asked.

"Talk about what?" Pyre bit out, still wrapping the female up.

"About the fact that you've taken a mate."

He jerked at the healer's blunt words. "I haven't."

Briggs guffawed. "You wreak of aggression and every time she's shown even an ounce of skin your scent gets stronger. I'm a healer, Pyre. I've seen many female parts while assisting with the birth of babes. Tempest doesn't have anything I haven't seen before."

Sweat beaded Pyre's brow, and he licked his upper lip, feeling edgy. "She's a private person. She wouldn't want anyone looking upon her person when she's so vulnerable."

"True, but you forget that I already have cared for her. I've seen everything the little Hound is hiding beneath her clothing and it's just flesh. Nothing more, nothing less."

A low growl rumbled Pyre's chest, and he glared at Briggs, hating that his friend had seen Temp naked. *You're jealous.*

Briggs held his gaze, not flinching. "I will not tiptoe around you. I've always spoken my mind to you, have I not?"

"You have," Pyre ground out.

"Then hear me now. The woman you guard so staunchly now has no appeal to me. Her scent stirs nothing."

Pyre's shoulders slumped. One less male to deal with.

The healer continued, leaning forward. "But if she had stirred my beast, I promise you that I would have made her mine before she left the cabin."

Pyre tensed, his upper lip curling at the idea of Briggs claiming the Hound. "She's *mine.*"

"I know, which is how I don't understand why you are letting her roam around unclaimed. Mates are a rare thing."

"We aren't compatible." He stared down into his Hound's face, her eyes flickering behind her lids. She was the light, and Pyre the darkness. "I can't afford to be distracted."

"That's rubbish, and you know it," Briggs barked.

"Even if I tried to court her, Tempest would refuse me." His gut clenched as he remembered the look on her face when she'd left him after he revealed his second human form. Betrayal. He knew the look well. "She will never fully trust me."

"She cares for you even though you've been an idiot. Come clean now, claim your female, defeat the king, and then give me nieces and nephews I can spoil."

Tempest cuddled into his side, and his heart beat faster. If only it could be like this always.

"You're being weak."

He glared at Briggs. "This is not just about me and my wants. My decisions affect an entire nation of people. She's working with the enemy. I cannot fully trust her, even if I wish to."

"You've mistrusted everyone around you for so long that you're going to miss out on the greatest gift anyone one of us could receive." His friend blinked at him slowly and then sank back into his chair, continuing to rock. "Tempest is special, and while I might not be interested in her, there are others who don't have your reservations. She will be snapped up by another from right beneath you if you tarry."

"Are you done?" Pyre asked, his tone cutting. His claws lengthened, and he tried to breathe slowly to calm himself.

Briggs nodded. "I've said my piece."

Pyre glanced away and then back to the female in his arms. "I knew you were trouble."

CHAPTER 26: TEMPEST

W hatever miracle Briggs and Nyx had created, it did the job. Tempest had never recovered so quickly. The next two days that followed passed by in the blur. Tempest did her best to blend in with the goings-on of the palace, listening to conversations and gossip and taking note of every person who came to stay for the masquerade. By the time the ball itself was mere hours from starting, she'd learned three things.

First: she wasn't alone in her doubts about the Jester. Several people were of the same opinion as her—that he was too brutal, that he had no plan past taking the throne from Destin. They wanted a concrete strategy for after the war was over, but there was none. Others, by contrast, thought Pyre wasn't being brutal *enough*. She'd have to look out for the bloodthirsty ones. They were a slippery lot.

Second: not a single person was willing to do anything

about their feelings of dissent. They were content to grumble and bicker in the shadows.

Third: supporting the Jester was their best—and, seemingly —only option. Which meant she had only to provide a viable alternative, and she could likely steal a chunk of his allies, maybe his whole operation.

That both pleased and unnerved her. Were people so easily turned, so easily won? And if so… how easily would they sell *her* out?

She shuddered.

"Temp?"

She turned at the sound of the voice. Nyx stood there, a gentle smile on her face as she held out a hand for her.

"What is it?" Tempest asked. Only then did she realize how low the sun was through the open balcony. "Oh. It's time already."

"Yes." Nyx laughed. "It is time to get ready."

"I… did not bring anything to wear," Tempest replied, bashful and somewhat ashamed. She had felt so proud, standing up to the Jester by refusing to bring a dress. But this masquerade was more than simply an opportunity for him to show her off; she needed to look like a calm, collected, striking queen if she was going to rally people behind her, not a tired and bedraggled girl in worn leather trousers.

Nyx grinned, her eyes dancing. "Trust me, I expected that. As did my brother. Come, follow me. I have a surprise for you."

She swallowed a gulp as Nyx led her to the bedroom.

Here's hoping she has good taste.

CHAPTER 27: TEMPEST

S he had no words when she saw the dress laid out on her bed, waiting for her. Tempest stared at the garment, then at Nyx, then back at the dress again.

"This is—wow, Nyx. Thank you."

"Don't thank me," she replied, an amused glint in her eye as she handed Tempest something she very much recognized—an elaborate, bone-white wolf mask. "This was all my brother's doing. Do you need any help getting dressed or would you prefer to be left alone?"

"Alone," Tempest said, a few seconds too late, so absorbed in the idea that Pyre had picked such an unearthly beautiful dress for her to hear the question properly. Nyx squeezed her shoulder and exited, the door closing quietly behind her.

It was stunning.

The dress she'd been given to wear to her Hound coronation

ceremony had been elaborate, but it did not hold a candle to the work of art gracing her bed.

It was sleeveless, with a tight bodice and a flowing, feathery, voluminous skirt that split down the front and would trail behind her for several feet. It was made of layers and layers of impossibly light, translucent blue and silver material. The bodice itself was constructed of dozens of interlocking snowflakes and was cut low in the back. Beside it was a pair of silken hose and a formal pair of snow-white boots.

Feminine and fierce.

It was too beautiful.

She ran her fingers along the fabric. To wear such a dress required more than putting it on. Tempest strolled to the vanity and sat. She cleansed her skin, the perfumed water causing her skin to tingle. She applied salve beneath her eyes that made her seem dewy and alert. Carefully, she used some silver from a pot to line her eyes and flutter through her eyelashes. It wasn't anything like the court fashions, but it was her.

Once finished, she unwove her braid and brushed her long hair, the waves tumbling along her shoulders. Tonight, her hair was her crown jewel of beauty. She'd not hide who she was. She pulled pieces up here and there, and finally decided to implement a series of small and thickly woven braids at the crown of her head, leaving the bulk of it to flow free and wavy down her back, and a few pieces to frame her face.

She glanced at the balcony. Someone had been in her room earlier to add new fuel to the lanterns, but they had also strung garlands of tiny snowdrops and bluebells across the balcony. Wandering over, Tempest plucked a few of the flowers and returned to the mirror, threading them into the braids. That would have to do.

Standing, she moved back to the end of the bed and eyed the dress. How in the blazes was she supposed to get it on?

You should have accepted Nyx's help.

Quickly, she shucked her clothing and slipped on the painted hose. Winter's bite, they were soft and comfortable. If only it were acceptable for her to wear them all the time. Her uncles had vetoed the garment years ago, claiming them to be indecent on a woman. Eyeing the mirror, she understood why. They clung to her every curve.

Next, she stepped into the gown, which was easy enough, but lacing the back was a bloody nightmare. It was only with some clever finger work—and constant glances in the mirror— that she managed to secure the dress in place.

When she caught her reflection, she hardly recognized herself. A creature of snow, ice, and liquid silver stared back at her.

"That is… really me," she breathed, touching the glass with her fingertips. The kitsune had done well. While the gown was the loveliest thing she'd ever beheld, it was also practical. The split at the front of the skirt made movement easy and gave glimpses of her painted hose. The boots felt like butter and hugged her calves and knees. There'd be no pinched toes or twisted ankles tonight from impractical shoes. A huge smile graced her face as she discovered hidden pockets with slits. The perfect way to get keep her daggers on her.

Pyre had thought of everything, that sly bastard.

That was when she noticed the pair of elbow-length, delicately embroidered lace gloves that were also set on the bed for her, as well as a plain white box that sat next to the mask. While the gloves were pretty, they were not practical. If a situation went south, she did not want anything to restrict her movement.

She moved to the bed, her dress rustling softly. With care, she opened the box and blinked. It was a silver choker adorned with opals, diamonds, and sapphires. She blinked again. How in the hell did he come by something so fine? It rivaled anything she'd seen worn in court, even the jewels the king had gifted Temp. Her fingers shook as she pulled it from the box and clasped it around her neck, the cool metal embracing her skin.

Next came her weapons. A garrote hidden in a bracelet Dima had gifted her when she'd won her first match against him. Poisoned hairpins from Aleks that he'd given Tempest when she'd managed to discern the top ten most deadly poisons in Heimserya. And finally, the daggers Maxim brought back for her when he'd returned from a trip to the Fire Isles. She strapped them to her thighs and hid one in each boot.

Feeling a bit more like herself, she reached for the final item.

"And now it's just the mask," she whispered, picking up the beautiful wolf mask and inspecting it. The mask was made of porcelain or something similar. It was fragile and liable to shatter, but that only made it more precious. With gentle fingers, she tied the silver ribbon of the mask around her head and hid it beneath her braids, so that it looked as if the mask was sitting on her face unaided.

She faced the mirror and studied her reflection. A warrior princess stared back at her. She spun on the spot, testing how much movement she had in the skirt, and was surprised further by how easy it was to move in the dress. The bodice was tight, but not rib-crushing like the dress she had worn at Destin's request. This was the kind of dress she could easily fight in, regardless of the several feet of feathery material trailing behind her.

Her gaze trailed to the necklace. It looked... like a collar. Tempest huffed. The Jester couldn't be trusted to be generous in everything.

Time to go.

She pulled open the door and half-expected Pyre to jump out at her, but no one was there. Tempest ran her hands down the skirt and then lifted her chin. Now was not the time to be self-conscious.

The corridors leading to the masquerade ball teemed with people. She ignored their stares as she worked through the crowd and entered the ballroom. While the masks hid everyone's identity, her hair gave her away. Masks swam before her gaze—swans, snakes, lions, dragons, cats and...

A kitsune.

The unmistakable figure of Pyre, dressed in the resplendent, deep claret outfit Tempest had initially seen him trying on weeks ago in his cave in the forest. His golden fox mask covered the top part of his face, and he paused as he caught sight of her, his goblet of wine hovering near his lips in his hand. A slow smile curved his lips, and his amber eyes seemed to glow behind his mask. Her steps slowed, and her heart beat a little faster.

Calm down.

He set his goblet down on a nearby table and excused himself from his company, the crowd parting for him as he made his way over to her. She took his arm when he proffered it to her, eyeing his costume and then her own. The color gradient they made together—white to silver to blue to lilac, to claret to crimson to gold—it became clear to Tempest why the Jester had picked this specific dress for her to wear.

"You are a vision," he murmured into her ear, a mischievous look on his face that told Tempest he very much enjoyed the attention they were gathering.

"Will I ruin the vision if I open my mouth to speak?" she asked, feeling just as mischievous as Pyre himself. There was something infectious about the night, and her dress, and the masked ball-goers, that made Tempest feel distinctly like another person.

You're not. Get yourself together. Focus on allies.

Pyre snickered, his lips touching the shell of her ear. "That entirely depends on what you say, Tempest."

He led her farther into the masquerade hall, which was full of elaborately dressed people, strange masks, and heartbreakingly beautiful music played by a string quartet on a central plinth. Soft lantern light glittered off decorations all around the vast, cavernous hall, from silvered candlesticks, crystal chandeliers, and ensconced torches alike.

There were spices on the air—vanilla and cinnamon and something floral beneath them—that Tempest eagerly breathed in. When a passing servant handed her a spindly glass filled with a pale gold, sparkling liquid, she gladly accepted, if only to do something with her hands. Drinking was not on her list of things to do. She needed her wits about her.

"Why am I a wolf?" she asked Pyre as they circled about the room, stopping here and there for him to say his hellos and to introduce Tempest to the guests she had not met before.

"Is it not obvious?"

"True," she murmured, taking a delicate sip of her champagne. A wolf mask was a fitting symbol of her status as

Hound. A wolf among sheep. "But you always have an alternate reason."

He shrugged. "The mask has been in my possession for a while. When I met you—the first time I met you in the tavern—I thought your face was perfect for it. I cannot really explain it; but it was meant for you."

"I'm sure Brine won't appreciate the dog being a wolf for the night," she remarked with a wry grin.

"Oh, you and I both know that he likes you more than he lets on." Pyre chuckled. "You're a part of his pack now whether he'll admit it or not."

A flicker of guilt licked Tempest's stomach, and she was reminded of her actual goal for the evening. She had to work out who might rally behind her… and tell Pyre about her intention to marry King Destin. Though she had convinced herself before that he could find out second hand, now that she was level-headed and no longer sick, she knew it wasn't the right decision. Pyre might be sneaky and underhanded, but she couldn't be that way. Even to him.

She allowed Pyre to essentially show her off to all the factions, using the introductions as an opportunity to put names to voices and masks. But, as they wandered, her skin began to prickle. It felt like her time was short.

"What is it?" he asked after almost an hour of snatched conversations and throwaway comments.

She shook her slightly. "I… Pyre, you told me this masquerade was about securing support. About maintaining goodwill between factions for the war."

He cocked his head to one side. "Your point being?"

"It seems as if everyone is already *prepared* for war," she said, waving around them. "Everyone is behind you—that was clear

as day to me. There is no support to gather. They're all...
ready."

"Dance with me," he murmured, pulling her toward the
dance floor before she had the chance to refuse.

"You really are like two completely different people," she
said, studying his jaw as he took one of her hands in his. She
gingerly placed her other hand on his shoulder. When he slid a
hand around her waist to the small of her back, Tempest
shivered in an entirely pleasant way. Damn it.

Pyre's fingers roamed just a little higher up her back, a
knowing smile on his lips, clearly enjoying her reaction. "I
could say the same about you, you know," he replied as they
began dancing, quickly becoming one with the rhythm of the
music. Tempest had never been one for dancing before, but it
always came naturally. She chalked it up to swordplay. It was
essentially the same thing. *Except for the killing.*

"I am not *literally* two people though, am I?" she countered,
raising an eyebrow that Pyre could not see behind her mask.

He laughed easily. "I suppose not. But still; when you fly into
a rage you are rather different than your usual self, Temp."

"What can I say? You bring out the best in me."

"I can think of a far better way to channel that energy than
merely *fighting*," he said, his tone dripping with insinuation,
before his lips caressed her skin. For a moment, she closed her
eyes, and a small sigh caught in her throat. This was the banter
she remembered, the Pyre she had grown to like, and thought
was her friend.

This Pyre isn't real.

She stiffened, and her eyes snapped open; the magic broken.
Dancing with him like this was a mistake. Flirting with him was
dangerous. He'd already proven he couldn't be trusted to tell

the truth, nor not to hurt her. If she let herself, she could lose everything to him. That couldn't happen. Too much was at stake.

"Tempest." She forced herself to meet Pyre's gaze, which was uncharacteristically serious. He pointed toward one of the balconies, which was unoccupied. "Could we speak privately for a moment?"

She nodded, not trusting her voice. Now was the time to tell him.

As they escaped through the throng of people, she tried desperately to work out how to word what she had to say. Each step they took up the stairs, her pulse leapt. By the time they reached the wintry air of the balcony, however, her mind had gone completely blank.

Pyre closed the glass doors behind them, cutting off the noise of the masquerade. It was just the two of them, surrounded by delicate, silvery lights and the darkness of a northern evening. She followed Pyre to the edge of the balcony, where an iron and stone wall protected them from a precipitous fall. A healthy fire roared in the pit, cutting the chill. She glanced down and gulped—precipitous was an understatement. She could not see the ground.

"Scared of heights, Temp?" Pyre teased. "To be honest, I'm not all that great with them myself."

"I've ridden a dragon," she said dryly. Her brows furrowed. "If you're not fond of heights, why build a palace in a mountain?"

Pyre pushed his mask up, an incredulous expression on his face. "Come now. You can't honestly believe that *I* built this place, do you? It's centuries old!"

Tempest felt foolish, and her cheeks burned at the comment.

"I didn't mean you, I meant why choose this place as your palace?" she admitted. "Has the Dark Court always been here?"

"As long as the capital has stood."

She shook her head. "Unbelievable. How has it managed to survive for so long? An organized underworld older than most reigning families in Heimserya and its neighbors. It's—"

"Definitely a bit intimidating," Pyre finished for her, smiling softly. He turned his gaze to the sky. The storms had cleared, leaving a pure, unfettered night-time sky littered with stars and a far, full moon. He sighed heavily. "I owe you an apology."

"You do."

He cracked a smile. "Never one to beat around the bush. That's what I like about you." He sighed. "Tempest, I'm sorry I lied about my other form. I should have told you about Mal before you arrived here. I just... don't trust many people."

"That doesn't make any sense," she said, pointing at her mask. "What about this? I thought you said that was a test of whether you could trust me. I didn't tamper with the box."

"If only things were so simple." He laughed. He turned to face her, molten eyes keen on hers. When he raised a gloved hand to remove the wolf mask from her face, she did not protest. "I do trust you, though. But I had... other reasons... to keep you at bay."

Pyre stroked Tempest's cheek tenderly, causing her heart to constrict painfully.

"Your presence here, among my people, has done more good than you could ever know," he continued, still stroking her face. "I know we do not always agree on my methods—we probably never will—but know that your decision to help the rebellion will bring positive change to so many people as a whole. Speaking of the greater good is always difficult, but—"

"War is difficult," she said, smiling sadly, leaning into Pyre's touch without truly realizing it. "You said that before."

"You must know I was speaking the truth."

"Yes, but the truth is—"

"Difficult," Pyre interrupted.

Neither of them spoke for a long, tense moment. Tempest's skin pebbled, and nervous energy churned in her belly. She wasn't sure if she was to fight, run, or kiss the dangerous man in front of her. The latter would be a mistake for the both of them.

"But, despite all this, I know the truth," he whispered. "I was naïve before."

Pyre leaned forward and kissed her. A press of warm, hungry lips on hers, the flick of a tongue, and the graze of pointed canines. She flushed hot and then cold. Her body longed to melt into the kiss. Longed for her to let the kitsune wrap his arms around her and make her forget about everything.

But her conscience was stronger.

"Stop," she mumbled.

"Never," he whispered, nibbling at her bottom lip, his hands framing either side of her face.

Tempest dug deep and pushed him away a few inches. "No more!"

He examined her face, and her pulse doubled its speed. "What is it, love?" he asked, his voice low and raw with desire. "After everything that's happened... I know this isn't one sided. You at least feel *something* for me—"

"Destin proposed to me," she said woodenly. "And I—I said yes."

Pyre grew as still as if he were made of stone. The air

thickened around them, and all she could hear was her own frantic heartbeat in her ears. Claws extended from his fingertips, and his gaze burned her. He growled, and his fox ears went flat against his head.

The hair at the nape of her neck rose.

"No."

CHAPTER 28: TEMPEST

"No," Pyre repeated, fury building in his eyes. "No, no, *no*! What have you done, Tempest? What have you—"

She held her hands up, her pulse skyrocketing. "I've done what is necessary."

"Necessary?" he spat.

"Yes, necessary. Look at me!"

The kitsune glared at her.

She stabbed a finger toward the ballroom. "I've allowed you to parade me around like we agreed upon, but what good has it really done? Nothing but make me a laughingstock. You promised we would work together, and yet you've kept me in the dark, had me just waiting for the next scrap you throw me."

"So, you want to seize power?"

"I don't want any of this," she exclaimed. "I've been thrust into the middle of a war, and I'm doing my damnedest to keep

236

the bloodshed low. Right now, I feel as if my hands are tied, but as queen of this bloody kingdom, I could make changes without sacrificing so many lives. Surely you can see the merit in that?" She reached out for his hand, squeezing it. His claws scratched her palm, but she didn't let go. "You know me. I'm just trying to do what's best for all of us."

A moment passed, and his fingers wrapped around hers. Hope soared in her chest until his upper lip curled, revealing the sharpened points of his canines. His golden eyes were cold and hard.

"Pyre—"

"How did he get to you?" he asked, voice steely. He tightened his grip on Tempest's fingers until the pressure hurt.

She met his hard stare with one of her own. "I don't know what you mean."

"Was it bribery?" he pressed. "A threat?" He reached into his jacket pocket and pulled out a familiar ruby necklace. She was sure it came from the box of jewels King Destin had given her— the ones that were supposed to be stored safely in her room. He shook his head. "I didn't want to believe Nyx when she said she'd found these in your possession." He chuckled, squeezing the necklace. "Are jewels—mere *rocks*—worth selling out those who want to see Destin off the throne?"

Tempest tore her hand from his and suffered a flash of pain as his claws scoured her palm. "He has not bribed or threatened me with anything," she retorted, feeling her own anger rising. How dare he? The choice to marry the monster king hadn't been a snap decision. It had been long and thought out. Even thinking about it now made her sick. "The jewels were a betrothal gift. I brought them here to use them for my own purpose."

"Which is?"

"To *thwart* the king! You know damned well that *your way* isn't the only way to bring change," Tempest retorted. "You must have heard what people have been saying within the palace walls. There are more than a few of your followers who accept your plans because nobody else has given them a less violent option." She lifted her chin. "We're going to give them one. *I'm* going to give them one."

He scoffed. "What, by whoring yourself out?"

Her hand flew through the air, and her palm connected with his cheek. He rubbed his jaw but said nothing. *Bastard.* Trembling, she took a step closer to the kitsune, hurt raging through her. Every interaction with the man repeated itself— bicker, flirt, grow close, insult one another, fight, repeat. She was done with it.

"How dare you?" she whispered, so angry she couldn't scream. "You know nothing about me. You know—"

"Not meaning to interrupt," came a silken, slithering voice. *Damien.*

Pyre growled, shooting a baleful look toward the doors. Tempest glared at his profile. Her chest clenched. She pressed her lips together, worried the pressure behind her eyes would manifest into ugly tears. Her uncles were right. The heart was traitorous. One could only trust their head and their kin.

"The gathering has begun, Pyre," Damien said.

She swallowed down her pain and faced the ballroom. Damien stood in the doorway, light haloing his form. The dragon king took another step onto the balcony, and paused, his gaze taking her in. A tear leaked from the corner of her eye, and she wiped it away, embarrassed. Damien's expression darkened.

"What have you done to her, Fox?" he hissed.

"It's nothing," Tempest rushed out, as the Jester glanced back at her. She avoided his gaze and stepped toward the dragon. "What do you need—"

The ground bucked, and she stumbled as explosions filled the air. Where had those come from? She ducked, placing her hands over her ears. Screams from the hall echoed in the stone cavern. Nyx burst from the crowd, her lush, black, velvet dress trailing behind her as she ran onto the balcony.

"What's happening?" Temp gasped.

"War, Tempest," Nyx said, out of breath.

"Looks like you have to pick a side, Hound." Pyre chuckled, the sound bitter. He smirked at her. "So, what will you do?"

War. The word rattled around in her head.

The time for plans was gone. She needed to get to the battle now. Tempest grabbed handfuls of her skirt and sprinted past Damien and Nyx. Sweat broke out across her forehead as she pressed through the crush of savage and fearful people. It was like swimming against the current. Someone stepped on the hem of her dress, and she cursed. Savagely, she ripped the skirt and continued toward her room.

By some miracle, she made it to her chamber, wasting no time in ripping off the beautiful dress that had cast a spell on her. She kicked off the dress-boots and yanked at the laces of her dress. They knotted. Tempest tore the dagger from her hip and sliced through what she could. The bodice gaped, and she wiggled it over her hips, left in just her corset and hose.

Hurry.

She kicked off the painted hose and yanked on her familiar, travel-stained trousers, linen shirt, sweater, and finally her cloak. She snatched her satchel, sword, bow, and quiver from beside the bed before rushing out of her room, straight into the arms of—

"Damien," she said, tilting her head up to lock eyes with him. "Please excuse me. I have to—"

He held a finger to her lips to shush her.

A wicked smile. "Need a ride?"

CHAPTER 29: TEMPEST

*H*er teeth chattered as the night wind tugged at her hair. Damien soared through the darkened sky, his approach completely silent. Another flash of light appeared as a ball of fire rose toward the heavens. The center of the fighting.

Her stomach twisted painfully. This was not in the plan. She'd had it all worked out in a plan where war was obsolete. Her fingers tightened on the dragon's harness, at least Damien had been prepared to carry a human rider this time. She wasn't ready for war. But was anyone ever prepared for such a thing?

"Are we sure this is a real fight?" Tempest bellowed over the roar of whooshing, freezing air attempting to blast her from her position. She clung tighter to the dragon's hulking shoulder blades.

He let out a rumble that rolled through Tempest and traveled deep into her bones. She knew he was laughing, which only made her feel sicker.

"What is a *real* fight, my lovely?" his deep, slithering voice asked.

"As in—is this really the beginning of a war? Or is just a skirmish… something that can be contained and controlled?" Maybe they could still avoid an all-out war. Even if Pyre was prepared, the Hounds would slaughter anyone who came across their paths.

"Almost all fights end in war, you know," Damien eventually said. His gargantuan wings beat at the air, bringing them ever closer to the lights and explosions.

Screaming reached her ears, and she couldn't tear her gaze from the fires below. All she could hear was her mother crying for her.

"Tempest?"

She shook her head, trying to focus on the dragon. "I'm sorry. What?"

"It might take a while—even years between *skirmishes*—but disagreements between two groups of people always end the same way. It is the way of things."

It didn't have to be the way of things. The notion that war was inevitable and that peace was only a result of somebody slaughtering the opposition wasn't something she necessarily agreed with. What did it solve? If women were in charge, would things be different? Her mind drifted to Nyx. She was level-headed and reasonable compared to the rest of the rebels, yet, even with the power she wielded, she still allowed the Jester to torture the shifters. Maybe it didn't matter. A person's worth was determined by their heart, not their gender.

Damien descended and heavy smoke curled through the air. She coughed, and her eyes stung. The dragon circled above the battlefield—for it *was* a battlefield, that much was clear—and huffed out a cloud of air that broke through the smoke. The warriors below paid no attention.

"Brace yourself, my lady warrior. We are about to land."

Tempest wiggled until she was perched on his back, fingers still clenching his harness. Damien swept low, and she inhaled. It was now or never. Her thighs tensed as she sprung from his back toward the battle. Her teeth rattled as she hit the ground, rolling through the snow. She popped to her feet and moved into the fray without a second thought. While she didn't condone war, she'd been raised for it.

Her pulse pounded in her ears as she strode among the chaos.

Calm yourself or you'll make a mistake. Madrid's words were a whisper in her ear.

For half a second, Tempest breathed in deeply and surveyed her surroundings, the firelight casting ghoulish shadows over the fighting men. Gunpowder, the metallic tang of blood, and the putrid smell of excrement washed over her. She dry-heaved once and then unsheathed her sword as a dark-clothed man caught her eye and charged. She swung, easily managing to dodge his blows, before cutting the soldier down.

"That's my girl!" Damien called, swiping his tail along the ground, throwing warriors into the air. The dragon launched into the night sky, his wings stirring snow as he disappeared into the darkness. He could have decimated the battlefield if he had wanted to, but he flew away.

Focus.

Tempest lowered her chin and swept her cloak behind her, scanning the battlefield. It would have been nice to have the dragon at her side, but she was more than capable. Another warrior darted in her direction. She met his attack and parried, slicing his Achilles tendon before moving on. Tempest plowed forward. She never outright attacked, only defended herself against any seeking to kill her, whether they were shifter or human. Her brain worked overtime to identify just what exactly was going on. Through the blood and smoke and darkness of night it was difficult to see who was fighting who. Another fiery explosion went off to her right. The ground bucked beneath her feet, and she flung up an arm to protect her face. The flames writhed like a temporary sun and illuminated the field.

She froze. *No.*

The crown prince stood among the fray.

What was the bloody prince and his soldiers doing here? *An ambush.*

Her jaw clenched. Why in the hell had Destin not mentioned that one of his sons was returning—least of all his heir? This was just getting worse every minute.

Figure it out later. Move.

Protect the prince. Protect the prince. Protect the prince. It ran through her head over and over as she fought to get to his side. Even though he was a worthless sod, he wasn't his father, and she'd sworn an oath to protect the kingdom.

The prince stumbled in her direction, bleary-eyed and clearly drunk, trying to hold his own. He was nowhere near her level of skill, but he wasn't terrible. What he lacked in finesse, he made for in enthusiasm.

"Damn it," she muttered as another of the prince's soldiers collapsed to the ground, leaving the crown prince open on his left. Heimseryan soldiers dropped like flies. The Talagans who were attacking them were not mere thieves or brigands. They were too efficient. Her fingers tightened on the pommel of her sword. This was the Jester's doing.

Another soldier rushed at her. She met his attack and gasped as he whipped under her guard, slashing her along the ribs. Tempest sucked in a sharp breath and staggered to the side, thankful she'd worn her corset reinforced with steel. He'd have gutted her without it. The man rushed at her again, but Tempest was ready for him. She met him, brandishing both sword and dagger. Their swords locked, and she growled, feeling her boots slipping. The man spat at her and then his eyes went wide. His mouth slackened, and his legs collapsed. Tempest skittered back, wrapping a hand around her ribs, wheezing. He'd been shot with three arrows.

Were those meant for her? She locked eyes with a shifter holding a bow. The woman smiled and twisted to meet an oncoming attack. She'd take that as a no. An ally. For now. Her gaze dropped to the man, and her heart clenched at the huge silver ring sitting on his finger.

A wolf ring.

A Hound. She'd fought a Hound. And he was dead because of it.

One of your own. Who are you?

Tempest hefted her sword, ribs screaming, and stormed forward. A shifter with ram horns bellowed and charged at her. She planted her feet and screamed back—a guttural, vengeful roar that Brine would have been proud of.

The crown prince turned at the sound of the scream. The relief on his dirt-streaked face was palpable when he realized who she was. *Thank your stars, boy, that I am protecting you.* She could do this. Protect the prince. Become the queen. Protect the people.

Her brain shut down until she was just a product of her training. One man. Two, three, four. Some of her attackers were skilled, of that there was no doubt, but she was a Hound, trained by the Dark Court. She was death.

The prince stumbled again, a sloppy smile on his face. "Tempest!" he cried, swinging his sword like a child. "I am so—"

A spear slid right through his chest. The young man gasped, blood staining his lips.

Tempest's vision went black, then white.

"*No!*" she screamed, dropping her sword and yanking her bow from her back. In a matter of heartbeats, she'd felled the prince's attacker. Tempest tossed her bow over her shoulder and grabbed her sword from the snow, already closing the distance between herself and the prince. The young man fell to his knees, and his hands went to the shaft of the spear, disbelief in his too-bright eyes as he yanked the weapon out.

"Don't do that!" Tempest commanded. The prince gasped wetly and dropped the spear to the bloody snow. She caught him before he fell. "Set up a perimeter!" she bellowed at his remaining guards, who were forming a circle around them. Tempest pressed the bottom of her cloak to the prince's wound but knew it wouldn't help.

Blood bubbled from his mouth and onto the snow beneath them, his face growing pale. A drop of water smeared the ash and snow, then another and another. She was crying. "It's going to be okay," she soothed.

"I—don't," the prince began, though the words were barely audible through his parched lips. "Don't want t-to die."

Tempest smoothed back his hair and lied; it was all she could do. "You'll be fine. You'll be fine. You can do this. Just keep your lovely eyes open."

The prince wasn't fine, and he didn't close his eyes, although it didn't help. His chest stilled, and his eyes glassed over.

The royal was dead.

She froze like that—on her knees, with the prince in her arms—for what felt like an eternity, though she knew that wasn't possible. The world slowed until it resembled a watercolor painting. A dull roar echoed in her ears, but she didn't move, slowly rocking the crown prince. She'd never liked the boy, but that didn't mean she wished him dead. The fear in his eyes before death took him would never leave her mind.

A hand touched her shoulder, and she flinched. A dagger found its way into her hand, and a foot soldier held up his hands. He was barely more than a boy. What was a boy doing on the crown prince's protection detail?

"My lady," he said, his voice wavering. "You are hurt."

Tempest dully looked down at herself. She was covered in gore. Wounds on her arms and shoulders sluggishly leaked blood. She couldn't feel them, whether it was from the shock or the cold, she didn't know. At some point, the sun had come up. Tempest blinked slowly and scanned the battlefield, illuminated by the morning sun.

It was a massacre.

Her gut clenched, and she twisted, violently throwing up. Tears sprung to her eyes as she heaved. Her body shook as she straightened and wiped her mouth with the back of her arm.

"Let us treat your wounds," the soldier said, holding out a hand to help her up.

Tempest shook her head and held onto the prince tightly. "I can't leave him."

"Tempest."

She vaguely recognized the voice. It belonged to one of the

battalion commanders—she remembered sparring him once, when she was younger.

The commander gazed impassively at the young prince and then nodded at her. "If your wounds are not treated, they'll become infected. Let us see to the prince and you to your injuries, then you can accompany us back to the capital."

Her fingers crushed the prince's icy, velvet cloak. What the man said made sense, but she couldn't get her body to do what he asked. She gazed back at the prince's face and closed his eyes. One finger at a time, she released his body and laid him gently against the snow. It took all her strength to stand and stay on her feet. The commander eyed her and held out a hand toward what remained of his battalion.

"You will find a healer among them as well as a horse for our journey."

She didn't smile or nod. It was a miracle she was able to put one foot in front of the other. The masquerade seemed like ages prior, but, in reality, only a few hours had passed.

And with them so many lives.

Her numbness hardened into an icy rage. The Jester had known this was going to happen. Their last conversation hung heavy in her mind. She would not go back to him—not after what he said. Not after the vile attack she had been thrust into.

You gave him the information.

Tempest brushed the thought away. The men of her world were determined to bring hell upon them. She'd have to save them on her own.

"You can do this." One tear tracked down her cheek. "You *have* to."

CHAPTER 30: TEMPEST

ing Destin did not cry when the lifeless body of his eldest son was placed before him in the announcements room. There was an emptiness in his eyes.

At first, Tempest thought it was grief, but then she reminded herself who she was looking at, and she peered harder. The lack of sadness and true shock wasn't surprising. Her expression didn't change as she concluded that he really didn't feel anything. He'd have to do better than that to fool his people. Tempest's uncles, by contrast, who lined the back wall with the rest of the Hounds, looked far more upset than their sovereign, all dressed in morose black, their shades of blue hair shining brightly against the mass of darkness.

On the journey back to the capital, she'd come to one conclusion.

The crown prince should have had more Hounds in his protection detail. The royal had been woefully exposed. Destin was a master tactician, and there was only one explanation: the king had *wanted* his son to die. How did it fit into his plan?

That's the monster you're going to marry.

Chills ran down her spine. Any man capable of murdering his own flesh and blood was no human at all. Her fingers twitched at her sides. He was a monster, one she planned to slay.

Destin swiftly moved over to the balcony which overlooked the palace courtyard. It was the place where palace decrees were announced. The courtyard was currently filled with scared and infuriated citizens of the kingdom, awaiting an announcement from their leader.

Her soul chilled further as the king straightened his back and prepared to give his announcement, not one ounce of weakness to his form.

"My beloved son, the crown prince, has died," he called out. Devastation saturated his voice, sounding so genuine that even Tempest was taken aback. One point to the murderous king. "My son, and your crown prince. My intentions were good in sending my sons as ambassadors to Kopal—to forge new alliances with our neighbors to allow Heimserya to flourish, for everyone, both Heimseryan and Talagan." Tempest almost gagged at his false words. "And yet, no sooner was my eldest on his way back to his home, our good faith in our neighbors was destroyed." The king paused, so deliberate but also so shock-provoking in his speech, that Tempest hated to admit she hung on his every word and every moment of silence.

Dangerous.

"We have yet to determine the identity of the vile creatures who attacked us," he continued, "but, nevertheless, we must fight fire with fire. We cannot allow the vagrants who ambushed our people and mindlessly slaughtered them to evade our grasp. We will have our vengeance."

Here it was. Another piece to the puzzle. The people began to cry out, whipped into a frenzy by his words, shouting unwavering support of his war. An unholy conquest under the guise of righteousness. She was going to be sick.

Her gaze strayed to the crown prince's body. He looked so small. She had never liked him; anyone honest enough to tell the truth would have admitted the same feeling. The man was older than Tempest, but he had acted like a spoiled, foolish boy, who was drunk on wine during most of his waking hours. He would have been a useless—possibly even dangerously so—king, but part of her wondered if that was just a way to cope with having such a father. No matter, he had not deserved to die. No one but those guilty of true evil warranted such a fate. What would he have been like if he'd been given the chance to grow as a person? Being an ambassador could have shown him just how fraught relations were with their neighbors. He could have made a change.

Now, he never would.

She shifted her gaze from the dead prince to his father, who was still busy, riling up the crowd far down below him. It was all in the name of his son, a son he cared nothing for. A son whose body he left on the white stone, alone and uncovered. She fingered the edge of her bloody cloak. The bastard hadn't even allowed her time to change before he addressed the people. Part of her wanted to storm across the room and cover the body with her own cloak, but she tamped down the urge. Drawing the king's attention would be foolish.

You caused this.

Exhaling slowly, she tried to ignore her conscience. If she

had arrived at the ambush just a few minutes earlier, or if she had gone straight to the prince's side the moment she arrived, she might have saved him.

Do not think about it.

"I think, in these fraught times of war," King Destin said, his powerful voice slicing through Tempest's head like a knife through butter, "we require hope now more than ever. And so, despite the tragedy lain before us today, I would like to make an announcement. As you are all aware, it has been a long time since my wife passed away."

Her skin prickled. He wouldn't. He couldn't.

"Though I grieve for her every day, I must accept that it is time for me to move on," Destin continued. "And what better woman to stand by my side than a warrior queen?"

Wicked hell. She was going to be sick.

Tempest risked a glance at her uncles, who had already worked out who he was talking about. She avoided their accusing gazes

Madrid stood stock-still, his gaze searing.

She looked away before he could catch her eye, but it was a pointless endeavor; King Destin was literally announcing her as his future queen. All of her uncles would know what Tempest had done within mere seconds.

Sweat beaded between her breasts, and the air seemed too thin.

"This is one of your own women," Destin called out. "One who refused to allow her social standing and gender to get in the way of what she wanted. The first female Hound: Tempest Madrid!"

A pause. And then: riotous cheering and applause. The crowd went wild, their roar of approval echoing inside the chamber. A roiling sickness tore through her stomach. She felt every pair of eyes on her keenly. Especially her uncles' eyes. She pinned her gaze to the balcony railing and kept her chin up, even though whispers among the Hounds had already begun. This was where she lost their respect—where she went from a warrior to another female to be sold like chattel.

Destin continued. "Tempest has worked tirelessly, fighting against prejudice and the expectations of her status as a woman, to become an exemplary member of the Hounds. She won a position on my war council fair and square, and, in the process, won my heart."

The room wavered, and bile burned the back of her throat. What would the king think if she puked all over his pristine floor? The crowd outside ate up every word he said. The king had missed his calling. He should have been an actor. Although nauseated, she plastered an equally actor-worthy smile to her face when a member of the king's royal guard made it clear that she should step forward and take her position beside Destin. She couldn't move though—her feet were rooted to the floor. Grimly, she thought of how lousy an actor she'd been when she'd met Pyre. If only he could see her now. The stinging in her heart told Tempest to bury said thought deep, deep down.

He has no place here.

Someone nudged her shoulder, and she found herself taking wooden steps to Destin's side. A smile frozen to her face, she gazed over the crowd, knowing what kind of monster she looked like, covered in the blood of their enemies and his son. Her clothing was ripped and disheveled. She looked as if she had come straight from a massacre—which she had. She supposed that was the point.

The king glanced down at her lovingly and wrapped an arm

around her waist, giving her a glowing smile as if her current state of dress was nothing. He'd announced her as his bride. His warrior queen. His equal. She kept her own careful smile plastered to her face as the crowd went wild. She had to look the part. Otherwise people would see through her ruse.

The king hauled her against his side, her breasts pressing to his ribs and the people's cheers grew even louder. Her heart beat in her ears, and she lay one hand lightly on his chest. He continued to address the people of Dotae, but she didn't hear the words he spoke, entirely focused on the way his thumb had slid between the edges of her shirt and corset, brushing her skin. What should have been a caress felt like he was running blades against her side. The urge to vomit emerged again. What had she signed up for? Had she signed her own death warrant in agreeing to marry the monster? Would she be the next victim in his war? The king had deemed his eldest son, the crown prince, as worthless, so how much more worth did she have?

No. Your worth isn't dependent on him.

Tempest glanced up at the king, studying his jawline. Destin had plans for her, she was sure. She'd play the part of being happily betrothed for now, but when he came for her, and he would, she'd cut his heart out.

The king's announcement came to an end, and she gently extricated herself from the king's arms before he could think to hold on to her for any longer. She strode back into the room. The Hounds' silence was louder than the crowd's cheers could ever be. Maxim broke the quiet and muttered out a garbled congratulations that he clearly did not mean at all.

Madrid shook his head ever-so-slightly, eyes infinitely sad, and Dima said nothing at all. Aleks stood at the end of the line as she moved for the exit. She'd been avoiding him for weeks, and he knew it. He locked gazes with her and squeezed her hand once before she shook him off and fled the announcement room. Her steps were measured until she rounded the corner, where she burst into a sprint, simply trying to find somewhere —anywhere—she could hide in a dark corner by herself and cry.

A child's sob broke through her panic.

Tempest slowed and frowned. At first, she thought she must've imagined it because that was exactly what she wanted to do, but no. The crying grew louder as she moved deeper into the castle, the sound full of genuine grief and sadness.

She rounded the next corner and spotted a small form leaning heavily against the wall, gasping for air, barely able to stand.

Princess Ansette.

Her face was puffy and red, though beneath that, her pallor was pale and sickly. Her shoulders were shaking.

"Ansette," Tempest said gently, taking careful steps toward the princess with a hand slightly outstretched. "Oh, lass, what can I do?"

The girl hiccupped and waved a hand at her but said nothing, tears streaming down her face.

Tempest approached her like a cornered animal and placed a hesitant hand on the girl's shoulder. "I was with your brother when he died, though I was too late to save him. I am so, so sorry. I tried my best." The last part was a whisper.

Ansette's sobs slowed to hiccups and then, finally, to long deep breaths. The silence was drawn-out, but it was better than the heartbreaking sobs. Eventually, the girl turned her turbulent gaze on Tempest and spoke.

"I suppose one member of the family dies, and another takes

their place," Ansette said, her voice cold and hard. She glared at Tempest. "Welcome to the family, I guess."

Tempest seized the royal's hand, trying to make the princess feel like she wasn't so alone. "And family we shall be. Your grief is mine. Your happiness, mine as well."

Ansette's eyes widened, and a fresh wave of tears ran down her face. She shook her head. "Run, Tempest." She spoke so softly Tempest hardly heard her. "Run," she repeated. "You need to get out of here. If you stay, you'll die just like my mother did, and all of my father's mistresses. You shouldn't die for him. You're too good for that."

Tempest stiffened. The string of deaths had been suspicious, but the murder of the queen... if that were proved true... "I can't just leave," she replied, her smile wobbly. "I have too much to do." There wasn't any other choice. And, looking at Ansette, she knew she couldn't leave the girl alone with the devil ruling the throne. Who knew what he'd do with his mouthy, opinionated daughter?

Ansette wiped her face with the skirt of her dress. She looked so pitiful that Tempest wanted to hug her, but something told her that she shouldn't. The girl wasn't ready for it. Perhaps not ever.

"I will do what I can for the people of Heimserya," Tempest murmured instead, "and for those who live farther out. I've never had any aspirations to become queen, but at least it will afford me this much."

"I hope you live long enough to see that come to fruition."

So did she.

Tempest bowed and then turned on her heel, her mind reeling. Her grief felt wrong compared to the princess's.

Tempest had not just lost her brother. Nor did she have a murderer for a father.

But you will have one for a husband.

She swallowed hard. If she wasn't careful, she'd become the king's next victim.

CHAPTER 31: TEMPEST

$\mathcal{A}$ few minutes into her journey from the barracks, a heavy hand fell on Tempest's shoulder, roughly pulling on her. She stopped in her tracks, ready to punch whoever it was in the face for getting in her way. Spinning, she shrugged off the hand and blinked as she came face to chest with Maxim. He reached for her arm, and she jerked back.

"Leave me," she said, voice icy. The Hounds were all working for the king. They did his bidding without protest. Mindless killers. She loved her uncles, but they had sworn an oath just like she had. The Crown came first, as it should. She wasn't beholden to them, even if they'd raised her. "Leave me alone."

"There are soldiers looking for you, back at the barracks. I do not think you will find peace there." A pained expression crossed Maxim's face. "What were you thinking? You will be taken back to the palace and watched every second for the rest of your life."

"What do you propose I do?" she exclaimed, feeling trapped and panicked by her ever-shrinking options. Tempest drooped her head, feeling useless. "What am I supposed to do?"

"You can follow me."

For a moment, Tempest didn't know what to do. Trust didn't come easy these days. Could she trust any of her uncles? They had clearly been part of the reason mimkia had spread. They were guilty through and through, whether they knew exactly what they had been doing or not. Even so, she didn't doubt they loved her, but was that enough for them to betray their king? She peered up at Maxim, scrutinizing him. He'd never lied to her before, and true concern colored his expression.

"Make a decision now, lass," he said softly. "There isn't much time."

"All right," she whispered. "Lead the way."

A fist squeezed around her chest when he reached out and lifted the hood of her cloak over her head and tucked her hair away. She felt like a child again, and heat pressed at the back of her eyes at the sweet gesture. Maxim pulled his own hood up and bid her to follow him. Snow and ice cracked beneath their boots as he led her deeper into the capital—the streets unfamiliar—but eventually she recognized the back entrance of a tavern that her uncle frequented. Out of habit, she scanned the area, noting a few drunkards who were lazily leaning against nearby buildings. Nothing too suspicious, but still, something set her off.

"This isn't right," she murmured, her gaze straying to Maxim's back. "I think we're being watched."

"We are. Now, hush," he said, voice lowered. "And let me do all the talking."

That sounded foreboding. She snapped her mouth shut and examined the street once again. Her uncle knocked on the back door with some impatience. After a few seconds, a silent servant with white, grizzled hair, opened the door and waved them in, taking them up a flight of stairs and then another. The scent of stew, bread, and unwashed bodies permeated the area. The servant lifted a broom and rapped on the ceiling. Tempest observed in silence as a trapdoor opened in the ceiling and a rope ladder was tossed down.

The servant stepped aside, his gaze averted to the wall. Why wasn't he looking at them?

"You first, Temp," Maxim said.

Her attention snapped back to her uncle. "What is going on?"

"Just get up there."

She frowned at her uncle and ascended the ladder, reaching the attic floor. Her mood soured when she spotted who awaited her. "No," she muttered and tried to go back down, but Maxim was already behind her.

He smacked her on the rump. "Climb, lass."

"Traitor," she hissed, her nerves on edge as she climbed into the room. The rest of her Hound uncles—Dima, Aleks and even Madrid—stood there watching her, faces ranging from concern to anger to complete desolation.

Maxim came up behind her and closed the trapdoor. Tension so thick it could be cut with a sword swelled in the room.

"What is going on?" she asked in a level tone.

"We should ask you the same thing," Dima replied, a bite to his words. "How could you do such a thing?"

Were they speaking about her association with the Jester or her betrothal to the king? Time to play stupid. "I don't know what you mean."

Maxim crossed his arms and rolled his eyes. "That won't work on us, lass. We raised you."

"You cannot marry the king." Madrid stepped away from the wall, his dark gray eyes narrowed. "It was foolish to encourage his attachment to you. Just what were you thinking?"

Oh no, he did not.

He did not get to deal out judgement when she knew his hands were soiled with the blood of their people.

"You think I chose this?" she hissed, stepping closer to Madrid. "All I have wanted is to be a Hound my entire life. If I'd had a choice, I would have run far, far away from the king. I'm not naïve. How could you expect me to turn down the king's proposal? I'm not suicidal. If I had refused him, my life and yours would be in jeopardy."

"Your life already hangs in the balance," Aleks said.

She glanced at him from the corner of her eye but made sure to stare down Madrid. "You and I know he gets everything he wants without consequence. I am no exception."

"Careful," Dima said. "Your words are sounding a bit revolutionary."

"Oh, come off it," she said heatedly. "I'm not stating anything that isn't true."

"You could have come to us," Aleks said in his soft-spoken way.

That was the last straw. She turned the full force of her

loathing on her uncle. "And when would I have done that? Between your mass poisonings of your people?"

"Tempest," Dima barked.

"No!" She held a finger up and glared harder at Aleks. "You cared for me when I was sick and were more of a father figure to me than anyone." Her chest ached painfully. "I'd always hoped you were my real father, now I pray to all that's holy that it's not true. I couldn't bear the thought to have the same blood as someone who kills innocents, children no less."

"That's enough," Madrid cut in.

"No, it's not nearly enough." All the pain, worry, and confusion were pouring out of her, and she couldn't hold it all back. She scornfully eyed the four men. "You four are leaders of the Hounds. I know you're not ignorant about the mimkia. I've seen the devastation it's brought to our kingdom. How could you do such a thing? We're supposed to be protectors, not executioners!"

"I had to do it," Aleks said. His eyes were mournful and full of shame. "At first, I did not know the full extent of what I was being asked to do, but I would be lying if I said I was still that ignorant now. I admit it: I am the one responsible for purifying all of the mimkia to be shipped into the villages. I am guilty of it all."

She'd known it was so, but to hear it was a different thing altogether. Everyone around her had been lying through their teeth this whole time—on both sides of the Heimseryan and Talagan conflict: Pyre, King Destin, and the Hounds. She couldn't trust anyone, not even her uncles. She snapped, a red veil slamming over her vision.

Screaming, she lashed out toward Aleks, with every

intention of attacking him where he stood. Dima grabbed her around her waist and lifted her from the ground.

"Calm down," Dima commanded.

"I will not!" she yelled. "He's a murderer. You are all *murderers*. You make me sick."

Maxim moved closer; his steps were quiet for such a big man. He held up his hands. "You need to calm down, lass."

"You're just as bad as the king!"

"We are not." A twitch of anger creased Maxim's brow. "Once you calm down, you'll realize that. The king has more sway and power than one man ever should. I'm sure you know that. There was nothing we could do in the face of his orders other than to obey them. Such is the life of a servant of the Crown."

"Then you are no better than him! You could have done *something*, even if it meant losing your life. You could do something."

"And where would that get us?" Madrid interjected, his composure skill intact. "The king would just replace us with pawns who would unflinchingly do his bidding, and then what? There would be no one left to oppose him."

Oppose him. The words rattled around in her head, and she sagged in Dima's grasp. "Is that what you're doing, opposing him? Because from where I'm standing it sounds an awful lot like justification for genocide."

Maxim sighed, and his shoulders grew slack. "Sometimes, Tempest, in the name of the greater good, there is no choice. You have to do evil things."

No. She didn't believe it. "But the children—"

"Think of how many thousands more children we have to protect!" Maxim said, grabbing Tempest's face as if the pressure of his fingers on her cheeks would make her understand his point. "You cannot know what is at stake."

Tempest bit her lip. She didn't agree, and Maxim could see that clear as day on her face. He loosened his grip, smiling sadly, and caressed her cheek. "I know you do not agree. In fact, it is in your nature not to agree with such a notion as doing something evil for the sake of good. Just because your intentions are honest, it doesn't make your evil acts any less reprehensible. But sometimes... sometimes, you really must do whatever is necessary to protect the little ones."

The fight went out of her, and she hung her head, wanting to cry. "Let me go, Dima."

Her uncle released her, and she collapsed on an empty wine barrel that lay on the floor, near a small window. She stared at her shoes and then out at the city, her gaze resting on the far-off castle. It was this sort of justification and lack of action that was tearing their kingdom apart.

"The little ones need protection from *the king*," she whispered, her voice hoarse. "And I intend to take on the responsibility."

"You think you can change him?" Dima sneered.

Tempest laughed hollowly. "No."

She turned from the window and examined each man.

First, it was Aleks, who looked so ashamed. She felt tempted to console him despite her anger, but she knew better. He deserved to wallow in what he'd done. Next, Dima, whose face was almost impossible to read, as usual, but Tempest knew him well enough to recognize the slight tensing around his jaw that meant he was on the verge of losing his temper. Then Maxim, whose eyes pleaded with her to take what he had said at face value and trust them.

"Has the king threatened you?" she said bluntly.

"In what way?" Dima asked carefully.

That was an answer in and of itself. What threats had the king made? What would be so important that they'd commit such crimes? "So, we're at an impasse."

"It would appear so," Madrid answered.

She stared at the infamous Hound. He held her gaze, and, for the first time, she saw a real emotion. Disappointment and something almost... protective. Fiercely so.

Oh. Winter's bite. You are stupid.

She thought of what Maxim had said about doing what had to be done to protect the little ones. She was *their* little one.

"How long has he held me over your head?"

None of the men answered.

A long time then, she gathered from their silence. Her stomach rolled. She had agreed to marry a man who had been using her safety and wellbeing as a means to force good men into doing very unspeakable acts. Acts she was fighting against.

"Tempest," Madrid said, very quietly, finally breaking the oppressive silence in the room. "I will only offer this once. We will hide you from the king. He will never find you. I'm certain you agreed to his proposal for the right reasons, but this choice will only result in your death."

"Not if I get to him first."

Madrid sighed. "I'm going to ignore you said that."

"We never wanted his attention on you," Dima added, nodding slowly. "I'm sure this comes as no surprise, but the king has a reputation of disposing of every lover he's ever taken to bed." His jaw clenched. "I've buried too many bodies and won't allow you to be the next one," he said raggedly.

"We tried to keep you from the king's notice," Aleks said gently. "But your trial secured his undivided attention."

"Oh, so it's all my fault," Tempest fired back, hackles raised at the insinuation. "It's *my* fault that he organized my opponent to be a lion—expecting me to fail and die, I might add. And then, when I unexpectedly won, it's my fault he sought me out, knowing that I could not escape." Her throat tightened. "And it's my fault he pushed his advances on me, knowing I could not refuse."

Maxim seemed to swell. "If he's touched you—"

"I've been able to handle myself." Mostly. But for how long?

"We never said this is your fault," Madrid cut in, calm as ever. "There was ultimately no way we were going to be able to stop his attention from falling on you, the first female Hound. We just... hoped otherwise. We wished for things to be different." His back stiffened, and his expression grew even more serious than it had been before. "But that's why you must leave," he said. "I know your intentions are good. I have no doubt you'll try to build your position and influence as queen to the best of your advantage. But Destin will see right through what you're doing, and you'll be dead by morning. You can't marry him."

Tempest glowered, feeling somewhat like a petulant child. "And why not?" she asked, expecting the answer to be along the lines of *we want to protect you.*

"Because you will undo all the work that we have already done," Aleks said, his voice so small Tempest thought she'd imagined it. "In the background. For years now."

She stiffened. "Excuse me?"

"You heard him," Dima answered. "You've stumbled into something that is bigger than all of us. Years of planning has gone up in smoke in a matter of months with you on the scene."

Tempest blinked slowly. She'd never considered that her uncles might have a plan of their own. How was she so blind? Over the past few months, in her haste to deem them traitors and monsters, she had underestimated their abilities as Hounds. Then again, she'd had more reason to believe them loyal to the Crown than not.

She ran a hand over her face and placed her head in her hands. For every layer she peeled back, more were revealed. The Hounds were essentially prisoners in gilded cages that were afforded status and luxury beyond what most people in the kingdom could hope for. They were respected. They were loved. They were feared. Yet they were prisoners nonetheless, stripped of their own choices and freewill.

Hounds work from the shadows. Darkness is our ally.

Just like the Jester. Like the Dark Court.

Then the similarity of what the Hounds and rebels were both trying to accomplish sparked a dangerous idea. If both sides were working in the shadows, then why not work with the shadow puppeteer himself? While she didn't want to put her uncles in more danger than they were already in, they were all dancing on the edge of a sword already. Hell, they'd been putting their lives on the line every day for only God knew how long.

You are the link between the Dark Court and the Hounds. Damn well use it.

"What would you say if I told you that I could provide you with more people? Ones that would escape the king's notice."

Madrid cocked his head, his gray eyes scanning her face. "I would say that you've been busy. Just what are you getting at,

Tempest?" The tone of his voice suggested very much that he did not like what he thought she was about to say.

She took a deep breath. "What if I said I could put you in touch with the rebellion. With... the Jester?" Tempest waited a moment for her words to sink in. No one moved, or even seemed to blink.

"He's alive?" Madrid said softly.

"There's always someone to take his place in the Dark Court," she said evasively.

"Ties to the Jester." Maxim chuckled. "You've been busy, lass."

"Not much of a choice."

Dima rolled his neck. "How is it that you managed to get yourself tangled up with the Dark Court when we've made sure you were kept away from all this while growing up? You're a bloody magnet for disaster."

An impish smile came to her face at the exasperation in her uncle's tone. "The fact that you raised me should be answer enough."

"You think they will work with us?" Aleks asked, turning to Madrid.

The stoic man studied Tempest, and she straightened under his scrutiny. "I think there will be rifts, but it could be possible," Madrid said.

Her attention turned to Aleks. "The drugs stop now."

He held her gaze. "I've long since stopped brewing them. Once my discovery was made, the king seized my work and sent it out to his agents. It's no longer in my control."

Did Pyre know? "I can't guarantee anything from the Jester."

Maxim smirked. "We raised you better than that. No daughter of ours will take no for an answer. This isn't just about Dotae, but Heimserya as a whole." Her uncle eyed Madrid. "What say you?"

"I still think she should leave." Madrid started toward Tempest, reaching out a hand before deciding against touching her. "But I don't think that's in the cards for you, is it?"

"I won't abandon those in need."

Madrid shocked her by smiling slightly. "Then, it seems, the choice is made." He bowed his head and dropped to his knee.

Her mouth gaped as her uncles followed suit.

"We pledged ourselves to the Crown. My lady, soon you will take up the mantel. Our swords are yours." The air rushed from her lungs as Madrid lifted his head. "Welcome to war, daughter of ours."

CHAPTER 32: TEMPEST

*I*t was amazing that one conversation could change her life.

Tempest gazed blankly at the tavern room the servant had led her to, her mind a whirl. Time was short until the guard hunted her down and *escorted* her back to the palace. It was the only rational decision to combine her uncles' forces with those of the Dark Court, but every time she thought of Pyre, all she could see was the empty gaze of the crown prince. The Jester had done that, and he'd used her to do it. She held her palms up and stared at the dried blood on her hands. Was she any better?

Unable to stand one more minute in her clothing, she hustled to the warm bath steaming near the fireplace. Tempest tore her clothing from her body and tossed the soiled items in the fire. She submerged herself in the bath and viciously scrubbed her skin until it hurt. The clear water turned musky and rust colored. Nausea swamped her again, and she launched from the tub, flinging water everywhere. Shivering and dry heaving, she wrapped herself in a towel and roughly dried her body. Her skin pebbled as she yanked on the rough clothing the servant had left her, the coarse fabric scratching as she adjusted her garments. She took one last look at the room, then pulled her cloak over her shoulders, and tucked her hair away beneath the hood, thankful that the cloak was black, so the blood didn't show.

Tempest tossed a small bag of coins onto the unused bed that Maxim had left her and exited the inn room on silent feet. She ghosted down the stairs and slipped past the kitchen without seeing a single person. Her breath fogged in the cold air, and she examined the alley and street. The fake drunkards were gone. Was that a good sign or bad?

Just to be careful, she slunk toward the slums, making sure to loop and weave through the shanties, remaining as inconspicuous as possible. With furtive eyes and keen ears, she took in the pale faces and anxious, fractured conversations of those around her. Talk of war was thick in the air, and nobody liked what that meant. The people were scared. Mothers clutched their children tighter. Men were drinking more. They all feared what the future would bring. King Destin's speech may have riled up the upper class—the ones important enough to have been within the palace court to hear it—but those that would actually fight, didn't know what this meant for them and their families. They would be the ones sacrificed on the battlefield if Tempest didn't figure out a solution.

Kill the king. That's your solution.

Ensuring none of her periwinkle hair was visible beneath her hood, she instinctively quickened her pace. When she saw a flash of movement out of the corner of her left eye, her fears were confirmed: she had been spotted.

For a moment, she veered right toward the city gates on instinct, then ground her heel into the gravel beneath her and began climbing the closest building. The damaged wall was still a safer bet despite the tail.

With a glance down below her, she saw three guards—no longer trying to hide their presence—were pursuing her. She bolted across the ramshackle roof and leapt for the next one, feet clattering across tiles, tin, and loose wooden planks. She was starkly reminded of another time she had navigated across roofs in such a manner—fleeing Pyre's gang only two months prior. Her shoulder had been damaged from her fight with the lion, and she'd hurt her leg during the pursuit, but she had still made it pretty far before she'd been caught. She was even stronger now.

Brushing aside the thought, she finally reached her destination—the crumbling outer wall. With a few creative movements, and some quick scaling of the shanties around her, she managed to make it to the tallest building unscathed. Frowning, Tempest glanced over her shoulder.

Half a dozen guards were in pursuit.

Damn.

She didn't have time to doubt as she launched herself at the wall, scrambling to grab the ramparts in order to fling herself to safety. For one terrible, agonizingly slow moment her grip faltered, and her left hand came loose from the wall. In a last-ditch effort, she pulled an arrow from her quiver and lodged it into a space between the bricks of the wall itself and used it as a handhold to haul herself up. She crouched on the wall, breathing heavily, her cloak whipping in the wind. The guards stared up at her, their expressions ones of satisfaction. A cold chill ran down her spine, and she flicked a glance to the other side of the wall.

The *very finished* wall.

The sheer drop made her head spin, and a filthy curse slipped passed her lips. How had they finished it so quickly? It had been ruins for as long as she could remember. Tempest eyed the distance to the ground. If she tried to jump, she'd lame herself, or possibly die. Damn it. She needed to get to the city gates. Now.

With no other choice, she fled along the city wall, knowing her only chance was to descend the stairs near the main gates and fight her way out. Her lips lifted into a grim smile as the guards shouted and began to chase after her, but the labyrinth of the slums slowed them down. Maybe there wouldn't be much fighting at all, as long as she didn't come across any more guards along the way.

Her boot slipped on the slick stone, and Tempest faltered— narrowly missing an arrow as it whistled through the air where she would've been. She yelled in surprise. That was too close for comfort. She kept running as two guards burst from the turret ahead, and she dropped to her knees, sliding across the ice between them. Tempest slammed the door behind her and locked it before sprinting to the other side and back along the wall. Her pulse pounded in her ears as she scanned the roofs around her. Where had that arrow come from?

As if summoning one from her thoughts, another whistle pierced the air, and she rolled. Popping to her feet, she kept sprinting, praying that she wouldn't lose her balance and fall. An enormous building loomed near the wall, the capital's flag hanging from the side. Time to get off the wall.

Tempest didn't let herself stop to think about it. She just jumped, and her fingers seized the long flagpole. Her hands burned as she slid toward the ground too fast, then she freefell. Even though she'd been trained to fall correctly, the impact still knocked her to the ground. She rolled and groaned as she clambered to her feet. That worked better than she'd anticipated.

The thunder of boots against stone warned her of the guards' approach. Tempest hobbled into a darkened corner and observed as the men ran by, none the wiser that she was no longer cornered. She moved with the flow of the citizens toward the city gate and stiffened because close to twenty guards stood near the exit. Chills ran down her spine as the gates began to close, their heavy hinges screeching in protest.

None of this made sense. Was the king closing the gates to keep her inside or did he have something else already in play? He couldn't know of her plans or her treachery.

Unless one of your uncles betrayed you.

Tremors moved up and down her arms. No. They wouldn't. She pushed away from the gates, determined to make it to the docks and the tunnel. That was her last resort.

The jog to the docks was a blur, and, thankfully, no one followed her. She slowed and purchased some nuts and fruit while surveying the area. It seemed like no one was lying in wait for her. Her steps quickened as the tunnel loomed closer, and she entered the darkened passageway. Her skin prickled as dark shapes peeled themselves from the walls, taking the form of soldiers.

They were cutting off her escape, her salvation.

With a short, sharp intake of breath, she rolled her neck. "Please let me pass."

"State your business," a soldier barked.

Relief washed over her. They weren't looking for her. "I am meeting with my family. I only came to gather some supplies." She held out her nuts and fruit.

Someone lit a lamp. She blinked. Fifteen guards. Another moved from the shadows, and she exhaled slowly. Wrong, there were sixteen, and the last one wasn't a guard at all.

Levka.

His lips pressed together as he stared at her. "Family, huh?"

She swallowed the lie on her tongue. "Family. Friends. They're all the same to me."

"Please welcome the Lady Hound, our sovereign's betrothed." He lifted his chin at her. "We've been tasked with assuring your safety."

"I thank you," she murmured. "But I assure you that I don't need protection. I am a Hound after all."

"But there have been rogue attacks outside the wall, and it's not safe."

Time to play nice. She batted her lashes. "Then it's good I have all of you with me. You'll keep me safe. Now, excuse me." Tempest strode forward.

Levka stepped up to meet her. "I'm sorry, but I cannot allow that."

So, this was the way it was going to be. Tempest sighed and pulled her sword from her scabbard. "We don't have to do this, Levka."

"You're right. We don't, but you're forcing my hand," he gritted out. "Seize her."

The men converged on Tempest, leaving her no choice but to fight. She slashed her sword at the closest soldier, wounding his calf. Twisting, Tempest removed her dagger from its sheath on her thigh and threw it at another soldier closing it. It sunk into his shoulder, and he grunted in pain.

"Stop this madness," she commanded. "No one has to get hurt."

But they kept coming.

In another life—two days ago, even—she would have felt remorse for hurting a man when he was simply doing his job. Such feelings speedily fled in battle. It was kill or be killed, and she did not want to die. Fatigue plagued her. The dash across the city had taken much out of her. A guard rushed forward and cut her arm with his sword. She cried out.

"Do *not* harm the lady!" Levka bellowed. "Every wound she sustains, the king will carve exact replicas on your flesh."

Another stepped on her cloak, and she released the clasp at the throat, spinning to meet her next attacker. A blow found her leg, and she crashed to her knees in surprise. She hadn't seen that one coming.

Her harsh breathing echoed in the tunnel along with the moans of the soldiers she'd wounded. Levka moved through the soldiers, his expression eerily blank.

"Give up this madness, my lady," he said. "You are the future queen of our nation. Come back to the palace quietly. Where you belong."

Not before she got word to Pyre.

"I cannot do what you ask," she replied, shaking her head emphatically. "Either come with me or drag me back."

For a moment, his face tightened, and then he closed his eyes. "So be it," he muttered, waving his hand. Four soldiers darted in, wrestled her sword from her grasp, and grabbed her by the arms. They hauled Tempest to her feet, and she fought, biting, kicking, and clawing.

She spat at Levka, her glob of saliva hitting him in cheek. He lifted his hand to his face, not taking his eyes from hers and wiped the spit away. His gaze strayed over her shoulder for a moment, just before a rumbling began, getting closer and closer until the noise was deafening.

The hair at the nape of her neck rose, and she craned her neck to look over her shoulder.

"A bear!" one of the soldiers cried, trying and failing to get out of the way when the monstrously huge creature bowled through the soldiers like they were toys. The soldiers released her as the bear approached and roared, its huge teeth longer than any of their fingers. Men scattered, their fear almost palpable, but she didn't move. A smile curled her lips, and she began to chuckle, so relieved to see a familiar face.

"About time you showed up, Briggs." She coughed, too full of adrenaline to care about the blood that wet her lips. Somehow, she must have hit her face.

Then another dark and furry shape joined Briggs, smaller than the bear but no less intimidating.

A wolf—Brine.

Relief washed over Tempest as the two shifters made quick work of the surrounding soldiers—except Levka—whose cries turned guttural as they either fled or were cut down by vicious teeth and claws.

Goosebumps rippled over her body when Brine released a haunting howl that echoed around them.

"You were almost too late!" Levka barked, his hand touching her shoulder.

Brine gave him a look with his sharp, amber eyes and let out half a snarl. It was a simplistic enough sound that Tempest took to mean, *You're lucky we showed up at all.*

She glared at Levka and shook him off. He was part of this too? Tempest struggled to her feet, ignoring his hand as she retrieved her dagger and sword from the cobblestones. Did no one among her family or friends know how to tell the bloody truth?

"Tempest," Levka began.

She held a hand up. "*Don't.*" Her attention turned to the wolf. "Brine!" she said, and the wolf snarled at her. "It's nice to see you too." She limped toward the formidable shifter and threw her arms around his powerful shoulders and buried her face in his midnight fur. "Thank you," she whispered.

He whined and leaned his wolf head against her own. Her fingers sank into his fur, and she breathed in his smoky scent. More soldiers would be coming, she knew, so they had to move. A mammoth nose pressed against her right arm, and she lifted her head to stare into Briggs's dark-brown bear eyes. She didn't hesitate to press a kiss to his snout before standing.

"You need to go before more soldiers arrive," Levka urged.

She rose to her feet and stared at the two shifters. With a sharp nip at her wrist, Brine indicated for Tempest to climb onto the back of Briggs.

"I appreciate what you've done but I can't leave yet," she said, and Briggs growled and slapped the ground with his huge paw. "I was only coming to relay information. I've gained an ally for the Jester."

Brine pressed closer, his eyes focused on her.

"The Hounds. *All* of them."

Briggs's maw dropped open, revealing all his terrifying teeth.

Her adrenaline began to wane, and it was difficult to fully control her bloody, shaking hands. "I only wish this information to be passed onto the Jester. He has a week to reply."

Brine dropped his muzzle to the ground as if he was bowing.

"They need to go, now," Levka gritted out, stalking closer. "We don't have much time." He inclined his chin at Briggs. "Make it look good, huh?"

Tempest squeaked when Briggs sliced his claws against Levka's arms and chest, knocking the man over.

Levka moaned. "Sweet poison, that hurts."

"Do you make it a habit of yours to get as close to death as you can?" Brine growled, surprising Tempest. She blinked and glanced away from his naked human form.

She grimaced. "But I didn't actually *die*, did I? I'm just a little banged up."

The wolf closed in on her and set his forehead against hers. "He will not like this. I was sent to fetch you."

Tempest chuckled. "Pyre's not my keeper, nor has he ever been."

Brine smirked. "So stubborn. I knew there was a reason I liked you."

"Aw, you like me? I knew it."

"You're okay," he huffed, "for a human."

"Real cute," Levka groaned. "We need to go, Temp."

Brine nodded at him. "Get your pup to a healer, Tempest. He looks faint." He stepped away and she turned her back to him, giving him privacy to shift. "Don't forget who your enemy is, dog. The city twists its people."

"I'll bear that in mind," she said.

"What should I pass on to him?"

Blurrily, she stared at the end of the tunnel leading into

Dotae. "That Tempest Madrid brings the Dark Court a pledge of allegiance from the Hounds to fight with you all and take down the menace of the throne." She paused. "And that I will not be manipulated. I'm not his subordinate, and that I know what he did."

"Anything else?" Briggs drawled.

"That he was right." She began to limp toward the city. "War is upon us."

CHAPTER 33: PYRE

*H*e swirled the fire whiskey around the glass tumbler, leaning against the stone balcony railing. The winter wind whipped around him, a haunting melody whistling around the craggy peaks, yet the chill didn't bother him. An advantage of being a shapeshifter. Pyre's gaze swept the forest below and moved toward the coast in the direction of Dotae—the direction of his greatest enemy.

Destin.

His lip curled and a low growl rumbled in his chest. Even thinking the degenerate's name angered him. He tossed back his spirits, the whiskey burning down his throat. One day soon the monster would be dethroned. *And dead.*

A sharp rap sounded at the door. There was only one person who made a single knock sound angry. Brine.

"Enter," Pyre said lazily.

Brine's woody scent hit him first as the wolf approached

silently and stood by Pyre's side. He slid a look in his second's direction and then turned his attention to the empty tumbler in his hands before once again taking in the breath-taking view. "Things went well, I take it?" he drawled.

"No one is dead."

Pyre couldn't help but smile at that. "And our Hound? I suppose she is sulking in her room?"

Brine chuckled. "When has Tempest ever sulked?"

"Tempest?" Pyre said slowly. That was new. He turned toward his friend and slung a hip against the railing. "On a first name basis, are we?"

The wolf huffed. "She has a way of growing on a person."

"That she does." He waited a few moments and then sighed when Brine didn't continue. He had always been a terrible conversationalist. "So... how is she?" Brine cracked his neck and faced Pyre; his expression unreadable. That wasn't a good sign. Tempest must be *really* mad at him. Well, angrier than normal. "I take it she isn't happy with me?"

"You could say that."

He rolled his eyes. Getting information from Brine was like pulling teeth sometimes. "On a scale of slap me to murder me in my sleep—how upset are we talking?"

"Honestly? I think she has hit her breaking point. Where she is normal fire, this time she was ice. A numb sort of rage."

Pyre pursed his lips and nodded. He wasn't surprised at her reaction to what occurred in the woods, but he hoped she'd at least give him a chance to explain himself. While he didn't mourn the loss of the crown prince, he didn't like killing any more than anyone else.

"Well, then... it seems as if I have amends to make." He stepped away from the railing. "As Briggs likes to tell me; best not to let it fester." A stewing female was a dangerous one. "Time to grovel."

"You won't find her."

He paused, his brows furrowing. There was something alarming in Brine's tone. Pyre swung around and eyed the wolf. "What do you mean I won't find her?"

Brine held his gaze, his silver eyes solemn. "She did not return with me."

The hair at Pyre's nape rose and goosebumps ran across his skin. She hadn't returned. He inhaled slowly. "Did I, or did I not, command you to retrieve her?"

"You did, but she did not wish to come."

"Then you should have thrown her over your bloody shoulder and hauled her arse back here!" Tremors began running down his arms and his nails lengthened into claws. *His* Hound was still in the grasp of the king. "She's just a slip of a girl! How could you do this?"

Brine's eyes hardened and he took a step closer to Pyre, his chest puffing out. "Because she didn't want to return to you. You don't own her."

The wolf's words echoed through his mind. *She did not want to return to you. You don't own her.*

Pyre snarled and tossed his tumbler against the stone wall. The cup shattered and glass exploded across the veranda. He stared at the sparkling shards of glass scattered across the stone floor and tried to get his temper under control. With difficulty, he kept from attacking his second in command. Barely.

"Do you feel better?" Brine drawled, looking nonplussed.

He didn't. He wanted to storm Dotae and drag his mate back to Dark Court where he could keep her safe from harm. She had no business playing games with Destin. Temp had no idea what she'd gotten herself into.

"I don't envy you," his friend said gruffly.

"What?" Pyre muttered, rubbing his forehead. How quickly could he get to Dotae? Surely, Damien could get him to the coast and then Chesh could smuggle him into the city. From there he could get to his Hound and talk some sense into her.

Brine crossed his arms. "Having a mate as feisty as yours will always be a challenge. She will never allow you to cossette or hide her away. Tempest is a warrior in every sense. I like to think she'd be a wolf if she'd been born from a Talagan line."

"She's not my mate." *You know she is.*

His friend snorted. "If you say so." A pause. "Mark my words Pyre. If you try to capture Tempest and force her hand, it will not go well for you. She will be owned by no man. She's a wild and free soul."

Pyre snarled at him, flashing fang before facing the south. He curled his fingers around the carved stone railing, his gaze once again moving in the direction of Dotae. Brine wasn't wrong. If Pyre pressed Tempest, she'd lock him out completely. His palms began to sweat at the idea. He needed to get his emotions under control. Now.

Emotional entanglements are a distraction.

"Did she leave you with a message?" he asked, his tone barely civil.

"She managed to gain the alliance of the Hounds."

Pyre blinked and glared at Brine. "You could have led with that, you bastard."

His friend shrugged. "You were more worried about the lass."

"Touché," he muttered, his mind already spinning with possibilities. "How did she manage that feat?"

"No idea," Brine answered. "She keeps surprising me."

"Anything else?" Pyre asked. He half expected the wolf to tell him the elves had come back from the dead and were offering military aid to the Dark Court.

"She told me to express that she knows what you've done and that she is not your subordinate."

He chuckled. How typical of his Hound to give him a verbal lashing whilst not even being there. Even while driving him to distraction, Tempest still managed to draw him even closer to her. He wanted her close. Pyre wanted all her secrets.

You'll have to give her yours.

Pyre stiffened and rolled his neck. "There's much to be done." Time was short to remove the tyrannical monarch before he discovered his bastard was still alive—alive and ruling the Dark Court.

A humorless smile curled his lips.

One last joke before our finale, eh father?

Continue the series with THE HEIR

ABOUT THE AUTHOR

Thank you for reading THE ROOK. I hope you enjoyed it!

If you'd like to know more about me, my books, or to connect with me online, you can visit my webpage https:// www. frostkay.net/ or join my facebook group FROST FIENDS!

From bookworm to bookworm: reviews are important. Reviews can help readers find books, and I am grateful for all honest reviews. Thank you for taking the time to let others know what you've read, and what you thought. Just remember, they don't have to be long or epic, just honest. ❤

Have you read REBEL'S BLADE?

It's an ENEMIES TO LOVERS epic fantasy series perfect for Sarah J. Maas and Holly Black fans.

Check out what readers are saying: "Frost Kay is absolutely one of my favourite new authors. Hands Down. Her stories are impeccably well thought out and her characters are solid. I can't wait for more!" Bestselling Author Tate James.

Made in United States
Troutdale, OR
01/13/2025

27913557R00192